Someone was shooting at her—but who'd want to kill her?

She heard a loud popping sound and her window shattered. The whizzing of air past her head made her jerk back, startled. Her heart hammering in her chest, she felt a sudden stinging on her right ear lobe. Blood dripped down onto her shoulder, and she realized she must have been shot.

"My God!" she screamed. "A bullet came through the window. Someone just took a shot at me!" She grabbed her cell and dialed 9-1-1. "Yes, operator, someone shot at me—right through my window. It's broken. There's glass all over inside my kitchen and I'm bleeding."

After hanging up, she surveyed the damage. Her scrub top was a mess. Blood was splattered on the floor and part of the table. "Oh my God, there's blood everywhere!" She put ice on the ear wound and pressed a towel against it to stop the blood flow. Then she huddled in the den to wait for the police.

"First, Ed threatens me, now this. The police will be swarming around, and he'll be one of them." *There's evidence I might have left behind and—oh, my God, the empty sandbag's still in the bedroom!"* She ran to the bedroom, grabbed the empty canvas bag, and shoved it into the laundry hamper. Then she took the bloody towel off her head and stuffed it in on top. *If they see blood in here it's because I tried to get this wound dressed before they got here.*

She wet a wash cloth and wiped off the closet doors where she'd left a smear of blood. *Everything's going crazy on me. Who'd be shooting at me? Munson's in the slammer.*

She's at it again—just can't seem to stop...

Widowed R.N. Martha Chance's futile attempts to rid the world of sexual predators takes her into the realm of terrifying, sadistic criminals, where she uncovers corrupt but powerful city officials who condone sexual crimes against defenseless children and don't appreciate Martha's interference. On behalf of the tiny dark-eyed and dreadfully abused little girl in the hospital where Martha works, the desperately lonely teenage girls who frequent online chat rooms and are prime targets for unscrupulous men, and the friend and fellow R.N. suffering horrific domestic abuse, Martha and her alternate personality Serena seek not only to avenge the abuse but to make sure it will not be repeated. Unfortunately, her thirst for vengeance makes Martha a target of men who will do anything to keep their evil deeds a secret—and unleashes upon her a man who plots her death to satisfy his own fiendish soul.

KUDOS for *The Avenger*

Ramona Forrest's *The Avenger,* the second book in her *The Vigilante* series, does not disappoint! *The Avenger* plunges the reader farther into the inner life and thoughts of its split personality, modern-day, well-grounded but not quite stable, saucy, super-hero, grandmother, and friend to those in need, Martha/ Serena...If you enjoyed *The Vigilante*, I recommend *The Avenger*! – *Mary A. Fuller, Attorney at Law*

Forrest's characters are well-developed and three dimensional. And this time she delves into the area of hired killers and dirty cops. As it turns out, her best-kept secret isn't all that "best-kept" and more and more people know or suspect what she has been up to. This leads to some exciting twists and turns. If you liked *The Vigilante*, you can't go wrong with *The Avenger*. – *Taylor Jones, Reviewer*

The Avenger by Ramona Forrest is every bit as good as its prequel *The Vigilante*. You have to love an author that makes a series of a hot, sexy grandmother vigilante out to castrate every sexual predator she can find. First there is the idea that a grandmother can be hot and sexy, and then the idea of that hot, sexy grandmother castrating sexual predators. I love the irony of it. Not that castration would stop most sexual predators, since rape rarely has anything to do with sex. But you have to appreciate the poetic justice of it. I enjoyed the book and the characters immensely. It is very refreshing to find a main character that is not a hunk or a bombshell, but a grandmother, of all things. And the fact that the author makes the woman, hot, sexy, and a looker, just adds to the charm of it. The plot is strong with some intriguing twists and turns. I found myself riveting from the very first page. – *Regan Murphy, Reviewer*

THE
AVENGER

Ramona Forrest

A Black Opal Books Publication

GENRE: MYSTERY/SUSPENSE/MEDICAL THRILLER

THE AVENGER
Copyright © 2014 by Ramona Forrest
Cover Design by Jackson Cover Designs
All cover art copyright © 2014
All Rights Reserved
Print ISBN: 978-1-626941-17-5

First Publication: MARCH 2014

Published by Black Opal Books **http://www.blackopalbooks.com**

DEDICATION

In addition to dedicating this work to all those who have suffered abuse of any sort, I dedicate this book to those lonely, unsuspecting, and foolish young girls who attempt to find love and excitement via online chat rooms.

CHAPTER 1

I'm not too comfortable in pediatrics, but I'll take it," Martha Chance said to the hospital staffing coordinator. She accepted the proffered shift although she felt she'd regret her words. Having and raising a child of your own didn't make you a peds nurse and, truthfully, Martha always felt a bit uncomfortable caring for the very young.

Today, she shrugged her worries aside, figuring, *What the hell, if they're running short, I can hack one night of it.* And she wished to accommodate her place of employment.

Arriving on the ward, she got a coffee, greeted the rest of the staff, and got a detailed report on her patients. A broken leg, a post appendectomy, one injured in an auto accident, and one other patient that sent shivers up her spine and her pulse racing.

Her heart sank to the depths. She'd be challenged emotionally with Aliya Pederson, a four-year-old female victim of obvious sexual abuse. For Martha, once, just the mere mention or appearance of such a thing would have brought back haunting memories hidden and safely buried from conscious thought. Two years ago, all that had changed, and it changed the person she always thought she was.

She made her rounds. Getting a tight grip on her feelings, she approached the child's bedside. The battered condition of this tiny girl was inescapable. Martha fought the anger rising within her. It soared to insurmountable heights as the seething torment within her mind brought back her husband's last, fateful words of warning.

"Martha, get a grip on your feelings!" In the face of his own fatal diagnosis, his greatest fear had not been for himself, but for her. "You let *her* out like that again and you'll end up in the damned penitentiary!"

As Martha approached Aliya's bedside, the little girl opened one discolored eye to see her caregiver and turned away. Sobbing, she cried out in her child's plaintive, high pitched voice, "No—fraid, no—fraid!"

Her small, dimpled knees curled to her chest, she wound her arms around them, with her head pressed tightly against those closely held legs. Tears crept beneath long silky lashes and her body shook in fear.

Hoping to soothe the child, Martha pulled a chair close to the crib, let the side down, and, with soothing voice and gentle hands, stroked the child's lovely black hair, and slid her hands carefully along the bruised little body to quiet her. With Martha's gentle approach, Aliya slowly relaxed enough for the initial exam. The report said her injuries consisted of internal vaginal tears and bruising in many stages of healing. The mother had claimed the father molested the girl, but then quickly denied it. Then she said a window was open in the child's bedroom, and they believe a stranger got in and attacked the girl. As to the bruising, the mother claimed Aliya was a very clumsy child and fell down a lot.

Aliya had long silences, interspersed with fearful cries. In her attempt to withstand the pain during the required treatments, the child held her small body stiff, her mouth and fists clamped tight. Her swollen, discolored little vagina would incite anger and a sense of utter soul-sickness in any decent person, Martha knew. Older, healing bruises bore evidence of physical abuse carried out over an extended period of time.

Martha shook her head and wiped her hot tears away. In private conversations, the charge nurse had mentioned that many a nurse had shed bitter tears after treating Aliya. Martha felt a sickening anger that this tiny girl had suffered such horrendous indignities and pain. A competent nurse, she understood her mission and gently completed the needed dressings. It hurt her deeply to cause further pain and the fear she saw in the girl's eyes sickened her soul.

As Martha gently rubbed lotion on the little limbs, she noted the presence of healed scars as well as bruises in yellow, purple, blues and greens, an entire range of slowly healing colors. The child relaxed slightly under Martha's gentle ministrations and opened her big, dark eyes. Her little private area covered again, she ventured a peek at her nurse, but offered no smile or words.

Martha fully understood, deep in her soul, the tortured hell that child had suffered. She gritted her teeth as she finished Aliya's care. Of the psychological damages, there'd never be a complete cure, never could be. This child would suffer for years to come. Her grandson Will was another poor child who'd never again be able to trust the male adults in his life.

During her shift, Martha observed the child closely. Aliya continually shrank away from close contact with the nurses and most other adults.

"The parents of this child have failed her miserably," Martha told another nurse. "Does she have any place of safety in her family setting? Will she be returned home to suffer the same things again?" She huffed in despair, then added, "Has Child Protective Services seen this child?"

"They're on the case," Allison, the charge nurse, said. "But it doesn't look good for this poor little one." A dedicated pediatric nurse, she gnashed her teeth in anger. "Social Services and the police department did the best they could. Unfortunately, while she's been here, that damned mother and her high-priced lawyer have gotten the father released—Aliya *will* be returned to that home. And all that after her initial claim her husband had molested the child." She wiped away a tear.

"I don't believe it!" Sickened, Martha felt her rage rapidly mounting until, choking with outrage, she swore, "Before God, I'll never work this ward again, never!"

"Honey, we see it all the time and it never gets any better," Allison said, trying to soothe her. She slammed a chart down, and the papers scattered. "Child Protective Services is a joke to us on this ward. We all feel that way."

During the remainder of her shift, Martha continued to observe the child. Aliya interacted shyly and with reticence with other children, uttering a few soft words and even a smile or two. Sadly, she was lost in her own painful world the rest of the time, and usually lay curled in a tiny ball in her white slatted crib. Martha sighed and a few futile tears escaped. Recovery for this child would be long and painful—if she lived.

The father, jailed on suspicion, had been freed on his own recognizance after the mother begged his release. She claimed he was a respected member of his community and held an important position in his company. The case fell through when she absolutely refused to bear testimony against him, claiming it was someone who got in through that open window. They had seven children to care for. She wanted him at home as they needed the income from his highly paid position.

Martha finished her shift and, in the privacy of her car, loosed her anger, nearly howling with rage at what she'd seen. Horrific memories of her own haunting and devastating past flooded her mind. She fought tears, driving blindly through the darkened streets, not seeing passing cars, trees, or bushes.

She tried to blot out the tormented cries of the battered child she'd tended and cried in anguish over things she could not control. "Why, oh why, do I ever work in Pediatrics?" Pain and anger ruled her mind as she barreled her way home, unseeing.

Reaching her house, she pulled into the garage. Once inside, she took comfort in her quiet, well cared for surroundings. Her rage slowly settled. As her thoughts ran wild, she voiced them to that alter personality who dwelt within her mind. "Serena, you want to clip that rotten bastard of a father! I know you do, and so do I!"

She frequently spoke to her alternate personality. At a fearful time in her life, she had sought a psychiatrist. In that office, she had learned a terrible secret from her past. After discovering her alternate self, Serena, Martha faced a continual internal struggle to confront and quell the desires of this other part of herself. Feeling herself the stronger person, Martha managed to ignore her other self for the most part, but after seeing the injustice to that small child, Serena loomed strong again. Martha believed her alter had right on her side and she agreed with her.

Serena, a being with absolutely no consideration for legalities, social mores, or consequences, could easily take action. In the distant past, she'd been the strong one for Martha and it was that impetus that drove her. Right now, Martha felt that commanding presence urging—pushing...

Within her mind, she reasoned, *After all the man can continue to work. What's a little clipping compared to what he's done to Aliya? It'd protect the child and who knows, maybe other kids in that family. He could continue to provide for his family—couldn't he?*

"You stupid, asinine fool!" Martha stared at her reflection in the mirror. "Bob knew your weakness—he warned you!" She sat on the bed trying to get her head straight. "I can't think this way, yet with all my heart, I want to avenge that poor child! Yes, I agree with you, Serena, you wild-hearted thing, but please, leave me and my body the hell alone!"

Martha was tired of dwelling in the past and being unable to sleep. "I need to do something to help me relax and get some sleep."

Getting out of bed, she stepped into the shower. The warmth of the water soothed her tired mind and body.

"Oh Bob, I need you now more than ever. I don't know what will happen to me. I can barely control my thoughts anymore, and when I see a poor soul like that child, I don't even want to." Her rage was soaring. She fought it down and growled again. "I've got to get some sleep and none of your sneaky tricks, Serena"

Martha felt terribly alone after the loss of her husband's big, solid body; his mind; his embrace; and his wonderful, good-hearted sense of humor. He'd had a way of making things right. In fatigue and confusion, Martha fumbled in her purse and helped herself to the mild sedative the doctor had ordered after her husband's death. She justified it, saying, "I've got to get some rest. This whole thing will drive me mad if I don't. After all, it is not up to me to solve all the evils of this world." But she smiled into the darkness with inner satisfaction. *We took care of a few of them when we could, didn't we?*

Martha lay awake going over the trauma of Will's molestation and her subsequent awakening to how her other self had taken care of the perpetrator. "I'll never be the same person I was before Will was attacked! That sick monster paid his price, and I'll never be sorry for what I did as Serena." She sighed and faced the truth. "I have no good reason to go down that road again. It isn't my family that's being harmed. Aliya will be like Will if she survives, and my grandson will never be the same joyous child he used to be because of that hideous gift-that-keeps-on-giving from that soul-destroying pedophile."

When she finally dropped off, Martha slept long and hard. Rising in the morning, she worried her other self might have gotten out again. Checking her image in the bathroom mirror, she saw that her face was clean of errant make-up. And there were no other telltale signs of Serena's activity. "Idiot, there's no way she can do anything I'm not aware of. After all, we *are* one person now."

Martha fully understood that any action she took would be her own, but her alter personality's influence frequently edged her beyond what she would ordinarily do, even encouraging illicit actions. With the full and conscious knowledge that anything she did would be her own responsibility, Martha held back.

She had been able to remain a law-abiding citizen with Bob's steady, calm presence. Losing him had been the toughest time of her life. She'd been brave for him and hidden her heartbreak the best she could, but he was gone now, and she was alone again.

Moping about her empty home after his death, she quickly discovered how easily the world kept right on spinning when hers had come to a screeching halt. Those who'd helped her mourn had quickly returned to their own busy lives. Her daughter Jeanne's problems with Will kept her endlessly embroiled in his recovery. It seemed that as he grew older each day, he also continued to struggle from the trauma of having been brutalized by a sexual predator.

Later in the day, Martha inspected her image in the mirror as she applied her make-up for another afternoon shift. She liked the quieter atmosphere of afternoons. Most of the doctors had gone home, orders were done, and the work atmosphere was generally more settled.

A grandmother, maybe, but Martha was a bit proud of her looks. A tall, slender woman with chestnut-hued hair softly curling about her collar, she'd always been considered a looker by her co-workers. Bob had always loved her looks, her great green eyes, everything about her, and he's said so often.

Seeing the lackluster look in her eyes, she grumped, "People say I'm nice looking, but what good has it ever done me?" The small nub at the end of her nose had always bothered her, but fit the rest of her well enough. "My heart is barely into what I do these days, either." Work usually brought her out of her funk so she told her mirror, "I'd better take a couple of shifts."

Most co-workers knew of and respected her sorrow, but the work did not. In a hospital, there could be no sorrows other than the patients'. They came first, and no one questioned that. Martha worked per diem as always and frequented several areas, preferring med-surg. She often worked psych, postpartum, neuro, respiratory, ortho, or wherever the hospital needed her skills and enjoyed the liberty of cancelling shifts as well. Not taking a regular shifts, five days a week, gave her the freedom for other aspects of her life. Right now, short on things to occupy her mind, she welcomed the hard work of nursing.

By habit, she overtly watched for abuse. The occasional adult abuse the nurses saw didn't set off that internal anger like that of the young. Eyes of children shadowed with pain, mistrust, and hopelessness tore her heart out. For Martha, it was too close to home.

CHAPTER 2

One reasonably quiet afternoon, Martha found the young nurse, Judith Munson, crying quietly in the med room where she'd found a moment of privacy. "What's wrong, Judith?" Looking closer under the thin scarf the woman wore, Martha cried, "My God, you've got those bruises around your neck, again!"

"Again," Judith gulped. "You've seen them before and never said a thing, haven't you?" Huge tears coursed down her cheeks as she begged, "Oh, please, don't pass it around that my husband is a miserable, rotten bastard. I don't know where to turn anymore." Her darkened hazel-shaded eyes were reddened. She dried her tears, but her streaked make-up and tear-reddened eyes were a dead giveaway. "I didn't want anyone to know."

Martha smiled as she rearranged the thin, gauzy material around Judith's neck and handed her a tissue. "Here, wipe your eyes and nose. Your face is a mess, too, and if you don't want anyone to know, you might want to keep that discolored neck hidden while you're at it." A surge of anger at this evidence of physical abuse flared, but with long years of practice, she hid it as she fussed with Judith's scarf.

"I don't know what to do. I can't go back there tonight. I just can't!"

"You don't *ever* have to put up with brutality like that," Martha fumed. An idea formed. "You have children at home?"

"No, thank God, we never managed that." Judith blew out a breath. "I'm glad, now that I've finally realized what a son-of-a-bitch I married. It's only been three years, but the last six months have really been tough. I don't know why I'm telling you this, but it helps, somehow." She sniffed back her tears. "I know you've lost your husband and have your own problems." Her eyes dried, and she began working on her make-up with a small mirror from her purse. "I wanted to come to the services that day, but he wouldn't let me leave the house."

"Why not come to my house and spend the night?" Martha found it easy to ask. She'd always liked this good nurse, though she only knew her in passing. Whoever knew what went on in someone else's life? She shook her head at the cruel realities. "I'm alone now and have tons of room to spare."

"If it wouldn't make trouble for you, I'd be glad to stay with you, at least for the night. But I have to warn you, if Marvin finds out where I am, he'll be in a hideous rage." She managed a sheepish smile. "But what else is new?" She hugged Martha. "Thanks. If I don't get these meds out, I'll be in trouble here, too, and I don't need that." She went about her work with a lighter step and shoulders straighter.

For some reason, Martha felt better, too. *Now what am I getting myself into? When that enraged man finds out where his wife is, there could be hell to pay.* Her inner self merely smiled at that prospect. Serena feared nothing and, these days, Martha shared those benefits, whether good or not.

Let the bastard try! *If he runs afoul of Serena, he'll certainly deserve what that soul-less miscreant has to offer.* She laughed at her thoughts, hoping no one heard her. It was an evening shift and Martha was endlessly busy with new post ops to stabilize and incidentals that always occurred. Vomiting to clean up, bloody dressings to change, medications to measure and give, kept Martha's mind off Judith's problems and, she realized with relief, her problems as well. She mulled it over in her mind. *Could be this situation of meddling in people's private affairs will bring big trouble into my life. But frankly, I don't care what her bastard husband tries.*

Martha frequently talked to herself, but only in her head, not wanting to sound like she'd lost her marbles. Some of her coworkers believed she hadn't completed her mourning and they might think she'd totally flipped out. She couldn't help a giggle at that idea. *If they only knew the real truth about crazy ol' double me.*

After the shift ground to a halt, Judith followed Martha home. "Put your car in the garage," Martha said. "With the door closed he won't find you by driving past." She'd given Bob's truck to her son-in-law and had room for another vehicle. "Does anyone at work know you're staying with me tonight?"

"No, I never mention personal things at work. If people see my bruises, they never say anything."

"They do think things—there's been some talk," Martha replied. "I've heard it."

Judith parked her car inside the garage and followed Martha into her house. Seeing the comfortable, warm interior, she heaved a sigh and flopped into Bob's big leather chair. "I can't thank you enough for this, Martha. We don't know each other very well, but I've always respected your work." She threw out her hands. "I don't want to bring trouble to you, but I'm afraid that's just what will happen if he finds me here. I'm worried about that. He follows me sometimes, too." She sighed. "He may have followed me tonight. I'm not sure what to do anymore."

"Are you saying that you're returning to him?" Martha looked at the young woman sitting before her. She was tall and shapely with bright gold-blonde hair and deep dark hazel eyes. *She really is a dish, to use an old fashioned term. The man must be an idiot to screw up his marriage with someone like her.*

"It's actually my house we're living in and I don't plan on giving that up. I'd like to divorce him, but he's threatened me several times with death or worse, if I try it. The police aren't any help—unless he kills me." Judith grimaced. "Wouldn't be a lot of help to me then, would it?"

"You've got a dilemma," Martha agreed. "Let's have tea and a snack."

She worked to lighten the mood and ease Judith's tenseness. The woman looked like a rubber band stretched to the limit. And Martha, tired from a solid eight hours at work, didn't feel like coping with tears.

"Yeah, sure. You're really a cool one, Martha. Please understand that I worry what you could face, taking me in, even for one lousy night."

Judith looked like she wanted to start crying again. Martha deflected it by sending her to the freezer to dig out some frozen sweets. *Maybe it'll cool her off.* She smiled to herself as she made the tea. *Am I a heartless bitch, or what?*

Sitting at the kitchen table, nibbling away at frozen biscotti and sipping tea, Judith visibly relaxed. So Martha decided to question her. "So what does your husband do for a living?" Somehow she needed to know more about this man because, unwillingly, an idea had formed in her mind.

"He's an investment counselor, or broker, or some-thing. He works for a large firm in downtown Denver, the

High Street Brokerage Firm." She shrugged. "He never tells me anything. I have no idea why he's so secretive about what he does. I really don't care anymore. He's an abusive heel, and I want out."

"Mmm," Martha mused. "Does he have family? You ever see or meet any of his friends or co-workers—at all?"

"If he has a family anywhere, it'd be news to me. It's like he popped out of the woodwork and into my life one day. We go to a few parties, Christmas, New Years, things like that, where he needs a wife on his arm. Well, if I haven't got too many obvious bruises." She winced. "I'm not close to any of the people who work there, and I've never heard of or met any family members." Judith looked intently at Martha. "Why do you ask?"

"There may be a way to help you in all this. No woman needs to put up with spousal abuse, mental or physical." Martha meant what she said and knew that no man would try to abuse her, in any case. She wasn't the type.

"I'd be afraid to face him in court, Martha. You have no idea how evil he is. No one he works with would believe it either. He said he'd kill me or, worse yet, scar me for life in some way. He's already made those threats, mentioning sulfuric acid. Wouldn't *that* stuff leave a hideous face?" Tears formed in her eyes. "What if he blinds me?" Her face went white.

"Scar you? He threatened that?" Martha couldn't prevent a sly chuckle and knew it was more Serena than herself.

"How can you laugh?" Judith cried. "It's abominable! If I try to leave him, that's his main threat and I'm terrified he'll do it."

"Don't you ever wonder how he'd feel if *he* woke up one morning with an ugly scar?" Martha asked. "Wouldn't it be justice?"

"My God, woman, what are you talking about?"

"Oh, just a wandering thought. I get so sick of hearing about abuse—kids, women, animals—you name it. It's always someone that won't fight back or is too weak to defend themselves. The bastards know they can get away with it." Martha sighed then added, "You know full well, people like that are nothing but cowards and bullies."

"You're right and I do know it. I guess he knew what a stupid wimp I was when he courted me so passionately, and, oh, so lovingly. He must have needed a new punching bag—the dirty bastard!" Judith smiled at that comment herself. "What a damned fool I am. I fell for it like a fish for a baited hook."

Martha silently applauded the anger rising in Judith's face, the tightened jaw and narrowing of her eyes. "Well, enough chatter. Think you'll be able to sleep tonight? If not, I have a pill or two to help with that."

"Thanks, my nerves are shot and I can't even think about tomorrow. I have to go back there. Yes, I'll take something and be glad to get it." Judith accepted a couple of mild sedatives. She smiled to see what they were. "Hum, *diphenhydrinate*, no narcs—good idea."

Martha showed her the bedroom and connecting shower. "You can decide in the morning if you're strong enough to go home. You're welcome to stay here longer if you need to. I'd be glad for the company, actually. It's beyond lonely with Bob gone."

"Gosh, thanks, Martha. I'll think about it and let you know. You know, I can't believe I've become such a miserable coward. I've never been this way. At first, he fills your mind with guilt that, somehow, it's all your fault," she went on, almost lost in thought. "The whole thing creeps up on you while you still think you love the guy." With a pensive grin, she shrugged her shoulders and wrinkled her brow in confusion. "What a mess my life has become," she said and closed the door to the second bedroom.

Martha lay awake. The words she'd heard had struck her with an idea. The man threatened a scarred face, if Judith tried to leave him. "He did, eh? I can think of a good way to put out this man's fire."

Martha usually relived the memories of Bob's last days before she found sleep, but less frequently as time wore on, and the pain had softened with the remembering. It was long before she found release in sleep. When she did, wild dreams filled her restless slumber for long hours during the night, and she tossed and turned in turmoil.

ᘓᘔᘓ

When Martha got up, she looked at her torn and twisted bedding in wonder. "What went on in my head last night? If it was something good, I wish I'd been a part of it and knew what it was. I need a lift."

She threw on a robe, ran her fingers through her hair, and put on a pot of coffee. The house was quiet with the sun barely inching up. Martha heard a faint noise and turned. Judith stood in the kitchen door.

"Good morning," Martha said, greeting the sleepy-eyed blonde. "I hope you were able to sleep."

"Actually, I slept like a baby, considering all I've got to face when I go home today. And I *am* going home, Martha. I've decided that much. It's *my* home and thank God, I never put his name on the title, so no problem there." She sighed. "Getting him out without his killing me, cutting me with razor blades, or throwing acid in my face, that's my problem."

"Why don't you set some recording devices around the house in places? You could get some choice evidence that way. You might need it one day. It'd come in handy for your divorce."

"Wouldn't the folks in his office get a kick out of hearing one of his tirades? How embarrassing would that be?" Judith uttered a hollow little laugh. "If only I could manage something like that. It'd serve him right."

Martha wanted to say, *And why can't you?* But she only asked, "Think you'll be okay going home today?" She worried more about Judith's survival than Judith did. What was the fool woman thinking? "Will he be there? Doesn't he work during the day?"

"If he wants to, he does. I guess he's successful enough to make his own hours. He could be there when I get home." Judith's face turned ashen. "I hope he won't be—I don't think I could face that man today."

"Call me and let me know how it goes." Martha looked deep into Judith's darkened hazel eyes, and silently wondered, *Will I see this woman alive again?* "You will call, won't you?" she asked again.

"Yes. I'll keep you up to date. Someone needs to know the truth and now *you* do. If anything happens to me, at least someone will know why."

She left via the garage door and Martha closed it after her. A sickness rose within her imagining the hell Judith faced in going back to her home. Was she brave? No, Martha didn't think so. For some unholy reason, the abused seem to reach out for the abuse, knowingly or unknowingly. Judith had never eaten her breakfast, either.

"What an ugly puzzle it is." Off duty today, she had time to let her mind wander lazily about a suitable revenge for a man like Judith's husband, Norman Munson. "Am I becoming an increasingly vengeful person these days?" she asked, continuing her thoughts. "And against those who've never hurt me or mine."

It's you, Serena, you're completely unprincipled and care nothing about legalities. I feel your insidious pulling at me, I always do. She laughed. *So what've you figured out about Judith's husband? How about a few scars for him, definitely one that shows*! Martha laughed again and felt better than she had in weeks. Forgetting for a while about her own losses made her feel normal for a change. She decided life still had a few good things to offer.

Feeling a burst of enthusiasm and energy, she decided she'd better get back to the gym and tone up. *For some reason I feel there's important work ahead of me and I'll need every ounce of strength I've got.* Bursting out in a laugh that was not entirely her own, she headed for the shower.

Later that afternoon, resting from the strenuous effort she'd made at the gym, Martha sat with her feet propped up, enjoying her favorite soap opera. The phone jangled and she picked it up. "Hello?"

It was Judith. "He caught me in the house and nearly killed me," she sobbed. "I don't know what to do."

Hearing the misery in her new friend's voice, Martha said, "Judith dear, come back over here. You can stay with me again."

"What if he follows me?"

"Hey! I don't care if he follows you. Believe me, I don't. Just get over here!" Martha assured her before they hung up.

The Serena part of her laughed in excitement. *The bastard caught her in the house and nearly killed her, did he? He'll need a lesson or two, won't he?*

Martha opened the garage and shortly the newly battered Judith pulled in. Martha gasped at her bloodied face as she limped into the house.

"Girl, you need the ER. Look at your face." Martha helped her to a chair, Bob's big soft leather one, and watched Judith painfully curl herself in to it.

Tears mixed with blood streamed down Judith's face. "I guess I should go in, but its superficial stuff. I don't think I need stitches. I'd rather no one knew what happened, Martha. I'd really like to keep this quiet."

Martha handed her a box of tissues while she went for her first aid kit. After numerous repairs, the bleeding stopped and ointment was applied, along with a few steri-strips and several dressings. Martha relaxed. Judith, sighed, said nothing, and appeared deep in thought. Martha despaired of this young woman ever having the courage to take action against her battering husband.

"It will help in your divorce if you have this documented, Judith. A doctor's report would be admissible as evidence in court, and your husband would have the embarrassment of it, too." Martha felt like a nag trying to get Judith to do something, anything, about this deadly situation.

"What good is that if I'm dead, Martha. You don't know him. The man's insane—I swear to God he is. He wasn't that way at first, but over the last six months I've come to believe he's either schizophrenic, maniac depressive, or something else. He laughed at me for suggesting he had a problem." She threw out her hands in futility. "He won't seek treatment, either."

"Maybe it's time for a bit of operant conditioning." Martha breathed the words with deadly meaning, thinking of how animals and people were trained by purposeful events happening to them. "I believe I have a great idea. You can stay here for as long as you like. I can help you that way at least." She winced and tried to soften what she had inadvertently said—and shouldn't have. Judith knew what operant condition was since it was in the course of study for nursing as well as a host of other classes.

"Aren't you afraid of him finding me here?"

With those words, Martha realized Judith hadn't heard or processed her statement about operant conditioning, and she heaved a sigh. "No, I'm not. No man would ever dare touch me that way. He wouldn't even try it," she went on. "People are different, Judith. Munson knew who to tie up with. Abusers always seem to. They seek out the meek and gentle, someone they can terrify and brutalize. He wouldn't have asked me for a second date."

"You're very wise, Martha. I wish I was more like you, and maybe I can be, if I ever get out of this mess." Her tears had dried. "Thanks again. You can't imagine what it means to me, finding a friend like you. You just can't!"

It grew dark. Martha called into work and scheduled herself off for an unspecified time. "I'll give you a call," she told the staffing secretary.

She made a soft meal for Judith and they ate together.

"I need more clothes but I can't go back there any time soon," Judith said.

"Don't worry, we'll make out. I'll find you enough to wear. You're not planning on going anywhere are you? Not for a while, anyway, the way you're banged up. We're close enough in size, I'll find something for you."

Judith uttered a painful laugh. "No, I have no plans, and thanks for the offer of clothes. I'm tired and worn out from this nightmare life of mine. I'd like to go to bed, sleep for a hundred years, and put it out of my mind." She went into the same bedroom and closed the door.

CHAPTER 3

Martha settled to watch a bit of TV but kept the sound very low, listening for sounds outside the house. She believed they'd have a visitor. One who searched for his favorite punching bag—his wife. She fought against her rising anger at a man who would treat any woman that way, especially one he'd vowed to love, honor, and protect. If he came pounding on her door, she'd be polite, oh, so innocent, and he'd never guess her hidden agenda.

Several vehicles drove by, but nothing happened. No one pounded angrily on her door. She slipped outside to see one who drove by in a nice white Escalade pickup and chuckled at the small, rather ridiculous, bed attached to the back. She believed it to be Judith's husband since she'd noted it passing the house very slowly with the driver looking intently at the house. If it'd gone by earlier, she hadn't seen it but decided Munson now had the place staked out. No surprise there.

After watching for a long time and seeing no further Escalades pass by, Martha decided Judith's husband had given up for the night. Unable to sleep, she decided on another plan.

Martha left several lights on in the house and, while her guest slept the night away, drove toward another part of Denver. She felt a good bit of curiosity about the home the husband wanted to take from Judith. After learning the address, she decided to take a look. *Maybe I'll catch a glimpse of him*, she thought then scoffed. "Then again, he might still decide to pay me a call if I've screwed up his marital battering. Meanwhile, I've got to see where this lady comes from."

As she had thought, this part of the city was definitely upscale. The home was located in Windsor Hills, a nicer section of Denver. When she found the place, it looked downright palatial. Judith hadn't said anything to indicate wealth on this scale, and that aroused a few questions in Martha's mind. "Makes a person wonder why she slaves away as a nurse. I'd say she didn't need to work at all. No figuring that one."

There won't be any sneaking about a home like that, Martha decided. "They might keep Dobermans for watch dogs behind that big iron fence. If anything happens to Munson at this home, it'd be taken as an act of vandalism or a home invasion." She drove home determined to know more about the man. *Maybe a computer check?*

Back home at her computer, Martha mulled the information over in her mind. *Marvin Munson, investments and securities, it says.* "I wonder if he works out at a gym somewhere. Maybe he sleeps around during his day at work. A lot to think about. It'll take a closer check on this bird," Martha sighed and went to bed.

໑໑໑

Judith stayed at Martha's. She slowly healed and began to relax—unless she heard a certain type of vehicle pass by. At those times, Martha would see her face blanch white and her hands clench in fear. Martha, on the other hand, was busy furthering her research on Munson.

With all the time she spent on the internet and moving about town, Martha began to feel more like a private eye than any other professional. She learned that Munson did indeed have a love interest. She happened upon that fact accidentally as she followed his Escalade to an underground parking area of a posh set of luxury condos. "Wow!" she exclaimed. "You need a code to enter this setup and I don't have one." She didn't try, but instead, laughed aloud. "There are other ways."

She decided to deliver flowers, as though from a nearby florist. She pulled out her lap top and punched in the address. Many names popped up. She tried to imagine which would be single females. How about this one: Poppy Montmorency? Sounds tarty enough. Could she be the one?

Martha took time to change her appearance. She opened the trunk of her car and hauled out her bag of tricks. Later, a blonde, heavy set woman went to the Daisy Fresh Florist and bought a bouquet of mixed flowers. With the posies in hand, she walked to the front lobby. Dressed in frumpy slacks, she attempted to enter the *Villas Capistrano Grande* luxury condominiums.

She met a guard who questioned her. "Are you one of our residents?"

"No, sir, I'm here to deliver these flowers to a Ms. Montmorency." He was about to make a comment when Martha added, "If you'd care to make the delivery, that'd work for me." She offered the bouquet to the man.

"That'd be penthouse number four, ma'am." He indicated the bank of elevators. Martha thanked him and took the first one that opened. Inside, she punched several floors up to the penthouse level, but got off on the fifth.

Tossing the flowers in the nearest trash can, she went down the stairs to the garage and sought a white Escalade with a small truck bed on the back. She had no real plans at the moment, but, after finding the vehicle, she made a decision. "Well, how about a nice calling card?" She pulled out an ice pick and punctured every tire, not once, but several times.

After climbing several sets of stairs, she took an elevator down and walked out of the fancy apartment complex of Munson's paramour, or she hoped it was. If not, poor Norman would have a few flats to fix in the morning or whenever he resumed his cloak of faithful husband.

Martha felt elated she'd done even this little bit.

It's not like a good clipping, but it's a start.

"Shut up, Serena."

Her other self, not satisfied with a few flat tires, believed it wasn't enough.

♥♥♥

One week later, Martha saw Marvin escorting a slim, elegant brunette into a secluded bistro, Andrei's Hideaway. Martha entered and requested a quiet, tabled nook. Slipping a small handful of bills to the young lady who seated her, she was placed near the errant couple. Martha poured over her menu, straining her ears to overhear any commentary from the cozy duo.

As they took a light meal, Martha listened in disbelief to their conversation. "Honey, as soon as I get rid of that sick bitch that's torturing me half to death, we can plan our lives together," Munson complained to his dining companion. "Judith had nothing until we married and now she wants everything. Every damned thing I've got—all of it! I've slaved away all these years and now that damned, greedy bitch wants to clean me out." He took the woman's hand. "I can't wait for us to be together. God! You are *so* damned hot!"

"Oh, Marvin honey, you mustn't do anything too rash!" the woman said, obviously voicing the fear that he'd get in trouble.

She also heard in the woman's hopeful voice, the timidity and subservience of a potential victim. This foolish girl, in her eagerness to take Judith's place in Munson's life, was in the process of committing a grave mistake. *Great going, Munson, another one waiting in the wings.* Martha listened in shock, hearing his sorry tale of woe. *That poor fool doesn't know the deep pit of hell she's looking at. This bastard is planning a convenient little accident for Judith one day soon. Sure sounds that way.*

"Would you excuse me for a few minutes while I check on my make-up?" the woman asked, and Martha heard the soft, well-modulated, yet plaintive sounds in her voice.

While the woman visited the powder room, Munson took out his cell phone. "Hey, how're things coming? Good God! You haven't even located the bitch yet? I told you where she's staying. What the hell more do you need?" He muttered, listened, then snarled, "You'd better, you bastard. I'm paying you enough!" He hung up quickly before his dinner companion returned.

Martha soon exited the restaurant and returned home. "He's planning something for you," she told Judith. "And it's not a nice surprise party. You need to find a new place. You're not safe here anymore."

"Oh God! What's he planning, and how did you find out about it?"

"He's hired someone to do something to you. I found out that much." Martha huffed in disgust. "He has a new fool on the string right now and he's keeping her in fine style, a snazzy penthouse suite, at that. The woman's just waiting until you're out of the picture," she added. "This new little cutie will make a nice new punching bag by the sound of her."

"Poor thing! I don't even know who she is and I pity her already," Judith said. "Marvin wants my house. He has from the beginning when we first started dating. He couldn't stop looking it over and commenting on how much he liked the layout. He's practically measured the rooms and ordered curtains! It's been in our family for years. He conned me into signing away my cousin's rights if I should die. My family died in a plane crash about six years ago. I have no one close but the one cousin, and I hardly know her." She stared at Martha in horror. "Oh, God! He wants me dead, doesn't he? In an accidental way, a few bruises and broken bones would fit right in, wouldn't they?" Her body shaking, she managed the last bit with a tremor in her voice. "But you know, I didn't put it in his name. Something told me not to." With a new look of horror, she added, "But as a survivor, he'd inherit my home anyway. Yes. He would, wouldn't he?"

Martha watched Judith's small hands curl into fists. Seeing that, she realized there was a tiny spark of survival left within the woman. "You should have gone to the ER when he first beat the hell out of you. You'd have absolute proof of his treatment of you then. No wonder he made those threats to disfigure you. No woman wants that. It'd be worse than death."

"What a damned fool I've been. If it wasn't for you, Martha, he'd already have been successful—he would have." She moved to the edge of her chair. "So what's next?" Her face had gone white and she sat there wringing her hands. "Where can I go now and be safe from Marvin?"

"Well, for one thing. Don't go back to work. He could certainly find you there. By the looks of your home, you don't really need to, do you?" Martha chuckled at the thought of anyone who owned such a wonderful home needing to work.

"Sure, I can stop working. I only work for socializing. I like being around a busy hospital, always did. I needed to get out. It's really lonely being the only one left in your entire family. Maybe that's why I was such an easy mark for a guy like Munson."

"Well now, that's not the only reason. Have you looked in the mirror lately? You're a very fine looking woman. Any man would take that second look," Martha told her encouragingly. "So you got the wrong guy. Don't be afraid to jump in and take another swim in the dating pool. I did when I met Bob and I thought I was through with men forever." She laughed, remembering her late husband fondly. "That man wouldn't take no for an answer, no matter how hard I tried to hold him off."

Martha had already decided she couldn't let Judith know about her second self. It was not a good idea to let people know about Serena.

"I'm sure you're right," Judith agreed. "But if I ever marry again, I'll be a lot more leery. It didn't take much for Munson to con me into marriage, and since I've been involved with him, any attempt I've made at having my own friends has been a disaster. He makes a point of being abrupt and short with them." She tossed her head. "They soon feel uncomfortable and never come back. Of course, I didn't want anyone from work to see that in my life, either." She smiled at Martha. "It turned out so good for you, I might think about it someday. That is, if I get myself out of the fix I'm in now—" Judith stopped speaking, peeking out the edge of a drape. Her face reflected the fear and horror she felt. "Martha, he's outside this house! He's coming to the door!"

"The devil, if he isn't. I'm calling the police. He could be armed for all we know." She called 9-1-1 and explained the situation to the operator. Switched to the nearest police station she had to explain everything all over again. After becoming three shades of frustrated, she turned to Judith. "The patrol car is on its way here now. Stay out of sight."

At the hammering sounds on her door, Martha swung it open part way, keeping the chain attached. She saw a big, solidly built man, with ruddy features. His irate look confirmed who he was. "Yes, may I help you?"

"You know a Judith Munson?"

"I do. I work with her." Martha stood firm behind her door. "If you're her husband, you need to know I have a patrol car on the way over. She's suffered enough at your hands, you brute. I've seen her cuts and bruises. You might want to hop in that fancy Escalade of yours, move on out of here, and be quick about it."

"Go to hell, lady! She's my wife and I need her at home. What the hell ever happened to 'until death do us part,' anyway?" His faced reddened further with his increased anger and frustration. "She's my wife!" His huge fists were clenched tight and Martha knew he was ready to knock her door in.

"Suit yourself, but you're not getting inside this house." Martha felt rage at this brutal man, but she hid it well and shrugged. "You'd better get out of here, Mr. Munson." She'd decided to be the meek little friend with no vengeful attributes to be remembered.

At the sound of sirens, Munson hurriedly jumped into his Escalade and, after a glance at her that would melt an iron girder, he sped quickly away.

"You lousy coward," Martha scoffed at the departing vehicle. "All batterers are basically cowards and you fit that pattern."

The two police officers came in. Martha introduced Judith and, together, they explained the situation to the police. Viewing what remained of her injuries, they made a detailed report. Then they took several photos of her fading bruises and healing cuts. "Ma'am, would you want protective surveillance? We could order it for you. For sure you need to get a restraining order against your husband."

"No—I think I'll be okay. He's a lot of hot air most of the time." Her tone was so offhand that Martha could only stare at her, finding it difficult to believe Judith would refuse police protection if it was available.

After the officers left, Martha exclaimed, "What's the matter with you? Why won't you let them help you?"

"Munson knows his way around every city official in Denver. Just how far do you think I'd get with a restraining order? My father was a big time lawyer and I know how things work down there. My husband's got his hand in every pocket that's open for a few extra bucks. Believe me, it goes on around there, big time." She looked at Martha, her features stricken with fear. "I'll find another place to hide, but I'd appreciate your help in that, too."

"I'm thinking." Martha wracked her brain trying to think of a place of safety for Judith. She thought of a certain gentleman and nodded. "I do have an idea." She chuckled. "How about returning home, not on your own, of course, but with a bodyguard. I know a guy who can more than handle that loving hubby of yours."

Martha remembered an old friend of Bob's, a body builder, Navy SEAL, and an all-around-mean son-of-a-bitch, especially if his protective instincts were aroused. He'd been a patient for GI surgery and Martha had come to highly respect the man. She knew him as a tough, independent-thinking sort, and a friend Bob had known from his Navy days. She'd met him several times. Duke Mason might be willing to take on this little operation. She was sure the man was unemployed and knew him to be a gentle giant sort of guy with the feminine gender.

Martha laid out the plan. "If you're willing, I'll make a call."

"Wow! Okay, go ahead. Maybe a big, old, Rambo kind of guy is what I need. Hired guts, if you will, since I don't seem to have any of my own. Marvin scares me way too much."

Martha picked up her cell, called Duke, and explained the set up. She'd last seen Duke at Bob's funeral and he'd been idle. Actually, he'd seen enough combat in his military years, that he'd had a tough time holding a job. This was especially true in the modern "politically correct" climate so prevalent of late. Too many scenarios simply made no real sense to his action-trained mind.

"He's coming over," Martha said when she hung up. "Wants to see what he'd be getting into with a job like this."

"Oh, my God!" Judith said. "What'll happen next? I'd better fix up a bit."

Martha detected a certain amount of excitement in her words, along with rising hope she might have an answer to her fearful dilemma.

CHAPTER 4

They waited with as much patience as the situation allowed until the doorbell rang. Martha opened the door to admit a tall, rangy dude with rugged features. A touch of gray streaked through his short sandy hair. The jeans and black shirt he wore clung to a lean, muscular body that appeared to be made of tough, dried leather.

"Hey, Duke, come on in," Martha said in greeting. She led him into the living room where Judith rose slowly from her chair and stood there looking at him, trying to take in the sight of this big, rough-hewn male. "Meet Judith Munson, the lady I mentioned to you over the phone," Martha continued as she watched him enclose Judith's small hand in his huge paw.

"Hi-ya," he said, his voice soft and low.

Then his face reddened a bit. Martha thought he likely hadn't expected a beaten and battered woman to be this well put together. And Judith, somewhat overcome by his huge male presence, couldn't take her eyes off him. His size threatened her. Martha readily saw that, but the warmth in his eyes rapidly overcame any apprehension Judith may have felt.

"Uh—I guess you weren't expecting a job offer like this one," she managed to say.

Martha noticed a flush, working upward through the healing bruises along Judith's jaw line, and smiled at the trembling of her extended hand, still clasped in Duke's. His pale blues continued to appraise the slender, blonde woman who stood before him. "Well, ma'am, no I didn't, but it sounds mighty interesting. Never could stomach a man who'd savage a woman that way, never could."

Martha found herself enjoying the encounter between the two. She also wondered how Marvin Munson would respond to this big, tough man living in his home and guarding his wife. *I'd love to be a fly on the wall for this one.* She laughed quietly. *What justice! Serena, you haven't had to do a thing. There are other ways—though not as much fun for the likes of you, girl.*

After Judith had left with her Iron Man, the house was lonely, but Martha had the time to think about things. She wondered how Ryan Mapus would see this latest event. Her last chat with the Detective Mapus, of Colorado Springs, had helped clear the air. Her crimes were committed against pedophiles and he'd declined to prosecute. She'd have been hailed as a heroine and the police cast as villains should he have tried to imprison her.

Martha was a different person now. Something had changed inside her. Was it possible a part of her had become Serena, no longer hidden away and unknown? Did she really care what Mapus would think? No, not anymore.

℘℘℘

The house seemed unusually quiet with Judith and her bodyguard gone. Awaiting news from her, Martha found life boring. She paced about the house like a felon in a prison yard until she pulled out her cell and pressed a button.

"Jeannie?"

"Oh, hi, Mom. What's up?"

"I just called to see how things are with you folks, and Will."

"We're all fine, I guess. I was just coming to see you, as a matter of fact."

"Oh, I'm glad you're coming over. See you in a few."

She hung up, made a pot of coffee, and got out a few biscotti. Her daughter liked them, too.

Jeannie rang the doorbell and Martha ushered her slim, fine-looking daughter into the house. "So how's everyone? I worry so much about Will—things any better with him, these days?" She tried to keep worry from her voice, but her daughter's troubled face only made her angry all over again.

"Oh, Mom, he'll never be our sweet little boy again. No matter how many sessions he has with the therapist. I see a different, dark little soul. It's in his eyes." Tears escaped and ran down her cheeks. "What you did to that devil was too good for him, I know that now, and Will wasn't his first either. You know what they found when they got his records from Pittsburgh or wherever. The man was a monster, though not as bad as his buddy, Denny."

"I know, honey. I swear I've never had the slightest regret over having done the things I did. It ought to be legal instead of a crime. It ought to!" Martha felt the thirst for vengeance rise within her. She realized all over again the frightening knowledge that Serena was indeed a good part of her, and she had grown stronger. She held those things back from Jeannie—her daughter didn't need to know about it. Jeanne had her own troubles with helping her son become a normal child and grow into a fine young man.

Will had become a known trouble maker at school from the beginning. In Kindergarten he'd broken all the rules. The next year, he'd been caught looking up little girls' skirts and nearly expelled. This behavior continued in spite of all the counseling he'd had. The entire family realized that he'd never be the same child. Will had been molested by an adult male. A crime that had destroying effects on an innocent child's very soul, be they male or female!

"It tears me up inside, knowing how easily these monsters get away with their crimes," Martha lamented. "With Bob gone, it seems closer to me, like it's all coming back."

"Mom! You can't let *that* get started again. You just can't."

"Of course not, Jeannie. Bob warned me about that on our last night together. He said I'd end up in prison." Martha laughed it off and served her daughter a cup of coffee. "Want a biscotti—anything?"

"No, and I can't stay long, either. Martin and I have another meeting at the school about Will." She looked at her Mother, eyes brimming, "I'm afraid for him. What'll he become as he gets older? We're scared to death, thinking about his future." Tears continued close to the surface of her big blue eyes and Martha's heart broke all over again for her daughter and her family.

"Makes you want to go out and cut the balls off everyone on that predator list, doesn't it? But no, we can't, they're *protected* and coddled by our laws!" Martha heard her own voice rise to a higher pitch, definitely a direct result of her internal desire to avenge all children who suffered as Will did.

"Mother! You sound too much like someone we both know is dangerous. Are you sure you're really okay?"

Jeannie's worried face made Martha regret her words and she retrenched, laughing. "Don't worry. Serena and I converse very often and she's under tight control. I know it

sounds nutty, but that's the way it goes when you are cursed with an inner being—well, for me anyway." Uttering a
light-hearted laugh, she tried to dispel Jeannie's worries.

"Mom, on another, and lighter, subject—I just have to
ask. Did you and Bob ever go to any sleazy dives around
here in Denver, you know, like The Paradisio?" Curiosity
in her eyes, she giggled.

"Jeannie, I have no idea of the sort of local watering
holes around here. And why bring that up? It wasn't really
me that did those things, you know that. Besides, it nearly
got me killed." She shrugged and shook her head. "And no,
Bob and I had no need to be looking for a place like that
sick dive, The Paradisio." She tried to sound indignant but
burst into a laugh. "You can't imagine the things that go on
in a place like that. Sometimes I wonder about Serena, why
she is the way she is—sort of slutty to my thinking."

Martha found she could laugh about that time in her
life, but she supposed she should feel ashamed. *If I'm not,
it's due to you, Serena, you unprincipled hag!* She'd always been able to converse with her inner self, Serena,
once they'd been brought together by the psychiatrists in
Colorado Springs. It was strange indeed, but her daughter
didn't need to know that either.

After Jeannie took her leave, Martha's deep worry
over Will held her in constant agony. She feared all over
again that Will's predator had scored a permanent hit on
that poor family. She was disgusted with the legal system,
knowing that in general, child predators spent less time
behind bars than a young, stupid pot smoker, and those ignorant kids were only hurting themselves.

With nothing else going on, Martha called staffing.
"What have you available for this evening?"

"Bored, huh? Well, come on in. I'll put you to work.
What floor do you want?"

"Anything but peds."

"Okay, we'll put you in ortho."

Martha laughed. "Thanks, Frannie, you're a doll."

Martha arrived at the hospital and took her assignment to orthopedics for the evening shift. She knew some of the staff there and looked forward to working with those patients who were basically healthy. They usually needed repair of worn joints or had sustained broken bones from accidents and the like.

She sat in the report room taking report. Hearing the name Aliya Pederson made her heart stop. Sick inside, she listened to the details of the savagely beaten little girl. Her broken bones were in casts and the child was being cared for in this specialty area before being transferred back to peds.

Martha knew some of Aliya's history from her previous admission. The father was at it again. The report said her injuries were from falling all the way down the steps into the basement. *Basement? Who in Denver even had one?*

Martha muttered under her breath. "Serena, you have some *real* work to do, and it's right up your alley." In a louder voice, she asked, "Does Child Protective Services ever even bother to get their asses out of the office and into some of these homes anymore?"

She jerked her head up as charge nurse, Susan Mitchell asked a question. "What was that, Martha? Do you know this child?"

"Not really, but I've heard the name mentioned on another ward, once. Some say the father has a history of child abuse. It made me wonder about these new injuries."

"We've had a few ideas about this case as well, but we cannot make assumptions unless we have the facts, now can we? The proper authorities have checked it out and believe the report from the family in this matter." Susan was politically correct to the letter and her tightly drawn lips told Martha the subject was closed as she turned her blonde head to answer a question from another nurse.

Martha kept her eyes and ears open during her shift, and hearing the terrified little child crying out, "No—fraid—no, fraid," tended to confirm her dark suspicions. But she kept her own counsel and completed her shift of drains, dressings, and pain coverage.

Leaving the hospital, Martha drove past the home of the Pederson's. She'd looked it up on the child's chart and it was nearby. It looked to be an upscale middle class residential home. "The man must keep a decent job to afford a nice home like this one, and seven children, too."

She felt her rage at a father, who would torture his little daughter, rising into a manic, swirling, inferno. Her need to avenge the child drove her nearly into a frenzy. *Down, Serena, you need time and planning for this job. How strange it is to be completely conscious of plotting to commit a criminal act and feeling absolutely no remorse at the thought of it.* "Serena, you are so very much a conscious part of me."

ᏋᎧᏋᎧ

Several nights later Martha/Serena, dressed as a street bum, moved slowly along the street where the Pederson family resided. She saw a long, low, ranch-style home with shake shingles and a three car garage. The landscaping and shrubbery were immaculate, as was the general appearance of the house. If they owned a dog, she didn't see it outside or any other telltale signs of a pet. With no water bowl, leash or doghouse in sight, she decided if they had such it would be in the back.

Lounging against a tree Martha, and her alter self, saw a big man, well dressed in slacks and blazer, come out to check the mail box located on the side near the front door. She heard a soft curse as he turned away empty handed and re-entered the house. Voices of young children came from within as the door opened.

Puzzled, she muttered to herself, "Sounds happy enough in there, maybe he only tortures the one child. That's been known to happen. Some people believe a certain child may hold an evil spirit inside them." She couldn't believe an upscale family like that would hold such strange beliefs. It certainly didn't fit in with what she saw tonight.

Martha decided she would see no more tonight and turned to amble slowly back toward her car, parked several blocks away. She halted her retreat, seeing the tip-up garage door swing upward and the man in question back his car hurriedly out. He sped away in a sleek, dark blue Buick Lucerne.

"Well, you drive a nice car, you torturing bastard."

He lived in a lovely comfortable home and was a solid member of the community. Underneath this appearance of normality, Martha knew, he was a rabid child abuser.

She went home, frustrated. This would not be easy. A man with an important job like his would surround his life with people, activities, and events. He wouldn't easily be found alone or isolated—except in a tiny little girl's bedroom, late at night while others in the house slept in their innocence. *Wouldn't they hear Aliya's cries of agony? Did they ever?*

CHAPTER 5

Two weeks later, Martha/Serena saw her opportunity. Pederson often worked late and went alone to his car parked in a dark, underground parking garage.

"How very nice." Martha uttered the words, but it was her Serena self who said them. "No more Gentian Violet. That did me in back in Colorado Springs."

Her mind swirling with ideas, planning, and preparations, Martha appeared to work and live her life normally to her friends and family. But inwardly, she plotted and planned for the right moment. On this fateful night she waited in the underground garage, hoping her target would show.

Pederson's car stood alone in the garage. Her own car was parked several blocks away. The lights were low at this late hour, and a furtive figure with a backpack was not easily seen sliding silently up to the long, sleek, dark blue Buick Lucerne.

Pulling out a long thin strip of metal, with a small hook on the end, from her pack, she slid it down into the door. Two quick pulls and the door unlocked. She opened it and crept inside. Remembering so vividly that tiny abused child crying in the night kept Martha, now totally

Serena, in a savage mental state. She slid into the back seat and crouched on the floor to wait.

She reminded herself she wasn't just Serena, but a morally upright, professional person of conscience. A small part of her ached with guilt over that fact, but another part of her seethed with the need for revenge against a dreadful man who willfully tortured a small girl. And because of that, Martha/Serena failed to see her purpose as wrong.

It was after nine when she heard her prey approaching. He walked with quick, heavy footsteps, clicking along the concrete surface as he neared his car. Her heart rate increased exponentially. It was time! Gripping the sandbag firmly, she brushed away the tiny trickle of fine sand that had leaked out of a small hole in the canvas bag. "Oh, oh, better sew this up," she murmured. "No need to leave clues lying about."

Anson Pederson used his clicker. The car unlocked, the headlights flashed, and he opened the door. Had he really looked, he might have seen a huddled figure lying quietly on the floor of the rear seating area, but he didn't. Whistling a tuneless melody, he shoved the key into the ignition. A heavy blow struck the side of his head and he immediately slumped sideways across both front seats.

Serena slipped out of the rear and opened the right front door to reach her victim. As the man was too big to handle from the driver's seat, she pulled him toward the passenger side, stretching him out enough to do her work.

Going to the left side, she struggled in the confined space under the steering wheel to roll him over enough for her purposes. She unbuckled his fancy leather belt. Then she tugged at his woolen suit pants, pulling them down along with the under drawers.

Seeing his male equipment, she exclaimed quietly, "No wonder he goes after little kids. That's one of the smallest, most pathetic willies I've ever seen. And yet he's

managed to procreate seven children! Another version of
immaculate conception? May wonders never cease." She
chuckled. "He's got enough to torture a little child, though,
but not anymore, no more, you hideous bastard!" Her rage
at the injustices committed by pedophiles shook her, and
she went to work.

Martha understood that this man's pathetic appendage
wasn't capable of the terrible injuries sustained by little
Aliya. It had been done by some other instrument of torture. As Serena worked on Pederson, she tried to imagine
just what else he had done to this poor little girl. She
couldn't.

When Serena left the garage, the bloodied man lay
groaning in the front seat of his plush Buick. His body bore
several other marks of abuse. Using a tire iron, she'd broken an arm. She wasn't sure which and didn't really care.
Hoping to disguise the real purpose of the attack, Serena
had inflicted several other wounds as well. The car itself
bore several marks of vandalism, including slashing of the
inside header and some of the fine leather seating.

Could she manage to emasculate the man and have it
look incidental to a crime of vandalism and robbery? She
wasn't sure of that, but she took his wallet, watch, and
wedding ring, along with his nifty Spanish-leather belt and
pricey shoes. Both cheeks and forehead bore marks of
slashing injuries, made to look like the real purpose of the
attack. Bloody drainage dripped down from his lacerated
face, staining the fine leather of his plush upholstery. No
attempt at antisepsis was made. *Trying to prevent infection
did me in the last time!*

Serena attempted to make this criminal act look completely unlike the events in Colorado Springs, hoping the
Denver police wouldn't connect what she'd done to this
man tonight with certain events in that city two years ago.

She'd already made her decision on that score in any
case. Whatever the price she might eventually have to pay,

it was worth it. No more would Pederson molest his tiny little daughter or any others in the family. She'd seen to that and it felt mighty damned good.

She wasn't sure anymore where Martha/Serena stood. Where did one stop and the other begin? *I don't know anymore—we are more one than ever.*

Outside the garage, as a heavily padded figure, she moved along the street with a backpack until she reached her car. Driving slowly along deserted streets to an area far outside the city, she deposited the items taken off Pederson. Tossing them into a vacant alley, she hoped a needy vagrant would find the items useful in his desperate life. Some poor soul would absolutely love the fancy, Spanish leather belt. She laughed aloud at the thought.

Martha took off the gloves she wore and placed the bloodied things in a plastic bag before tucking them in her pack. "Bed time, lady, you must be worn out from all the work you've done tonight. But was it enough?" She drove into her garage, pressed the opener, and shut the big rolling door.

CHAPTER 6

Pederson slowly regained his senses. Reaching a semi-conscious state, he tried to gain some idea of what had happened. Moaning in confusion, he cried, "What the hell?" Pain emanated over most of his body, his head ached, his cheeks and forehead stung like fire. He struggled to put things together. "Have I been attacked?" He groped about, touching his legs, arms, and, after bumping into the steering wheel and column, realized he was in his car. The blood dripping onto his shirt made him touch his face and pull away a bloodied hand. "Oh shit! What's happened? My face is all bloody!"

The keys dangling in the ignition brought him farther into consciousness. He'd been on his way home—he remembered that much. Looking about, he realized he was still in the parking garage. "I was going home." Struggling to sit up, he looked in the rear view mirror, the light was dim but enough to see the ugly abrasions scoring both cheeks, and his forehead. He avoided touching his ugly torn flesh, as salty tears of pain rolled down his cheeks to burn in the abrasions. "Son of a bitch!" he gasped, reeling in shock and horror at the sight.

The blood flowing down onto his once white shirt and nicely printed tie went unnoticed as the pain radiating down the back of his legs made him reach for his genitalia.

Only his left arm obeyed the command as the right was useless. He realized, from the excruciating pain radiating down it, that it must have been broken.

Shocked, he saw his trousers were down around his ankles and the sight of that made him sick with a terrible fear. "What the hell?"

With his left hand he reached down to seek the source of the aching pain that radiated down his legs.

"Oh, God in Heaven! What the fuck has happened to me?" Blood ran down from the area of his crotch and the sight of it froze the marrow in his bones. "Son of a bitch!" He screamed his fear and pain aloud and heard it echo throughout the empty garage.

"Say, mistah! What's happenin' heah?" A large black man stood outside the car, a half-fearful expression on his face as he surveyed the severely battered man. I'm here to clean up 'round the place and I hear you a yellin' for help."

"You've got to get me some help here, man. I've been attacked and beat all to hell." Pederson saw the man's eyes widen in terror at the sight of his bloody, torn face, and the disarray of his disheveled and bloodied clothes. "Look at this blood on my hands."

"Where'n hell are my damned shoes, my belt. God, I'm bleeding my life away and I can't use my arm! Do something, man!" Pederson yelled at the janitor. Then he found his cell, and threw it at the big black man.

"Yes, suh, I'm callin' 9-1-1 right now." The janitor grabbed the phone and fumbled with it until it lit up. He punched in the numbers then blanched in fear as he saw blood staining his hands. When the operator came on, he shoved the phone into Pederson's hand. "Sorry, suh, you do the talkin'. I don't know what to say." The man quickly grabbed one of his cleaning rags and wiped his hands.

"Shit!" Pederson took the phone and saw with distaste that it was bloodied. "Yes, operator? I've been attacked in the parking garage of the High Street Brokerage Firm. I'm bleeding all over! Hurry, please!" He gave the needed answers and punched off, looking about for the janitor but he didn't see him.

After what seemed like a lifetime, Pederson heard the wailing sirens as they heralded the arrival of the ambulance accompanied by two police cars. The janitor hurriedly unlocked the entrance gate for them and stood out of the way, unsure what else he needed to do.

The two EMTs quickly examined Pederson and ascertained he had no spinal injuries, then they gently removed him from his car and placed him on a gurney.

One man muttered low to his cohort, "Good God, Luke, look at his face!" He saw the man's trousers had been pulled down. He turned to Pederson. "I'm Jake Wells, EMT. So what happened here?"

Luke nodded, indicating Pederson's crotch area. He turned the victim over, examined the source of bleeding from that area, and murmured, "He's been assaulted down here, too." He shot a meaningful look at Jake and mouthed quietly, "'Doesn't look too good."

"God!" Jake exclaimed. "Who in hell would do a thing like this?"

They quickly cleaned and packed the area with sterile dressings. The severity of his wounds in that area shocked and sickened both males.

Pederson, confused and nauseated, turned his face away and vomited forcefully off the side of the gurney. He moaned in pain. "I was getting in my car to go home. I don't remember seeing anyone but they sure saw me."

A uniformed police officer stood close by awaiting his turn at questioning the victim.

"We're checking you out completely before we transport you to the ER," Jake said. He and Luke removed what remained of Pederson's bloodied clothes, cleaned the facial wounds, applied sterile dressings, and put a splint on his right arm. "You've got a fractured arm here, sir. We'll splint it for transport and let the doctor tend to it in the ER." After asking about allergies, Jake offered a mild pain reliever.

"Don't give him much until we get his story," the officer in charge said. He stood close by, waiting to question Pederson.

"You've got a pretty serious wound down here too, sir," Jake said to Pederson. "We'll wrap things up right quick. You need to see the doc, pronto."

Pederson already had a strong idea about the extent of his injuries. "Will I be okay?" He heard pathetic pleading in his own voice. The looks on the EMTs' faces confirmed his worst fears. "Son of a bitch!" he screamed as tears started down his cheeks and soaked into the fresh dressings over the cheek lacerations. The salt from his tears stung the wounds all over again.

The police officer stepped up to his gurney. "I'm Sergeant Bruce Milasky. I won't keep you now. We'll take your statement in the ER after the doc has attended to your injuries."

"Shit, officer, I never saw who it was. Nothing! He jumped me and I went out like a light. Now look at me—ruined for life! These damned criminals run the streets and you guys sit on your asses doing nothing!"

The officer waved the medics to go ahead and transport the patient. "We'll catch you as soon as the medics take you in. Be right behind the ambulance."

The EMTs loaded him into the ambulance and took off with one police car following. The other set of officers fine-combed the area and spoke with the janitor.

"Nasty sort, eh?" Milasky said. "Well, don't appear to be much visible evidence around here. We'd best impound the car so we can do in-depth forensics on it. It's actually the crime scene. The perp must have left us something. Jesse, can you believe what he did to that man? How can anyone hate that much? Or is that someone just a sick bastard?"

"It looks like Pederson might have made somebody mad as hell. Don't believe we've ever had an attack that included emasculation. Brutal as the rest of it was, it takes a special kind of mad for something like that." An older officer, Jesse Miller, put in, "Ever seen its like?"

"No, can't recall anything quite like this," Milasky replied, frowning in confusion. "There's something different about the case, but it's hard to get a handle on it. Something smells damned foul in several strange and weird ways, don't you think?" He shook his head as he pondered the facts. "It appears this was the particular dude they wanted. They waited until they had a good shot at him, alone and isolated as he was. We know that much about this case."

"Interesting, that's for damned sure." Miller studied the scene. "Wonder what the detectives will make of it."

Milasky ordered the tow truck. While they waited, they looked the car over thoroughly from the exterior. "See this slight scratch here?" He pointed to the front door on the passenger side. "Perp got in that way and laid in wait for that poor, miserable, cut-up man. Looks like he's kind of a big-wheel-sort-of guy, too. If he works in this building, it's mostly hot-shot financial dudes, you know."

The tow truck came and removed the vehicle to the police impound lot. "Better check in at the ER," Milasky said. "Where'd they say they went?"

"Riverside, wasn't it?" Miller headed for the patrol car. "Let's go see what the docs find out."

⁊ↄ⁊ↄ

The doctor came over to Pederson's gurney. "I'm Doctor Sellers. Sorry to lay it on you like this, but you have several very serious injuries. You'll need plastic surgery for your facial wounds. Ortho will tend your arm, and I've repaired your scrotum as best I could." He stopped and drew in his breath before adding, "I'm afraid your injuries will cause you to be sterile from this day on and impotent as well." He laid a hand on Paterson's shoulder in sympathy and added. "I'm really sorry to have to tell you that, sir."

Pederson emitted a choking sob. "I'm ruined for life! Why me?" He tried to gather himself up. "I'll have to call my wife and let her know what happened." He lay on the gurney in total misery—contemplating his life, how it would be from now on, while wondering, "Who in hell hates me this much?" He shivered. He knew in the darker areas of his heart that someone did, and justifiably so.

The staff called his wife on his behalf and an hour later, she hurried into the ER department. Locating his gurney, she rushed to his side. "What's going on, Anson? What happened to you, for God's sakes? Who did this to you?"

"I don't know, Shari, but somebody either hates my guts, or is a goddamned sick son of a bitch!" Pederson's fear and temper flared. "They gave me something for the pain, but it's sure as hell not enough, stingy bastard doctor! Those useless cop sons-a-bitches questioned me for a whole damned hour." He gritted his teeth in frustration. "They asked a million questions, trying to do their job from my bedside, the lazy bastards! But I didn't *see* anyone, I didn't *hear* anything, and I don't know *why* in the damned son-of-a-bitchin' hell this happened to me. I never saw who did this."

Fighting tears, he let his shoulders slump in despair. "Somebody must really have it in for me or hates my guts enough to do this to me. But why me, anyway?"

While moaning with fear and pain, he took a sidelong glance at his wife, wondering, *What the hell is she thinking?* Lost in misery as he was, Pederson still noticed a faint smile creeping slyly over his wife's face.

She had reason enough to hate him, the good Lord knew, but that was a private issue between them and a family matter. A man had his needs and he brought in a damned good income. His life style was his business, and she'd damned well better believe it. Anger only added to his misery.

He groaned again. "Go home, Shari. Wait until tomorrow to come back. I can't talk anymore tonight." He thrashed his legs about until his scrotal area shocked him quiet with pain. "God, I wish I was dead! Get the hell out of here. They're admitting me and I don't feel like dealing with you anymore tonight."

"Me? What have I done?"

"Nothing, but if I see you smile like that again, you won't want to be around me anymore." His voice held the low menacing growl she knew so dreadfully well. "You can't hide anything from me, you bitch!"

"Well, all right, Anson. I'll see you tomorrow then." Her voice shook with tremors, her shoulders were stiff and her head held high, but he was pleased to see her face turn white as a ghost.

With a sigh of relief, he watched her walk away. "Who'n hell needs the damned, cold-hearted bitch?"

༄༅༄

Officers Milasky and Miller remained in the ER, hoping to glean a few extra bits of information. Standing unobserved in the background, they'd watched the scene between Pederson and his wife. "Interesting little byplay there, eh?" Miller remarked. "Did you see that tiny smirk come over her face?"

"Looks like trouble in Paradise. There's always more hidden than revealed in any case and this one's no different." Milasky shrugged. "The man was downright nasty to her, but they've got a bunch of kids. They must get along some of the time."

"Wonder who wanted revenge on the man?" Miller asked. "I can't get the idea out of my head that this is payback of some kind. The tip of this particular iceberg is only one tenth of what's below the surface."

"Guess we'll have to see how this plays out, huh?" Milasky said. "Let's get on back. We're done here for the present. We'd best see what the car reveals, since the poor guy can't remember anything, no sounds, odors, or what the hell ever else might have been around in that garage."

෴

Martha, her conscience clear as glass, slept well. In the morning, while the coffee was brewing, she got the paper. Looking for news of the attack, she scanned it from front to back and saw nothing. "It should be big news but it hasn't made headlines yet, apparently. He might not want something like this to get out." She shivered. "If I were a man, I sure wouldn't."

The phone rang out a musical tune and she grabbed it from her purse. "Hello."

"Oh, Martha, I can't tell you how thrilled I am that you suggested having Duke as a bodyguard. Marvin is terrified of him and is moving out."

"You don't know how happy I am to hear things are going well for you, Judith. Serves the bastard right. I'm glad things are getting settled. And you're getting along with that tough nut Navy SEAL, eh?"

"Oh yeah, we're getting along just fine."

After she hung up she laughed out loud. "Serena girl, we didn't have to do a thing outside of a phone call to fix that battering husband. She's getting the divorce she wants, and I suspect she may be getting a permanent bodyguard along with it." With a satisfied smile Martha fixed her breakfast and sat down to eat.

Before she finished her toast the phone rang again— the hospital staffing secretary wondering if she could pull a shift. "Hey, sure. I can be there at three. Where am I working?"

"Med-surg."

"Yeah, sure, okay."

Martha drove to work with expectations of learning the details regarding her recent victim. Her pulse quickened when she heard the name Pederson during report. "The man was brutally attacked last night and has serious, though non-life-threatening injuries. He's got a fracture of the right ulna, repair of facial lacerations, and missing gonads. He has a number of bruised areas as well. I think he'd prefer a male nurse, but we're short of men today. How about you, Martha? Want him?"

"Sure, I'll take him. Anything more on the guy?"

"His meds are on the med sheets and his treatments are in the treatment book. We don't know much except that he was really nasty to his wife over the phone, I hear. His family situation may be suffering from this attack." The charge nurse, Betty Pell, tapped her pencil on the recorder and report went on.

Martha figured she could get anything else of interest from his chart and certainly when she examined him. Doing quick physical assessments on of her patients took several minutes for each one. She outlined each patient's needs, then set up her IVs, and straightened the med cart.

Martha was careful not to pay overt attention to Anson Pederson. She cared for him in turn and tended to any immediate, as well as routine, needs. The dressings to his cheeks and forehead were sopped with pale, bloody, serosanguinous drainage. She changed them per the doctor's orders and took that opportunity to survey the devastation to his handsome face.

With deep pleasure she noted the lacerated tissue was angry and red but had begun the healing process. In spite of the plastic surgeon's fine job of repair, scars would remain since the cuts had been so deep. Within the wounds, a few pale lines, spelling pedophile, would bear testimony to the bastard he truly was, for all time to come.

His fingers moved well enough and the warm radial pulse told her his circulation was intact and his arm would heal completely. He cried for pain relief as often as his medication could be given. *God, what a whiner this bastard is.* She smiled and offered comfort along with the medicine. *I should get the Academy Award for this performance.*

Pederson's wife came in and, without showing overt interest, Martha stayed as near as possible, hoping to learn how his injuries had affected his family. She heard a series of vicious snarls emanating from his room.

"Goddamnit it all to hell, Shari, wipe that smirk off your face. Someone will see it!"

"Anson, watch your language!" Shari whispered then asked, "Will you be able to hold your job with your face all cut up like that? Of course, I can't get a good look at it with all those bandages."

"Hell, yes! I'd better. They owe me big time. They'll have to have me. Hell, I've brought in more accounts than any other agent they've got." Then Martha heard a muffled sob. "My God, Shari, what if they fire me for having my face disfigured. It's all screwed up! They'd do it if it hurts their goddamned business. That plastics guy didn't help near enough. Outta sue the bastards!" Martha heard him moaning. "Who'n hell had it in for me, Shari, who?" The whine of his voice made Martha believe some deep inner fear had overtaken his conscious thought.

"Well, they better not can you, Anson. We've got seven kids to feed and educate and I can't do it on my own."

"Shit, Shari, is that all you ever think of? Self-serving bitch, that's what you are."

The unbelievably ugly words to his wife bore testimony that the marriage had severe problems. The horrible things Pederson had done to his tiny daughter must be known to the wife—she'd have to be deaf and blind not to know. To Martha that remained a great mystery. How could any mother stand by and let something like that happen to one of her own children?

"I'm leaving, Anson, or maybe I'll start calling you Annie. I've put up with your evil monstrosities and ugly threats all these years for the kids' sakes." She lowered her voice. "You'd damned well better keep that job, that's all I know. I'm out of here and I don't know if I'll come back here tomorrow, either." Her face appeared white with anger as she left the room, not seeing or acknowledging anyone on her way to the bank of elevators.

Well, Anson, your little world's crumbling, isn't it? Things aren't all peachy keen in the Pederson household, are they? Martha smiled in satisfaction at the fine job she'd done, altering the primary driving force of his depraved, pedophilic life.

He'd completely destroyed the very fabric of his tiny daughter's life for all time. "No child can survive such evil depravity," she muttered under her breath, still angry. "That child will never be normal after what she's suffered, just changed forever, like Will," she huffed to herself. "And even worse, he'll never be our sweet innocent little boy again."

She'd seen her daughter Jeannie's tears too often. Her grandson Will could never return to the innocent little boy he used to be after his rape and sodomy, and neither would little Aliya after what she'd suffered.

After hearing the wife's angry words, Martha wondered, *Why wouldn't the woman testify in a courtroom to save her child? Is the nice salary Pederson makes all that important?*

When, later in the shift, he complained of wet scrotal dressings, Martha applied new sterile bandages to the wounds, all the while noting the devastation to his child-destroying privates. *Girl, if you get away with this...*She felt exaltation at the success of her venture. *If only the castration part doesn't cause the authorities to point the finger my way. I don't suppose they have many cases of that.*

Martha continually thought of the serious nature of Aliya's vaginal wounds and decided, to her horror and disgust, that Pederson definitely couldn't have done that kind of damage with what he'd had. The monster had to have used some sort of instrumentation to torture his little girl. *Could his small male equipage have led him to compensate in this sick way?* The thoughts augmented her contempt for a man like Pederson. *Have I done enough to stop him? If not, what more would a person have to do?* She knew the terrible and final answer to that, too, and refused to consider it.

She completed her shift and reported off. On her way home, she couldn't stop crowing over what she'd done. But she had doubts. Rethinking her actions, she worried, *I'm becoming hardened to the commission of criminal activities. Does that make me one of them?*

CHAPTER 7

At home she tried to watch TV. Finding nothing to hold her attention, she picked up her cell and called her long-time friend, Lizzie Marin. Since leaving Colorado Springs, she seldom saw her dearest friend, but they kept in contact by phone. Lizzie had helped her through the trauma of facing her alternate personality. They came from different social levels, but Lizzie was always ready to step into Martha's life, finding her own devoid of excitement.

"Hey lady, I need to see you. Any chance—"

"Martha! You're not in trouble again are you?"

"No, I'm not in trouble—not yet."

❦

During the night, Lizzie knocked on her door, and Martha sprang up from Bob's old leather chair to open it and greet her. "Oh, Lizzie, come in." She hugged her close friend and confidant.

"Okay, dear girl, out with it." Lizzie's deep hazel eyes bore into Martha's dark green ones and her curiosity knew no bounds as she held Martha by her shoulders. "What's going on?"

"I'm at it again and this time I've no one to blame for my actions but myself." Martha took a deep breath. "I feel driven to do these things by the horrible things I see, Liz." She felt the sting as tears formed in her eyes. "Serena strengthens me and aids me. I have to do it. I'm guilty as hell, and I don't even care the tiniest little bit!"

"What have you done? God, Martha, this is so damned exciting!" Lizzie tended to add fuel to the flames of Martha's alter personality, Serena, a being whose thirst for revenge on offending males had proven endless.

Martha launched into the story of her recent activities with Lizzie sitting in Bob's big leather chair, nodding silently. *Is she agreeing?* Martha wondered.

"Darling, what you've done is wonderful," Liz finally said. "I applaud everything, But, Martha, please—you've got to be careful. If you get caught this time, moving away again won't get you off the hook, you know that."

"I do know it, but honestly, when you're so closely exposed to some of these things, how can you not take action? That poor child is ruined for the rest of her life and she's not yet five. Why do these awful things happen, Lizzie? Why?" She sighed then added, "And why is nothing ever done to help these kids? My God, the mother has to know what her husband is doing. In fact, she said it in front of witnesses. Yet, she's never said or done anything to stop the fiend. If it was me I'd have killed that monster a long time ago!"

"You are not the morals police, dear heart. I'm only thinking of you. I'd sure hate to see you in prison for defending some poor child. That'd make the whole thing a travesty, wouldn't it? She grimaced. "You say the man had almost nothing when you got ready to do the deed? Nothing?"

"Well, almost. I'm thinking—a slightly generous Gherkin!" After they shared several healthy giggles, Martha continued. "He's got seven kids, Lizzie, so what little he has—well, had—must have been very potent." Martha couldn't suppress a snort. "Notice I used a past tense in my referral. Wonder how he managed with his wife, big question there, huh? I always thought that a shortage like that, if you'll pardon the expression, it was just plain cruel for our Creator to pull a trick like that on a guy." She shook her head. "But after he was so nasty to his wife, she said she'd call him Annie, instead of Anson." Martha broke into a series of helpless giggles. "Oh, Lizzie, what have I done?"

Lizzie laughed so hard, she gasped for air. "Martha, you worry about the craziest things."

"Oh yeah, the wife had a smirk on her face when she first came to visit him," Martha recalled. "So I'm more than curious about their relationship. Maybe having so many kids made him feel extra potent or whatever."

"Well, maybe so." Lizzie, not one to dwell on one thing overly long, changed the subject. "So when do I get to meet the big Navy SEAL? Sounds like some kind of guy."

"I'll give them a call in the morning. I guess Judith's nasty husband has moved out of the house. She said he wanted to scar her face with acid and, not only that, the bastard had a guy hired to do away with her, so he could get Judith's home, which is rather palatial. It was something I just happened to overhear one night, so the big guy needs to stay very close to her for a while."

"What a devil her husband is!" Lizzie shuddered. "That's scary as hell, Martha, and I'm beginning to think you are, too." She squinted her eyes. "And just how was it that you overheard this business?" She paused then repeated her warning, "Martha, you've got to be careful!"

"The world's a dangerous place sometimes. I'm just trying to help, Liz, or do I just see things I shouldn't?"

"Maybe you're just supersensitive. After all, what happened to you as a child must have changed you. It does to other poor, molested kids. You ever think of that?"

"Lizzie, I know why I asked you to come. Having someone to talk to helps put things in order for me. I don't want to continue down this path, I don't! But when I run across another situation, Serena goes wild with wanting to fix things.

"Martha, you've got to lay low for a while. Doing too much too soon will get them asking other police detectives, maybe in Colorado Springs about...er...emasculation. Is there a better word?" Lizzie looked stern. "Think about it, Martha. It's the one thing that might lead them to you. So watch it, will you?"

"I think Serena hates you right now, Lizzie."

ℰↄℰↄ

"Damn, Marcus, take a look at this case. Hell of a twist to it and one we don't usually see." The tall, dark-haired detective, Harry Johns, offered the folder to the older man at an adjoining desk. "Well, I never have."

"What so different then?" Chief of Detectives Marcus Ebert replied.

"How many cases of assault do we get that include castration? Whether it was done accidentally or by design, we can't be sure." Frowning, he added, "Nobody does that—nobody! Ever hear of anyone with an MO like that?"

"Let me see that." Marcus shifted in his chair and mopped his brow. Sitting wasn't his thing and his comfort zone didn't exist if he sat at a desk too damned long. He frowned as he studied the report. "Not much information here." He turned toward his fellow detective. "Anything from forensics?"

"It happened in this dude's Buick, right in the parking garage, if you can imagine that. They found a few scrape marks like from a man's boot in the back seat, blood splatters, but so far it's all from the victim. Another detail that seems funny as hell to me, they found a small amount of finely grained sand. No idea of its purpose or how it got there." He sighed. "Not a hell of a lot so far. Why castrate a man? That's the strange part and something we don't see that much, if ever. If it wasn't accidental, how could something like that happen unless it's a hate crime?"

"What does the wife say, or family members?" Marcus asked.

"The wife was all cooperation itself, but somehow I got the funny feeling she wasn't that upset over what happened to her husband," Harry replied. "They have a bunch of kids, ranging from three years to junior high and he holds an important job with his company." He chuckled. "Most women would be damned mad to have their husband clipped that way. Makes you wonder, huh?"

"Looks like we'll have to scratch this dog a little harder to find those fleas, eh?" Marcus paused, thinking. "How about the family, anything wrong there?"

"Need more digging on that one. I had an eerie feeling something was very wrong inside that house. Just one man's opinion, but I get these hunches and, you know, sometimes they're spot on." Harry chuckled at his idea of intuition, but he felt a slight shiver up his spine, remembering how he'd felt in the Pederson home. The icy chill that something was not right in that house had nagged at him all the while he'd been there.

"Well, man, have at it." Marcus shuffled the scattered papers on his desk into a neat bundle. "Try for information from the hospital staff, anything that doesn't set right with you. You know, this case is unlike any other I've ever seen as well."

"Heard the Pederson's four-year-old was in there for quite a spell, but so far they haven't said why. I'll give that a shot." Harry sniffed. "If there's family trouble, that'd be a good place to look. I'll do that right away and re-check with the ER doc while I'm at it." He paused. "Maybe the family doctor would be a place to start as far as the family goes. But you know that damned HIPPA thing the medical profession has invented puts a crimp in everything. They can't say anything, even when they know they should, without a court order. Best get one of those, too, and make it cover everything."

෴

Martha took another shift. Lizzie had gone home, and the empty house echoed continually, mocking her with the emptiness of life without Bob. At the moment, neither Martha nor her inner being had a pending project and time lay heavily upon her.

Assigned to med-surg again, she watched to see who had Pederson. He was set for discharge in the morning and this shift would be the last chance to overhear anything of interest. She had a full load this afternoon and quickly got her work organized.

After report, while sorting through her charts, she saw a tall, solid-looking man with a touch of gray in his hair walk in. Dressed in a casual business suit with the neck of his shirt unbuttoned, he wore no tie. He approached the head nurse, and Martha, standing down the hall, took notice.

My, oh my, isn't he nice. Feeling a deep inner stir of interest, Martha was amazed at herself and decided she'd best quiet that raunchy inner person. *Serena—down girl.*

She heard his deep, soft voice as he spoke with the charge nurse. "I'm Detective Harry Johns. If I could speak with a nurse or other staff caring for Mr. Pederson, it might help us in our investigation regarding his assault."

"Well, sir, we hold to a very strict code of privacy in this hospital called HIPPA. We are not allowed to give out information such as you suggest without a court order at the very least." Randa Harmon, RN, was emphatic and stood her ground with the detective. "You'll have to find that information elsewhere. I'm sorry, sir."

The detective turned away from the nurse in futility, asked for Pederson's room, and went in. Martha edged as near the room as possible, curious to learn what went on between the patient and the detective. She felt cold shivers of concern and a bit of guilt zipping madly along her spine at the sight of the law. *Already, the vultures circle. I must take care not to be noticed.*

She moved about her duties, showing no more interest in Pederson than any other patient. As far as the investigating officer went, to Martha it was as though the detective had never appeared. But the fact that he'd come onto their floor had turned her insides to frozen mush.

Passing the room with Pederson and the big detective, she heard the murmur of voices.

"No, I never had anything like that in my car, officer. I have it washed and detailed nearly every week. My office expects us to uphold certain standards and that includes a decent looking car."

"Well, thanks Mr. Pederson," the detective said. "I guess this is just one more question, without a decent answer."

Then, she heard a chair scrape, and the big man exited the room with the look of frustration on his nicely chiseled features. Her idle thoughts returned. *That detective is a real fine looking dude.*

ফৈৎ

Martha's shift ended. She reported off and left the hospital. On the way home she decided to drive past Judith's house. She'd planned to stop for a visit several days ago but had put it off. It was rather late tonight, but she decided if she saw lights on, she's stop.

"Am I being nosey or overly concerned about Judith's relationship with the Navy SEAL?" she asked herself. "Is everything the way Judith stated? Is her devil husband really out of the picture? She sounds so sure these days."

Martha had frequently wondered about these things, since it was her doing that put the Navy SEAL together with Judith.

She looked through the fancy wrought iron fencing and across the manicured lawn, as she drove slowly past the home. Cedar shingles covered the sides of the house. Even in the softness of moonlight, she could see they were aging and had taken on a soft, weathered patina. The soft shades on the windows of the home added a rather old-style elegance to the longstanding residence in this fine upscale neighborhood.

When she noticed a figure moving furtively through the shrubbery next to the home, Martha felt her pulse surge. "Oops, what's going on—who's sneaking about the place?" Seeing the man's arms, raising and moving in sweeping arcs, and the shining metallic side of a container, she was struck with horror. "Could that man be splashing something on those dry shingles?" She gasped. "God in Heaven, he is!"

She stopped her car and, grabbing her phone, dialed 9-1-1. When the operator came on the line, she exclaimed, "Ma'am, I have just seen a man splashing a liquid substance on a house located at 4573 Terrace lane. Oh no! It's blazing up! Send a fire truck quickly—quickly, please!"

After another word or two to the operator, she saw the man's shadowy figure running away down the block.

The flames quickly shot upward, as if fed by some flammable substance, and reached hungrily toward the heavy cedar-shingled roof. Martha watched in horror, as the licking flames swirled upward toward the very flammable roof which appeared to carry a layer of dried pine needles as well. "That dry stuff will burn like gasoline! I've got to warn them."

She ran to the door, knocked rapidly, and waited. The door burst open. Duke Mason stood there in his bare feet, wearing faded jeans and an old sweatshirt.

He wore a happy grin on his face at seeing her. "Hey, Martha, what's happening?"

"Well, for one thing, this house is on fire! I just saw a man pour something on the outside walls and set it off. He ran away down that way." She pointed down the street. "Hurry! You've got to get out of here. It's getting to the roof!"

"Holy shit," he yelled. "Get Judith out of the house!"

He ran out, grabbed the garden hose, and started spraying water on the raging flames as the fire truck came screaming down the street.

Martha ran through the house, yelling, "Judith! Where are you?"

The interior seemed so quiet and peaceful it was difficult to believe a fire raged outside.

Judith appeared wearing a bathrobe about her trim figure. "What's all the excitement?"

Seeing her so casually dressed, Martha couldn't help but believe she and Duke had gotten *very* comfortable with each other, to say the least.

Martha explained what she'd just witnessed and watched her friend crumple into tears. "Hey, Judith, it's going to be all right," she offered, trying to comfort her. "Duke's out there, spraying water on it, and the fire truck is here, too."

"Oh, no it isn't all right, Martha. I knew it was all too easy. I just knew it!" Her panting breath came in gasps as her face tightened in fear. "He'd rather burn this house to the ground than see me happy in it. He's a devil, that man—he is." She turned her tear stained face to Martha. "If it hadn't been for Duke, he'd have thrown acid in my face already. He screamed that much at me the day he took his stuff and left." She tightened her small fists. "What's wrong with a man who thinks evil things like that?"

Duke came in and took Judith in his arms. "It's okay for now, Jude, but you aren't out of danger. The police are here and want to speak with you, Martha, about what you saw." He gestured at the door that stood open.

Two officers entered, bringing with them the odor of smoke and burning cedar. It emanated off their clothing as they approached. Speaking to those officers might open the way for further inquiries. It worried her a little, but Martha was determined to be a normal person and not a hidden, avenging angel. She met the men with a cool, helpful persona—one she did not feel.

The officer introduced himself as Sergeant Herbert Martin. "Ma'am, you made the call to 9-1-1?"

The other officer stood nearby, his seeking eyes looking around the home. Did he look for evidence of smoke damage, or what?

"Yes, I happened to drive by after work. I wanted to see how Judith was getting on but decided it was too late to stop for a visit..." She went on to explain what she'd seen.

"Could you possibly identify the man you saw running away?"

"I saw very little of him, except he seemed like a big man, maybe six feet or so. Had on dark clothes, but I never caught a glimpse of his face at all."

"We found a tin in the shrubs, probably used it to carry the gasoline he used. It smells of it. Must have tossed it in the bushes as he ran. Might find something there." He turned to Judith. "This is your home, ma'am?" His eyes softened as he looked at the pretty, blonde young woman

"Yes," Judith said. "It is and the man who did this could very easily be my husband." She choked off a sob. "We're divorcing. He's terribly angry and has made some very ugly threats against me."

She went on to explain her present situation and introduced Duke as her personal bodyguard. Martha hoped to play down her part in helping the woman, but Judith said enough to make them fully aware of her part in everything.

They suggested Judith not stay in the house until the danger from her husband had been resolved. If indeed he was found to be the person who attempted to set fire to her home, he'd be arrested. Unless he posted bail, she'd be safe enough. The police appeared oblivious to her bodyguard, but Judith wasn't. Martha had the renewed feeling they'd gotten rather close in the few days he'd been protecting her.

Judith spoke up. "Wait a minute! I have my own protection, sir. This man has been hired to be my personal bodyguard." She motioned to Duke, and he stepped closer to her.

Sergeant Martin uttered a derisive laugh. "Didn't stop the fire now, did he?"

Duke bristled, flushed red, and stepped into the officer's personal space with both fists tightly clenched. Martha thought the sergeant was headed for the floor but Duke managed to keep his cool.

"Listen, Officer, this woman's husband is a sick son-of-a-bitch, and I'm here to prevent bodily harm to this lady."

His voice came out as a low growl. His deep anger at the personal insult from Sergeant Martin, held at bay for the present, made his chest expand. By the way the officer moved back, Martha knew he'd quickly realized his mistake.

"Hold on there, mister, no insult intended," Martin said, quickly amending his brash comments.

Martha smiled to herself, seeing that the officer hadn't missed the hammering set of muscles behind Duke's clenched fists, poised and ready to defend his honor in front of the woman he'd sworn to protect.

CHAPTER 8

With some of the immediate fire taken out of Duke as well as the house, they sat down to decide how to proceed.

The fire danger had been taken care of by the fire department and the all clear given. Martha offered her home once again.

Judith, her face ashen, had her fists clenched tight. "He'll know where to find me, you know that, Martha. I can't bring that sort of trouble into your home, not again." Adamant in her refusal to further involve Martha, she looked up at her protector. "What do you think, Duke?"

"Hell, Jude, we'll use my place then. He'd never find you there. He sure as hell wouldn't know where I live. It ain't much, Jude, but it'd do for a while." His face had reddened at his suggestion, but he meant his offer. No one doubted that.

Judith flushed rosy to her hairline. "What do you think, Martha?"

The look on her friend's face left little doubt in Martha's mind as to their budding relationship. "Sounds like a plan, but he'll probably stalk my house thinking you'll be there, Judith." She looked at Sergeant Martin. "It's a possibility, isn't it?"

"Yes, it certainly is, ma'am, so if you see anything, give us a call. And that goes for you two as well." He handed each of the women a card bearing the needed information. The call would go directly to his department. "We're ready for anything. We'll get the word out. This man is a danger to more than you folks if he's the one who tried to burn your home tonight." Sergeant Martin turned to leave. "Be careful, Mrs. Munson." He flushed. "Looks like you're in good hands, though."

Martha waited until Judith and Duke left in his ratty old pickup, then she drove to her own home and pulled into the garage. "Wow! What a wild night!"

Feeling worn and very tired after all she'd seen, she planned to hit the sheets as soon as she checked the news channel. But entering the house, she stopped just inside the door from her garage. *If I was a dog, my hackles would be at full salute! Something's wrong, I feel it!* She flipped on every light switch she encountered, hoping illumination would dispel any ghosts. She checked behind doors and looked in her closets but still, the sensation lingered. Shrugging the eerie feeling away, she made a cup of tea and, with a few ginger snaps in hand, settled in to watch the news.

While trying to heed the details of what the news of the day provided, she let her thoughts drift off. Musing on recent events, her mind settled on little Aliya, wondering what effects would result from Pederson's injuries. *Is that little child safe, even now*? The man possessed such a cruel streak, her life could be in danger still. But if his abuse of her stemmed from sexual aberrations alone, she certainly ought to be safe.

❧❧❧

Martha drifted off, curled in Bob's big leather chair, but her inner person did not sleep. Suddenly, her pulse rate sprang alive at the presence of a dark shadow moving through the hall into the kitchen. Martha was all Serena now, still as a waiting cat, readying to pounce on her prey. The figure in the recliner chair lay quiet as if asleep.

Allowing her eyelids to rise only slightly, she saw the figure move furtively toward the body of her physical host. Her deadly resolve strengthened at the sight of a bright metallic flash from one of Martha's large kitchen knives clutched in his hand. Quietly—as if still asleep—she waited.

Seeing the knife increased Serena's anger and gave her a renewed and incredible strength. Carefully, the dark figure of the man neared Martha. His upraised hands clutched the gleaming knife as he prepared to plunge the sharp blade into the soft body of a sleeping woman.

Serena knew that, in his crazed mind, she'd become his nemesis. She caught the faint whisper of his threatening voice, "I'll teach you something, you fucking, meddling bitch!"

As the knife began its downward plunge, Serena slipped sideways in the chair, thrust her fist into his midsection, and rammed her knee solidly into his crotch. The man crumpled into an agonized ball of pain at her feet and lay groaning on the floor. She heard his muffled, furious curses.

"Oh, goddamn you, you filthy rotten bitch!"

Feeling the dampness, she saw blood dripping from her right shoulder. "Damn, he got me," she exclaimed as she flipped on a light and took a look. Upon examination, she knew the knife cut was superficial, but enough to cause profuse bleeding.

Martha once again picked up her cell to report the incident. After explaining the events to the 9-1-1 operator, she hung up. She'd be forced to deal with the authorities once again. This time she was the innocent party, just a good soul trying to help out a fellow nurse. *This should look good on my record, if I get one.*

She'd never met Munson, except when he'd come to her home, hunting for his wife. Martha congratulated her inner being for a job well done, all the while marveling that the Serena part of her possessed the strength to do such things. In spite of how well she'd integrated with her, Serena remained a mystery to Martha. She viewed her as a separate entity and always had.

She wrapped a towel around her shoulder to soak up the blood and turned to the man on the floor. Finding a rope in the garage, she bound his hands while awaiting the police. The knife lay nearby but she knew not to touch it.

"Why come here and try to kill me?" she replied to his groaning. "I only tried to help your wife. You beat her half to death every few days, and she finally had a bellyful of you, mister. I had to help her."

She sneered at him in both shock and anger. "You damned fool, the cops are coming. So how'll that look to your little sweetie you got so neatly stashed in that nice condo? Maybe she won't look so fondly on you now, eh? Ever think of that?"

Suddenly, Martha knew she'd said too much. If he was alert enough, he would know she'd shagged his trail from what she'd just spilled. *You stupid fool, keep your mouth shut,* she chided herself. *How much trouble do you want, anyway? Maybe he didn't hear what I just said.* At least she hoped so.

The police sirens screamed to a halt outside her home. Martha hurried to the door, opened it, and waited. *Put on a good act now, girl. Your life depends on it.*

The officers filed in. After greeting Martha, they introduced themselves and then turned their attention to the situation at hand. Looking for further threats from her attacker, the men checked everything out. Their investigative actions were impressive. Martha soon believed they were trained to see clues everywhere and find suspicion in every detail.

She pointed to the groaning man lying on her floor. "This is the man who attacked me, Officer. I happened to see him coming and fought back the best I could." She hoped her words sounded appropriately helpless.

"You all right, ma'am?

"Just a little scratch, he got my shoulder with the knife." She pointed to the bloodied area of her blouse. It had stopped bleeding and the towel had fallen off.

"You'll need to go to the ER and have that looked at, ma'am."

"No, Officer; it's only a scratch. I'm a nurse and I can bandage it well enough. I had to tie this guy up first, though, and call you people."

"Okay, I guess you'd know best." He motioned one of the men to get the camera. "We'll get a picture of your wound for evidence, if you don't mind."

They took a look at Munson, bound and moaning on the floor. Officer Miller happened to be in the group. He knew Martha and the situation with Munson's wife. "Hey, lady, you did yourself proud I'd say." He grinned at her. "So he did come here looking for his wife, just like you worried he might." He pulled Munson up and set him in a chair. "All right now, let's hear what you have to say, sir."

"This interfering bitch has done all she could to separate me and my wife. She had my wife over here for two-three weeks before she set that Navy SEAL bastard on me. He's keeping my wife away from me, too, and it's all her doing!"

Obviously seeing no fault in his own actions in the matter of his wife, Munson nodded his head in Martha's direction.

Explaining the situation, Martha said, "I work with his wife and I did offer her a safe place to stay after he beat her half to death. After the second beating, she hired a guy my husband and I knew. He needed the work."

"Work, my ass!" Munson had worked himself into a righteous rage. His face was flaming red and bloated with rage. "For all I know, my wife's shacking up with the guy and this meddling bitch right here is responsible for that, too."

Miller did his best to hold back his humor at the preposterous stance Munson had taken. "Didn't it occur to you that invading a private home and attacking a defenseless woman with a knife might be just a tad illegal?"

"Defenseless, hell—the bitch liked to killed me. Some things might be against the law but a man's got his rights!" Munson's shrill voice couldn't hold back the fury he clearly felt at his ignoble situation. "I'm a man of high position and blowing this little incident all out of proportion could destroy my career."

He quieted then and Martha wondered if he'd finally realized the stupid mess he'd gotten himself into. His wife had ample cause for a divorce after what he'd done tonight, although, more wasn't really needed. Abuse alone would do the trick.

"Marvin Munson, we are arresting you for premeditated breaking and entering, attempted murder, and bodily harm—some *little* incident!" Miller read the man his Miranda rights as he replaced Martha's ropes with a set of gleaming handcuffs. "I'm sure there will be other charges as well, maybe charges of assault and battery and arson will be added later if your wife chooses to press those charges, but that's it for the present."

Munson plodded stiffly between the officers as they led him outside and within a short while the police left Martha's home. Trying to settle down after the ruckus, she wanted to call Lizzie or her daughter, but the hour was late. *Who'd want to be awakened to hear this kind of news any-*

way? Sighing with fatigue, Martha made a cup of hot co-
coa and sipped it slowly as she settled to watch TV again.

"Well, here I am again. It was all so insane just a little
while ago, but it seems like a lifetime. I can't keep going
on like this. I'll go crazy if I do."

She sighed. "Serena, leave me the hell alone. We can't
solve all the problems of this screwed up world. I just want
to get some sleep." Sinking into her bed, she cried out in
the darkness, "Right now, I feel so all alone." Futile tears
slid down her cheeks. "Oh, Bob, why did you have to leave
me when I need you so terribly?"

CHAPTER 9

After the excitement of the fire and her encounter with Munson, time dragged slowly, day after day, until Martha cried out in exasperation, "Ye Gods! Has the world gone nice all of a sudden?"

She called Riverside Hospital for a shift or two to break her state of ennui. Of Pederson, she heard nothing and rarely thought of him. "Maybe his pedophile days are over for good. Dear God, I hope so."

Serena's wrath lay quiet and Martha thought that maybe her other self had gone silently away. *Not bloody likely!*

A TV series about trapping pedophiles caught her interest. Her heart rate increased while listening to the tales of foolish young girls talking to strangers on the Internet. "Serena girl, we need to check this out."

None of these people had hurt her or her family. Wasn't it wrong to give thought to the entrapment of these predatory males?

Story after story dealt with a motley assortment of males who passed themselves off as young boys looking for female companionship. As a mature adult, Martha easily spotted a few respondents that she'd have highly suspected of being far older than their messages implied. "My good Lord Almighty, some of these girls were no more than twelve years of age, some even younger."

She wanted to scream at the TV screen, seeing the gullible replies of potential victims. To Martha's consternation, a man of fifty could be the "boy" who answered a young girl's innocent chat-line e-mail with an unimaginable bag of sexual tricks on his mind. Once in his control, the poor child would find herself trapped and at his mercy. Another unsuspecting little girl would suffer for her foolishness, lured by false pretenses and promises of fun and excitement with a nice young boy her age. She would become an older male's next sexual conquest, and if she fought him, so much the better.

Martha, and even more, Serena, couldn't stop thinking about ways to put a few of those devils out of commission. According to the stories she'd seen on TV, one after another, innumerable men sought sex from gullible young girls in this manner. She felt her excitement rise, thinking of her next target and maybe several after that. Who knew?

Careful planning would be needed. *If I travel far enough away from Denver to meet these men—a quiet, lonely place like a cheap motel maybe, somewhere, anywhere, away from here would do. I live and work in this town and can't pull anything around here.* Martha knew she had to avoid the law. They wouldn't be so forgiving the next time.

"The law seems to protect those predators, anyway. Let them sweat it out, hunting for a phantom avenger, one who never strikes in the same area twice. Would the authorities even realize what these devils had been up to? What predator would ever admit to police what he'd been doing at the motel where he was so brutally attacked?

Carefully considering all the angles, she doubted her victims would reveal their illicit activities after their assault. "So much the better for us!" Martha laughed, hearing Serena in her voice. "I've got to learn the lingo these kids use when they talk on these chat sites. From the little I've seen, it might look complicated, yet it's rather simplistic, like crude phonics." She turned to her computer, hoping to learn how to get into the game. "I believe they are called chat lines."

She began looking on chatlines.com for information. She enrolled and began a long dismal search through multitudes of anguished teen missals of inane thoughts and ignorance. *My God, do parents really know what their kids are doing these days?* In her horror at how easily young teenage girls exposed themselves unthinkingly to the dangerous minds of predators, she searched for that certain one that suited her purpose.

One night, she spotted an e-mail that appeared to be written by a decent young man of early high school age. His e-mails said he was lonely, a boy who wished to meet a young lady, looking for friendship and adventure in a safe, controlled environment.

Carefully posing her answer, Martha connected with Tracker. She played the part of an ignorant thirteen year old, Teenie, who hated her mother and had no father. Left alone too often, she childishly played on the Internet instead of attending to her studies. She earned money baby sitting and that gave her a certain sense of independence. By subtly relaying these facts to Tracker, Martha believed he might see her as a potential victim.

In turn, she came to believe this respondent was no young boy, but a sly, malicious, predator of young females. "What young boy drives a delivery truck? What a fool! He doesn't try to hide it either, and tells me he lies about his age to make money." She chuckled. "I wonder if he wants poor little me to meet him somewhere, far away from his hometown. I'll let myself be talked into that—if he tries hard enough."

In her mind she already knew what to pack and her big, long, sandbag was part of the package.

"I'd best mend that little hole along the side of it. Maybe it's had too much use lately." Martha fondly remembered the soft *thunk* as it'd crunched heavily into Pederson's head that lonely night when she'd waited for him in the dark parking garage.

"Oh, well, I don't need it yet."

She had a shift to get ready for and signed off on her computer.

ↄ৹ↄↄ

At work, nothing happened to get Serena inflamed. Martha listened carefully to any bits of casual talk she was near enough to catch, hoping to hear news connected with Pederson, Munson, or little Aliya. She burned with curiosity about the fate of the little girl, including why any father could hate his child enough to do the things he did to her small body. *Will I ever know the reasons for him doing something so horrendously evil to that little girl?*

How any parent could feel that way was beyond Martha's understanding. She remembered how she and her first husband had cherished their own little girl. But strange things like that often happened and she knew it. Somehow, little Aliya had touched her closely and caused her to take an illegal action of vengeance, trying to help her. Had she been successful? She didn't know how to find out without bringing undue attention in her direction.

Leaving a patient's room, she heard an aid named Fred say to one of the other aides on duty, "Hey, remember the guy who got the shit beat out of him a while back?"

Martha halted and pretended to work on a chart at one of the mobile nursing stations outside an occupied room.

"Why? What have you heard, anyway?" a lanky male orderly asked, edging closer, primed for any juicy tidbit of gossip.

"Well, just that his wife was laughing like hyena when she left the hospital that first night he was here. I saw her outside the ER, before I came to work that night. I know people who live around there and they say he's a real bastard to his wife and kids when no one's around to see it." His voice dropped into more confidential tones. "Some say he went after one of the little girls in the family, too, said they've heard her screams in the night more than once."

"Hell, you say. That's sick! Wonder why the wife never calls the cops on him. Has her scared shitless too, wouldn't you guess?" The lanky male snorted. "Guess his sex lights are out for good from what I hear, eh?" He paused and voiced a warning, "Don't forget, we have ears in this place, too."

"Yeah, you know, mum's the word around here even if it's Charlie Manson." Fred laughed at his own wit. "Kids be damned, I guess. It's crazy how they let this kinda stuff go on, yeah?"

"It sure is," the other one huffed. "Well, better get this bod in gear or Nurse Ratchet will be on my ass again."

The tall young man walked away and Martha approached Fred. "You know, we had that little Pederson girl in here for quite a while. Sorry to overhear what you were saying but I've been concerned about her welfare myself. I can't help wondering how this incident will affect her treatment at home, if what you say is true."

Martha already knew what he'd said was true, but hoped to hear him say something that would tell her how the child was being treated now after the vengeful and emasculating strike she'd made against Pederson.

"He sits in the house all day, not doing anything, just whining around, according to their cleaning woman. She lives next to us. Woman's got a big mouth and no HIPPA standards." Fred looked closely at Martha. "Why do you care? It happens all the time to kids, don't it?"

"God, I hope not, but the little girl was my patient one night in peds." Martha knew discussing the child was out of bounds but couldn't stop her curiosity. She hoped she sounded casual enough. "Just wondered how she was doing, is all."

"Makes me wonder why the man was castrated, though. That's not a common thing, the cops said. Did that person know what was going on? Hey, maybe his wife did it. Not such a bad idea to my way of thinking. Well, that is if the guy was after his own kid, that way." Fred shuddered. "Well, got temps to take, see ya." He stalked off, tossing his head and flirting with a young female aid that passed by.

"Martha, you'd better keep your nosy mouth shut or somebody's going to wonder about you," she mumbled to herself and tried to do just that.

The shift ended without any more input on Pederson, but she never stopped listening for news on the man while hoping her work had put an end to his child molesting ways.

Remembering how poorly the man's male parts were set up she giggled. *Maybe it helps their creative genius. Or does it make them find some evil way to compensate?* Could that explain a man who tortured his own little daughter in such hideous sexual ways? She shuddered, remembering the night she'd had care of that poor child.

Sickened by thoughts of Aliya, Martha left for home. The streets were dark and slick from a recent rain shower. She whipped around to avoid a fallen branch as she drove. Unmindful of much besides her need to settle down in Bob's old leather chair with a nice, hot cup of chocolate and catch the latest news, she noticed, but didn't pay a lot of attention to, a car following. It wasn't close, just consistently behind her at every turn.

"Is that car following me?" Finally taking serious note of it, she tried to catch the color and make, but it stayed too far behind. "I wonder if Munson has turned his henchman on me now, since Judith has the SEAL watching over her and he can't get at her?" She frowned. "I don't want to become noticeable or need the cops helping me at every turn and yet here I am, being tailed, just like in a gangster movie or something!"

She drove slowly, hoping she was wrong, but as time went on, she realized the person following was very consistent, dogging her through the rain-slicked streets. It made her angry and afraid. Finally, after numerous twists and turns on side streets to see if the vehicle still followed her, she drove into her driveway and turned off her lights. Waiting in the darkened car, she wondered, *Will this person stop and make a move on me? He's certainly followed me close enough.*

In a short while the car moved slowly past her home. Martha tried to keep her head down and still get a close look. Sure enough, it was a white Cadillac Escalade pickup. If so, it had to be Munson. Martha believed he'd developed an unreasoning amount of hatred for her. She'd interfered in the deadly plans he'd made for his wife. Judith had filed for divorce and the man stood to get nothing from her, certainly not the home he was after.

"You stupid fool. Judith's on her way to making you a near pauper, in spite of your nice, high-paying job." She laughed and it lessened her tension at being followed. "And why are you roaming the streets when they had your ass in the slammer for trying to kill me? Nobody should have that kind of influence down town—no one!"

Martha wondered how well the man dealt with his divorce. Had his personality changed enough to interfere with his ability to make a living? She chuckled, realizing she was not afraid anymore. The swelling of confidence she felt came directly from her inner partner. "I wonder what evil plans that man has for us now. He's basically a damned coward, so let him come. Serena can and will deal with him."

Martha pressed the opener and drove into her garage.

℮ɔℇɔ

Nothing happened that particular night yet Martha felt exhausted by morning. "It's just a wee bit difficult to rest well when you're being stalked." She yawned, laughed, and put on a pot of coffee. "So what are we going to do?" she asked her inner self. "This can't go on. I won't be dogged this way, not by a wife-beating insect like Munson." Her jaw tightened. "I've decided I must put a stop to it. I have to. He's screwing up my chat line predator plans, big time."

Martha showered and went to the gym, knowing she'd need nearly super-human strength to implement her plans. She remembered her own traumatized grandchild, Will, and finally faced facts: *I have been handed a higher goal in life. How many unknown others are out there with no real protection from our politically correct laws?*

Without further adverse thought, Martha reached a conclusion: she had the will, cunning, and strength to eradicate any and all child predators from this earth. Certainly as many as she could possibly manage.

Feeling strong and filled with purpose, she told her alter self, "So, Serena, you've won your battle to take over my will. Pretty easy, wasn't it? I can't get over my bitterness against those who prey on the innocent, ruining their lives forever. Together, we can make a dent in them and if I should go to prison, it will be with a heady sense of accomplishment and my head held high." She laughed. "And I'm talking to my inner person again."

Feeling the strength of her decision flowing through her, Martha drove to her favorite gym. More aggressive than usual, she took deliberate chances by cutting into traffic where she could but shouldn't have. As if set on fire, she fought the feeling she had to drive fast, very fast. "Whoa now, girl, we won't live to do our deeds if you don't quit this stuff!"

Pulling into the gym, she saw the white Escalade drive past and felt certain it was Munson trailing her. *He's still on the prowl. How on earth did he get out of jail? What hatred, the man is sick in the head!* Shaking with nerves and a lot of anger, she parked and went inside. She decided to keep an eye on her car instead of doing the usual workout routine. Her vigilance was rewarded.

She watched as the white vehicle pulled slowly into the parking lot. A good sized man got out, casually walked past her car, and turned back to do it again. Glancing furtively about to see who might be watching, the man slipped close to her vehicle and she caught a full shot of his face. "It's Munson. He really is out. How does he do it?"

I won't be driving home in that car today. She observed him quickly open her locked vehicle and, bending down, he appeared to be placing an object beneath the steering column. "Whatever that thing is, I'll have the police check it out. If that bastard was in the slammer where he's supposed to be, this wouldn't be happening." She heard her own voice take on a low growl. "He should be in there from his arson caper and his home invasion on top of that. Why can't they keep a creep like that behind bars?"

She drug out her cell and dialed the number of Sergeant Herbert Martin, one of the men who'd come to her home the night Munson had attacked her. He'd given her his card with instructions to call him at any further attempt on her life.

Another voice answered and she noted how soft and deep it sounded. "I'm Sergeant Ed Gilmore, answering for Martin today. What can I do for you?"

Martha explained the circumstances. "Please send a bomb squad or whatever you do in a case like this. It could be a bomb. Munson's been following me all over town, and now this. I thought he was locked up. What happened?"

"I'm sorry. His lawyer got him released."

She sighed, clicked off, and settled down to wait for whoever answered in cases like this. "I won't get the bod toned up this way, but I'll be alive at the end of the day," she huffed. "This is more than serious! If they don't put this dude in the slammer after this trick, he'll end up killing me. Or maybe Serena will get him." She smiled as she said it.

The police arrived with sirens blaring. After assessing the situation, and interviewing Martha, all cars were removed from the area of her Buick. The bomb squad painstakingly examined her car while a crowd of curious onlookers gathered, much to Martha's dismay.

"No low profile for me, thanks to Munson. Why won't he leave me alone?" she muttered to herself while carefully avoiding the local news truck, thankful they were more interested in what the bomb guys worked on.

But unfortunately, Martha knew she'd be next. Those people tried for every slant, including one from the perpetrator if they could get it. Everyone had his chance to speak, it seemed.

CHAPTER 10

The officer approached, his voice gentle and comforting. "Officer Ed Gilmore, Ma'am. This guy shoved a high grade explosive down under your steering wheel. If you hadn't seen it, we'd have been picking up the pieces by now. What made you suspect you were being followed?"

"He's been dogging my trail for days. He's attacked me in my home, and now this. The man was under arrest for arson as well as his attempt on me right in my home. What happened?"

"Released on his own recognizance." He sighed. "This guy's got a lot of pull downtown, so I hear. Hey, you didn't hear that from me, now."

He laughed and Martha saw a smile so like Bob's, it took her breath away. She took another look at the officer—tall, well built, with a sort of heated animal warmth emitting from his dark blue eyes. His face bore the look of what Martha privately referred to as Western rugged, a face she'd noticed before on outdoor people from the desert heat of the Southwest. Lines from that wasteland lay etched across his forehead and those deep wrinkles around his eyes came from squinting into the sun. His big hands bore markings of the outdoors as well. She couldn't help but notice.

"You're not from around here, are you?" Martha found herself asking the personal question though she had no thoughts of getting close to any man again. Yet she'd taken that second look. Something about him caught hold of her in some strange way she couldn't help.

"Why, no, ma'am. Why do you ask?"

"I don't know, just idle curiosity, I suppose." The heat of a blush burning upward across her cheeks made her clench her fists, furious at her interest in the man.

He shoved his officer's cap off his head of sandy hair touched with gray and smiled. "I'm from Benson, Arizona, of late. Got tired of the heat and thought to try a higher altitude." He grew serious. "Well, back to business. You say you can identify the vehicle that followed you here?"

He deliberately bent his electric, dark blue eyes on her as he spoke and she knew it.

Martha fought back a blush. "Yes, it's a white Escalade pickup but I didn't see the driver." She told Officer Gilmore how many times she'd seen one like it and the circumstances of each occurrence.

"Thanks for your input. We'll put out an all points on the dude. Sure glad you weren't hurt, ma'am."

He bent another warm glance on her and she couldn't mistake the meaning she saw within it. She'd see this man again somewhere down the line, she knew that much. The police had impounded her own car, and Martha pulled out her cell to call a cab.

"Ma'am, let me give you a ride home," Gilmore said, coming close and gesturing to his squad car. "And you'll need to get a rental for a few days. We can help with that, too."

"Why, thank you, sir. I'd appreciate it very much."

Martha gratefully got into Gilmore's patrol car. She had on work-out clothes, but they fit her trim form very well, and she guessed he'd noticed that by some of the glances he'd shot in her direction. She chuckled. *This old gal's still got it—at least most of it.*

"You're in good humor for someone who could be lying on a cold slab at the morgue," Gilmore noted. A quizzical expression crossed those rugged, outdoorsy features and gave him a look of solid masculinity.

"It's nothing. Just a passing thought I had. This stuff is all so bizarre to me. I can't grasp the reality of it." *Better sound like a helpless female. They love it and I sure as hell wouldn't want this cop to know the real me.*

"Well, you're certainly handling it well. Not many women would, you know."

She heard appreciation and approval in his tone. His voice purred like a big tom cat—deep, yet with a softness to it. The sound of it went zinging through her like a fiery whirlwind, churning and burning.

They arrived at her home and pulled into the driveway. Martha, feeling mesmerized by the officer, wanted desperately to get away from that enticing atmosphere. She slipped out of the patrol car and murmured, "Thanks for the ride, Officer, really appreciate it." Purse in hand, she turned to leave.

"Hold on, lady, I need a few more minutes of your time." He exited his side of the patrol car and came toward her. Something in his looming presence startled her.

"Yes, Officer, what is it?" The nervousness she felt seeped into her speech. *What the hell does this bird want from me anyway?*

"Well, nothing, except I wondered if you might like to have dinner with me one night?" His low, purring voice soothed her fluttery feelings of idiocy.

"Er—well—sir, I just lost my husband only three months ago. I haven't done anything like that—I don't know." She felt the blush creeping up her face and the burn of it made her angry. *What am I, a stupid teenager?*

"Just askin' ma'am. You seem like a nice sort and I'm new around here. Anyway, give it some thought, and I'll check back with you." He handed her a slip of paper. "You can use this form to rent a car for a few days." Before he turned to enter the patrol car he gave her another glance. "You might enjoy a night out. I know I sure would."

She saw his eyebrows rise, and the smile that crossed his face as he drove away looked so like Bob's it made her heart ache with renewed loneliness all over again.

Just what I need to complicate my life right now. Wouldn't it be fun trying to clip a few child molesters with that guy hanging around? Martha laughed at herself, but enjoyed the nice glow suffusing through her body from her interaction with Officer Ed Gilmore. It felt good to have a man's appreciation again. *Serena, you really went for him, didn't you?*

She knew Ed Gilmore would be back, one way or another. And she had the worry of Munson still on the loose. *Why haven't they apprehended that devil? And how much pull does he have that he keeps getting out of jail? How can I rest with all this crazy stuff happening?* She sighed. "My life is completely screwed up with Bob gone, Serena in the driver's seat, and now this!"

Martha knew better than to get involved with an officer of the law. On the other hand—how long would it be before she heard from Ed Gilmore again?

And she would. He was way too interested. "Ye Gods, I don't need a man in my life right now. I don't care how much he caught my interest. Yet, I can't stop my thoughts. Something about the man draws me. It's you, Serena, you man-hungry, over-sexed thing!"

She huffed in frustration, though her heart beat faster as she remembered the tall, rangy, and rugged officer. "I think I just called myself a slut! What would Lizzy make of this new complication?" Then she laughed. "That nut case would think it's exciting and wonderful!" Tossing her purse on the kitchen table, she added, "Of course, it doesn't have to become a complication now does it?" In her mind, her thoughts turned to pursuing her activities as Serena, all the while entertaining a handsome stud of a police officer. Could she handle the excitement of a crazy thing like that?

Martha had to rent a car for transportation, and thought of asking Ed to help her. *I'd be an idiot to fool with that guy with all the irons I have in the fire.* She pulled out the phone book and tried to find auto rentals but gave it up in frustration and turned to her computer. After a short time, Enterprise was on the way to her door to deliver a nice Buick Century, just like her own, only newer and probably some other color.

On the Internet, Martha continued on to read the inane messages put out by girls too young to know which end was up. In shock, she nearly howled, "My God in heaven! This stuff is put out there by girls far too young to realize how they endanger themselves?" She sighed and checked for a message from Tracker.

"Oh, oh, here we go!' She clicked through his message. "He wants us to meet. I wonder what he has in mind. As if I didn't know!"

She replied: *idk, mayb—i'd luv 2 cu face 2 face. I'm x-cited! Luv, teenie.*

In time the answer came back: *just 4 fun, have 2 cu soon, K? Ttyl, tracker.*

Answer: *Yes, asap just 4 fun, ttyl, teenie.*

"Now he needs to say where and Teenie, the little teenage me, will be there with her trusty sandbag—just waiting." All other concerns forgotten, Martha drew herself up tight, her jaw tightening, as a hard resolve swept over her. She contemplated her next action against those who preyed on the young, innocent, ignorant, and definitely stupid. *The filthy predatory monster! He's really got it coming!*

After a couple of hours, a maroon Century was delivered to her. She completed the deal with the script Ed had given her and her own insurance papers. She drove it into the garage. Unable to find her opener, she sighed. "Left it in my car, I'll use the spare until they return it. Wonder how long that'll be?"

ଔୄଔୄ

She waited several days for the next proposal regarding a meeting place with Tracker. It would have to be fairly close, but not too close. She checked her computer often, waiting anxiously for that predator's return message.

Finally, Martha read the words she'd waited for. He wanted to meet her at a Motel 6 in Greeley. He would rent the room and she could meet him there. He would leave the door open so she could enter without being seen with another person.

"Perfect!" Martha cried, her heart racing with excitement and apprehension about the deed she planned. *It's only a couple of hours away by car and on good roads. I can get there and back in a short while, no longer than a shopping jaunt.*

Two days later, dressed as close to a teen aged girl as she could manage, Martha neared the motel. She wore sneakers, old jeans, a sweat shirt, and a floppy, cloth print cap to aid in hiding part of her face. She allowed the thick glossy, blonde ponytail she'd bought at K-Mart, to hang down enough to be to be seen. The art of disguise came into play once again and served her well. *Glad I've kept really slim, it sure helps with this get up. A grandmother mimicking a teenager has got to be inventive.*

Martha parked two blocks from the Motel 6, and walked toward the motel doing her best to look casual, and appear like any young school girl carrying a heavy backpack. Martha had often seen school kids loaded down and leaning forward with their burden of books. She knew the look.

It was already late in the day and the darkening sky came as a blessing to aid in being less identifiable, should any casual onlooker happen to take notice.

After ascending the cement stairway to the upper section, nicely located far from the front office, she sidled toward Room 248. Outside the room, she listened. Hearing no sound, Martha took a deep breath and entered. Though dark inside, enough light emitted from the doorway to see it contained the usual bed, dresser, bedside table, and those things meant for a night's rest. *Good enough. I need dim lighting in here for this meeting. Wouldn't want the poor slob to see the real me, now would I?*

A faint musty smell mixed with cleaning agents and moth balls, common to low-rent motel rooms, matched the scant amenities afforded here. He was not there as they'd arranged. Neither of them wanted to be seen entering the room together. He'd left after taking the room so she could enter alone. He'd come in later.

She waited for her prey. It wouldn't be long before the predator came seeking the innocence of a lonely young girl-child. She drew out the long sandbag, tensed her body in readiness, and waited.

Within minutes, Martha's heart slammed into her rib cage, hearing heavy steps nearing the door. *Tracker's no young boy with those heavy footfalls.* She'd left it ajar as planned. He stopped outside the door then, slowly shoved it open. The fool had begun to wheeze from his climb up the steps and his breath came in heavy rasping, respirations.

"Teenie? Are you here, Teenie?" he whispered.

Martha heard the depth of maturity and age in his voice. He'd tried to make it sound younger and lighter, but she knew for certain she'd found a child predator who posed as a teenage boy. *Not with those pipes, you aren't, you filthy sick bastard.* She felt her anger rising to a fever pitch. *Not in real good shape, either, are you, mister?* she thought, slipping backward into the shadows behind the door.

The man pushed the door open carefully, his ear tuned for the soft sounds of the young girl who awaited him. Hearing nothing, he came farther into the room, seeking his prey. Stepping back for enough room, Martha swung the sandbag with all her strength and saw the man crumple into a mass at her feet, dropping the bag he carried. She heard bottles clinking, and one smashed emitting the acrid odor of alcohol. As the odor of it pervaded the room, she growled low, "Whoa! Booze party, too, eh?"

Quickly grabbing his collar, she dragged him farther inside and closed the door, lest her actions be seen. She closed all the drapes and turned on a nearby lamp to get a look at Mr. Tracker. The teenage Romeo proved to be a man approaching fifty, slightly overweight, with a paunch, and partly balding, with grizzled, iron-gray hair. His eyes were closed, but she noted they were close-set. She was amazed at his protruding, beak-like nose. He resembled far more a human rat.

And he was, wasn't he? "You rat-faced, ugly man, my God!" she snarled at the inert figure on the floor. "What a hideous shock awaited some foolish, unsuspecting thirteen-year-old girl, if you'd gotten hold of her. Oh, you filthy, predatory monster!" She fought against giving his body a hard kick and decided just to get the job done.

This dude's strong enough to do whatever he wanted with her. She giggled slightly. *Serena, this pred's* really *got it coming. Let's fix him real nice and quick before he wakes up and finds out I'm really not thirteen!*"

She quickly pulled the man's trousers and shorts down past his knees and stopped in surprise. *Wow, a monster set! He'd have torn a little thirteen year old to bits with his equipment.* Shivering in disgust, she turned him on his side, pulled out her scalpel, and grasped his scrotal parts. With a few quick cuts, she altered his sexual ability for the rest of his sick life. She tossed the bloody parts in the commode and flushed them down. *Bye bye*! *Bet he won't be pulling this stuff again.*

Not wanting to appear medically practiced, she crudely dressed the wound with wads of toilet paper to prevent excess bleeding. "No more Gentian Violet for this business and no more long maternity napkins either." She wanted to savage him a whole lot more, but decided it might look too much like what she'd done to Pederson. *This much clipping ought to put this particular beast out of commission without any broken or shattered bones or slashed face. He's ugly enough as it is.*

Martha uttered a contemptuous laugh, that was pure Serena, and quickly packed her backpack then slipped out the door and down the stairs. Aping the walk and look of a young girl, she casually sauntered away to her car. Always careful to check the area for anyone who might note her movements, she smiled. "This run-down place doesn't get much business—nobody around. How nice."

Home was only a short hour or so away, hopefully far enough for comfort. After a while she stopped at a small roadside café for a bite to eat. Once again dressed according to her age, Martha believed she attracted no undue notice regarding her appearance. *I feel good about what I've done. I really do. I'd like to know that man's history. It can't be pretty, and poor little Teenie couldn't possibly be his first victim."*

At home, she slipped into Bob's big leather chair. The hour was late, but she flipped on the TV. *I wonder if they'd put it on the news if they've found him. Of course, he wouldn't want a thing like that known publicly, would he?* She watched for a while but saw nothing about it. *Will I ever know how this came out? Maybe the police reports would be on the computer. I'll check there.*"

Pulling up the Police reports for the past four hours of the Greeley Police Department, she searched for answers. "Oh, oh, here we go." She read a report about a severe attack on one of the city officials at an undisclosed motel in Greeley tonight. *Our rat-faced predator, Art Delavan, is a city dignitary, on the mayor's council no less! Wonder how this will play out in the news. He won't want what happened to him made known, why would he? Nothing may ever be done about it due to embarrassment.* She laughed. "Man, you never know who the devils are in any community. But I know of one who *was* in Greeley."

More relaxed after her busy night, Martha sought her bed but lay awake for several hours. Her mind busily detailed all the events of the evening. Did she leave any clues? Any fingerprints? No one had called to leave her a message, so no one would have wondered at her absence.

CHAPTER 11

The next morning, she found no mention of the man in Greeley in the papers. Frustrated and bored, she picked up the phone and called the staffing office. After a short conversation, she had a shift in psych. *Okay, I'll take it, but I really don't like psych that much.* She hoped and prayed not to face another Aliya Pederson on any ward.

Martha left the house and headed for work. "I suppose I should hate myself for the things I've done. It's criminal and not right." She fretted over it, then after a time she chuckled while driving down the semi-quiet afternoon streets. *But look at me. I feel good about it.*

She considered other ideas she'd often had. Every man walking along the sidewalk might be a child molester and every small child a victim. "Stop thinking that way, you fool," she chided herself. "Whatever you've done, my dear wimpy Martha, is not nearly enough. Nothing will ever be enough. Don't you get it?" Her inner self let out a derisive snort. "Idiot."

Martha shook her head yet again at the realization of how strong Serena had become. *My God, she really has taken over.*

"Look, Serena, back off. You can't possibly have total control just yet," Martha scolded her other self. "So, my dear, would you like to spend a nice long hitch behind bars? Maybe *you* are deficient in social consciousness, but I still have part of my mind left. This has to go a lot slower than you might like, old girl. Get used to it!"

Her temper had risen several degrees as she considered the dangers Serena willingly entangled her in. The right or wrong of it made no difference to Serena, and Martha knew she had a long, continuing fight on her hands.

Then, glancing out the car window, she saw a small girl walking down the street with her daddy, or was he? *Damn, every man I see looks like an abuser to me these days. If this doesn't stop, I'll need to see a shrink again. Yet I don't think I'd ever find the courage to learn anything more about myself.*

She passed the man and child but not before she saw the man jerk the child's arm and haul her along beside him. She saw how his face reddened and how he mouthed angry words to the little girl. Seeing the child burst into tears, she wanted to stop the car and stomp the cruel bastard into the cement. *Whew. Everywhere I look, that's all I see anymore.*

∽∾∽

In the offices of the Denver Police, Detective Harry Johns sat frowning as he read a report. "Hey Ebert, get a look at this. Some dude over in Greeley was found in a sleazy motel with his gonads neatly clipped. No sign of them were found in the room, but a few drops of blood found on the toilet seat let the whole world know where those babies went. What do you make of this?" He handed the report to his chief, Marcus Ebert.

"Let's take a look at it." Ebert perused the sheet from the computer. "Well, it's another castration for sure, but everything else is different, except—whoa there, here's an item that rings a bell." He put the sheet in front of Harry. "See there, they found a small bit of fine sand at the scene. Now where did we see that before?"

"Pederson, wasn't it?" Harry asked, puzzled. "Why sand? And why the emasculation bit? What about the victim? What was he doing in the motel? Do we know anything about the man's activities? Motels without family are always interesting—lends a lot to the imagination." He frowned. "The whole deal sounds damned shady if you ask me."

"To me, a low-cost motel usually means some kind of sexual meeting. The man in question is a city council type, so they're keeping that part quiet while they investigate the crime. I'd like to know more about this dude, too. Something really stinks about this." Ebert paused, thinking. "And finding the sand, who knows why on earth we'd find a thing like that? Looks like we have someone in the loop that's into male bashing, but for what reason?"

"If so, that makes two so far," Harry concurred. "If that were the case, someone either has, or thinks they have some reason for what they did. We need to find out who had something against both these two gents. I'd venture it would be very serious, probably of a sexual nature. It'd have to be."

"Like getting even, settling a score, maybe? For what, I wonder."

"Maybe. Why not?" Harry shook his head. "Makes you wonder what secrets the two men had that would set a person after them with such a hatred or vengeance. The damage was deliberate, and sure as hell permanent? What do these men have in common?"

"I think I'll have a chat with the guys at Greeley. See what they have to say." Ebert shoved a stack of papers in a pile and stood up. "Johns, how about let's get some coffee? My ass is tired of this damned chair."

ℰↄℰↄ

The mere sight of the hospital parking lot came as a welcome break in Martha's increasingly wild thoughts. *Whew, I've got to put the brakes on Serena before she lands me in prison, like Bob said.* Martha gathered herself into a moderate semblance of sanity and entered the hospital. The sounds and smells were familiar and the normality of it came as a balm to her troubled soul.

She reported to the psych unit after a short chat in staffing. The off-going nurse, Virginia Kreske, gave a short report. "Nothing wild tonight," she said and laughed. "God, some shifts are just plain murder around here, though."

"How so?" Martha asked.

"Oh, nothing much really, druggies, abused children, and a new schizoid to thicken the mix, but tonight should be nice. Only one demented Alzheimer's guy to gum up the works." She gathered her purse and jacket. "He's threatened everyone, so far, with a dinner fork, the handle from his over-bed table, and his shoes." She laughed again and went on to complete the shift report. "Oh, yeah, you'll hear an occasional scream from the schizoid."

"Man, what else?" Prepared for the usual night of psyche patients, Martha wasn't overly interested in the other patients until she heard the name of Pederson. *Is it possible we have that devil's wife in here?* Martha's ears perked up hearing a name so well known to her. *It must be a coincidence. It's a common enough na*me.

Without expressing undue curiosity, she took note of this patient's problem more than the others. "She was admitted yesterday, complaining of seeing things. She described them as animals inside her home, weird noises, and moaning coming from the walls. You name it and she's seen it or heard it," the off-going nurse reported. "She's no trouble except for the occasional scream or two." She reached for her jacket. "Sounds to me like she's got big trouble, though, working through being a schizophrenic."

"I guess we'll have to see how she does. Do we have a diagnosis yet?"

"Not yet, but the doc believes it could be acute sexual trauma. He's handled several patients with this sort of thing, he said." Virginia grabbed her purse off a high shelf in the drug room and turned to leave. "Stuff like this makes you wonder what goes on around you anymore. This world is getting sicker every damned day, if you ask me."

"Yes, you're right about that, Ginny."

Alone, Martha checked her charts and her meds. Making rounds with her aide, she entered the Alzheimer patient's room. He sat at his bedside table, waving the handle of it around, and punched out at Martha. "Git away, you heathen bitch!" He lunged at her but his restraints kept him in the confines of his Gerry chair. The aide, Herman, laid a gentle hand on the man's shoulder and it seemed to sooth the patient. "Got to keep away from them goddamned females. They'll cut the balls off ya, if'n you ain't careful, son."

Martha smiled at the old man's unwitting accuracy. Herman had a way with the fellow and took his vitals without incident. Martha decided physical contact on her part wasn't needed and went on her rounds.

She entered Mrs. Pederson's room. The patient appeared to be asleep but as Martha neared her bed, she suddenly sat up, wild eyed and fearful. With relief, Martha saw she was not Pederson's wife. Earlier, she'd found out the first name wasn't Shari either. Looking at her chart she noted the woman lived in another town and was a widow.

"Well, nothing about her to get me in an uproar. Why am I so relieved?"

Later when Martha had settled at her work station to do some charting, Herman came by and sat next to her, putting his bit into the charts. "Say, that old guy sure hates females. Wonder what's got into him that he's so down on women?"

"He's not the only one," Martha replied. "But he's certainly more visible."

"Yeah, I guess." He got up and grabbed his stethoscope. "Gotta catch a few vitals," he said and walked away.

Martha watched him go. "Nice kid. Can't figure women either, but then most men can't," she said with a smile and returned to her charts.

The evening went as usual and the shift ended. Martha relaxed as she drove home, the streets shiny with rain. She kept watch behind her for signs of a vehicle following and saw nothing, but that didn't ease her concern, "Whew, am I becoming paranoid, or what?"

She'd formed the habit of watching for anything that appeared to follow her through the dark of night. Since the run-in with Munson, she was exceedingly diligent in her observations. *Is the man still in jail, and if not, why not? Did he use his considerable influence with the authorities down town? Is he once again out on the streets with revenge against me on his mind?* "I'm really sick of that man's threatening presence. Maybe we need to meet him again, eh, Serena?"

C/SC/S

Martha slept fitfully, rising from her bed at intervals during the night and peeking out her windows. "What am I doing?" she scolded herself. "I can't stop wondering when

I'll be hearing from Munson again. If I call that romantic officer, he'd tell me if the nut case was out again, but I won't." She giggled a bit. "Just like a silly teen, aren't you, you idiot. But he was good to look at—oh, so good!" In reality, the police had a duty to forewarn her if the man was on the loose. She wondered if they'd remember to do it.

Then she felt her spine tingle. *Whoa now, he's here. I know it.* Martha slipped toward the garage door and pressed her ear snugly against it. She heard no sound. She returned to the bedroom and stood very still, listening. *Could that madman be in this house, figuring to clobber me while I'm asleep?"* She looked for her cell and remembered she'd left it in her purse which lay in the big leather chair of Bob's.

Hells bells, I've got to get my hands on that phone! She deliberated about calling the police when she had no evidence of Munson's presence. *'I have a feeling' won't do it for them when they are so busy, but they'd have a good laugh over it. So basically, Serena, it's just you and me against that sick fiend.*

Martha mentally prepared herself for a confrontation of a violent nature. *He wants revenge on me, and won't stop until he gets it—or I get him.* She felt the strength of Serena boiling within her body. And working out at the gym four days a week hadn't hurt anything, either. *Well, you fool, come on, then. I'm more than ready.*

She kept the lights off and waited where she felt she had the advantage. The moonlight was waning but gave a faint glow to the room. She'd placed a few rolled-up blankets into her bed, forming them into a human shape and whispered, "Here I am, you sick fool, laying here waiting for your lovely visit."

Standing back against her wardrobe door, she held a small baseball bat ready in her hands. It had been one of young Will's that he'd outgrown. Her back pressed against the closet, she waited as a lioness awaited her prey. That stance left three sides for his attack. "At least he can't sneak up on me." Her breath scarcely moved in her chest as she mouthed the words.

A tiny creak of her wooden flooring in the den identified his approach. The noise moved steadily toward her. He entered her bedroom and looked down on the sleeping form in the bed. He moved closer, muttering inaudible words. In his swiftly upraised arms, Martha saw a knife shining in the dimness of the room. *That devil is still bent on murdering me*, she breathed silently—waiting.

As the knife slashed downward, Martha stepped out and brought the bat down across his head. She saw his big body crumple at her feet. The knife had slipped from his fingers, but remained imbedded in the lump of blankets she'd arranged on the bed. "That could have been me, you slimy devil." She wondered if he heard her exultant taunt.

Now I must call the cops when I really don't want them or need them. This idiot belongs in a mental ward, but I wonder if this additional attack will be enough to keep him in jail. She quickly dialed the number on the first card she grabbed off her desk and heard the deep tones of Ed Gilmore.

"Please, Officer Gilmore, that crazy man has tried to kill me again, but I got him first."

She gave the address, hung up, quickly got a bit of rope from the garage, and bound the man's arms behind his back. Then she tied his feet to the bed so he couldn't come after her in case he got up.

Hearing the wailing cry of sirens in the night, she hurriedly donned a robe and met them as they reached her door. She opened it to see Ed Gilmore and another officer she remembered, Sergeant Jesse Miller. Officer Gilmore sent an intensely deep look into her eyes that sent her head spinning. *How can I be thinking of a guy at a time like this? Maybe it's the excitement of what has just occurred.*

She tried to calm her racing heart as she led the men into her home.

"So what happened here? Are you all right?" Gilmore asked in a hushed tone, far deeper and way more personal than required.

"Yes, I think so. Please come in, I'm so relieved to see you." She noticed they'd come in separate cars. "That crazy man must be out of jail again because he broke into my house and came after me with a knife, almost like the last time," She trembled and fought her tears, believing it made her look helpless. But inside, her elation at what she'd done to Munson had her riding an emotional high. "Can't they keep this monster in jail?"

Martha acted like she was losing it and trying not to burst into tears. "I'm a light sleeper, thank God, and heard something in the house." She led them into her bedroom and pointed to Munson, trussed up like a Christmas turkey. "I fixed my bed like I was sleeping and hid in the shadows with my grandson's baseball bat. Just as he thought he was stabbing me, I hit him as hard as I dared—didn't want to kill anybody."

"Good God, woman, isn't this his second attempt on your life?"

"Yes, and he tried to bomb my car. Remember? That's three attempts. Why isn't this man in jail?"

"Oh, yeah, I remember everything, ma'am."

Martha did not mistake the meaning in his eyes and it lit her insides into flames. She held her thoughts and feelings in check, she had to. *I dare not get involved with this man!*

"Looks like he's still out, I guess. I tried to tie him up. Hope he won't get loose." She did her best to sound helpless, but a man unconscious and trussed up like a turkey told another story, and Ed Gilmore was no fool. She pointed to the inert figure on the floor. "What will you do with him, now?"

"Wow, lady, you sure know what to do in a pinch. Are you sure this is the same man who tried to stab you a few weeks ago?"

Miller turned Munson over and Martha took a good look at him. His jaw was slack and spittle ran out the corners of his mouth. He'd been drinking. The odor coming off his clothes and breath confirmed it. There was no visible blood on his scalp and Martha felt relief seeing that.

"Yes, it's the same man. He blames me for breaking up his marriage when I took his wife into my home after he'd beaten her within an inch of her life." She paused and took a deep breath. "She went home the next day and he worked her over her even worse. Then she stayed with me until he found her here. I accidentally overheard him plotting to have her done away with. It was at a restaurant, and I happened to be in the next booth. He's hired someone to do the job for him. I heard him talking to the man on the phone that night, Officer Gilmore."

"And they let this bastard out of jail? I don't quite understand this town and how things work around here."

She heard the exasperation in his voice, but there was a strange hesitation in his manner she couldn't figure. It puzzled her but there was no time at present to worry about it. Martha kept trying for the helpless bit, hoping it worked. "His wife, or ex-wife by now, said he had a lot of pull downtown, whatever that means."

The figure on the floor moaned and cursed. "Son of a bitch! What the hell happened?" He looked up and, through bleary, bloodshot eyes, spied Martha. "It's you! You fuckin' bitch! You've ruined my marriage and my life. I've lost a damned good job, and that's your fault, too!" He sobbed in frustration. "My wife's left me! She's divorced me! I've been kicked out of my house and everything I've worked for all these years is gone." He raised his head and winced in pain. "Ouch! Go to hell, you bitch! What the hell did you hit me with?"

"Settle down, Munson—keep a lid on it. We're taking you in for attempted murder, again." Gilmore squatted down to the man and whipped out his handcuffs. He read Munson his Miranda rights then, untying the ropes Martha had used on him, brought the man's arms behind his back and handcuffed him. "Can you stand?" He was gentle, but his soft tones were backed with cold, hard steel.

Munson somehow knew it and Martha heard it in his voice. Now that the danger was over, she trembled violently inside her thick bathrobe. *This Gilmore is no man to fool with. Don't get involved with the likes of him!*

CHAPTER 12

ell no, I can't stand." Munson glanced at the bat lying on the floor in plain sight and Martha heard the whine rising in his voice. "She damned near killed me with that goddamned bat!"

Gilmore called Miller to come assist him in raising Munson. Together they hoisted the man to his feet. Martha heard him moan in pain.

"Careful now, enough of your damned police brutality. My head's already bashed in by this interfering bitch standing right there, gloating over me."

"We'll have you checked out when we get you to the station. Now let's go." Gilmore assisted the culprit out her front door, into a squad car, and sent him off with Miller.

She saw Munson crumpled in the back seat behind the metal security mesh as they drove away.

Her mind whirled with new thoughts of this man's hidden influences downtown. If he still had his pull down there, could he bring her up on charges of assault with a deadly weapon? *Isn't that the way the law works these days?* She didn't voice her thoughts.

Gilmore turned to Martha. "Sorry you had to hear all that. Now let's get your full statement." He bent his dark blues steadily on her, sending heated messages she easily understood. "You all right, ma'am?"

"Yes, I—I think so. I'm kind of shook up, though. That man is so full of hatred, it's hard to listen to him. He makes me shiver inside." She trembled, hoping to look a whole lot weaker than she was. "I only tried to help his wife. She's a real nice person. I guess he had her fooled until after they'd married. She told me it was all downhill from the wedding day." She wanted to make it clear who owned the Munson home. "What he said about losing the house wasn't true. It's *her* home and he wanted it. That's what she told me. He began checking it over, measuring, and trying every way he could to get her to sign it into both their names, right after they first married. After she went home with the Navy SEAL, Munson tried to burn the house down with her in it. I happened to spoil that for him, too." She managed a half-laugh as she told him her story. "No wonder the man hates me."

"Lady, you're one brave person. I believe that man was set to kill you." He looked at the knife plunged into the pillow. "Don't touch any of that. Forensics will do a complete on it in a bit."

"I can't sleep anymore, anyway. I feel kind of sick, now that it's over."

"Here, sit down." He ushered her into Bob's chair. "What can I get for you?"

He squatted in front of her as she sat in the soft leather chair and took her hands in his big paws. She felt the warmth and strength of them. It felt wonderful and made her feel safe. Brave as she was and strong as Serena could be, she'd been attacked and could have died tonight. That awful realization finally had finally begun to sink in. She began shaking and shuddering at the thought.

"Sorry, I don't know what I need right now. Why does this keep happening to me?" Martha quickly realized she'd best keep quiet about things that had occurred in her past.

Too much had disrupted the quiet in her life, way too much, and this man didn't need to know about it.

"What are you talking about, Martha? Tell me. I'm a damned good listener, maybe I can help. You can trust me, you know that."

His deep, dark eyes mesmerized her, and she felt herself weakening. *Oh, how easy it'd be to lie in this man's encircling arms.*

Imagining how it would be, she caught herself just in time. "Oh, it's nothing really. This thing tonight has me upset and shaken. It's like doing a good deed can get you killed anymore. Has the world gone crazy, or is it me?"

"I know one thing, my dear. It's because you separated him from his favorite punching bag, not because you befriended his wife. I'd consider it a real deal if I had you for a friend."

He still had a firm grip on her hands and she didn't try to remove them. It felt so good! She had the feeling that, as he knelt there in front of her, he was ready to leap up and devour her in the wildest way. He looked like a big cat, ready to pounce, and his eyes had grown so dark they looked almost black.

She had to break the mesmerizing spell the man had cast upon her. *Is this guy real?* He'd gotten way too close and it made her nervous as a cat on a hot plate. "Please, Officer Gilmore, I need to make coffee or something."

"Sure thing, ma'am." He loosened his clasp on her hands and rose to his feet. Then he bent down, like the finest gentleman she'd ever imagined, to offer her his arm as she rose from the chair.

"Thanks, I can manage." She didn't understand why his nearness made her feel defensive. "I'll just make a pot. Care for some?"

She walked ahead of him into her kitchen. She knew he took in the layout, how she'd decorated it, and lord knew what else. Maybe that's the way he'd been trained.

She hoped so. And she was absolutely certain he'd checked out her backside as she moved.

"You bet. I'd love a cup. It's been a long night for me. I usually do the day duty, but they were shorthanded tonight. I'm just filling in." He cleared his throat and said in low tones, "Sure glad the way this night's gone, I'll say that."

"Why do you say that?" But Martha knew what he meant.

"I wanted to catch sight of you again, for one thing. You've been on my mind a lot lately, but I've tried not to call, giving you some space."

Oh God, he's going to ask me for a date again. "I believe I've told you how I feel about things since my husband died. "

"I know that, but you have to take up living again too, don't you. You're too special to shy away from life, Martha. You've got a lot of living left to do."

"I suppose so. Actually, I've thought of you, too," she admitted as she brought cups to the table and set out cream and sugar. "Coffee's ready." She poured him a large mug, one that Bob so often used, and watched his big hand reach for it.

He mixed cream and a lot of sugar into his brew and sipped it. "Hey, lady, you sure know how to make a fine cup." He smiled at her, and the look of him sitting at her table seemed right somehow.

They sat in silence, drinking their coffee. Martha felt safe with him sitting on the other side of the table and relaxed a bit. "Do you have family here?" she asked more to break the silence than to learn more of him. A man like him would likely have a woman around.

"No, lost the wife about three years ago. We had a special kind of bond and it's been tough going without her."

She noted his look of deep sadness. It lay etched in lines around his mouth and eyes. "I'm really sorry to hear that. I've lost two very fine men in my life, too. I don't think I could stand anything like that again. It leaves you so dreadfully alone. I have a daughter close by, but she has her own worries." She sighed. "I guess you know what I'm saying then."

"You bet I do, ma'am. You might call me Ed, if you would." He grinned at her right then and it made her heart flip clear over. "How about having dinner with me one night, Martha? We know each other well enough after all that's happened tonight, not to mention the bomb thing."

She had to laugh and heard the joyous sound emanating from her throat. *Down, Serena, you're over doing this thing.*

"You've got everything, lady! So how about it? Like to step out some night?" He bent his eyes on her with his question.

"Yes, I think that would be fine. We know each other a little better. I'd enjoy a night out with a great-looking man. And you are, you know." Martha laughed in her embarrassment, but she felt good about taking this step.

"Well, how about Friday night then? About seven?" He rose to leave.

She smiled at him and tried to sound hesitant. "Sure thing—Ed."

"See you then." He left for his patrol car and she caught the flash of his smile in an overhead streetlight as he drove away.

"Well, you crazy fool. You've gone and done it now. Dating a cop and not any old cop, but one right up there with that Navy SEAL guy. He misses nothing, and I mean nothing!"

Martha often chatted with herself, because she'd become comfortable with the fact that she was basically two people and included Serena in her conversations as someone to talk to. "How can I keep up with everything I need to do and work? And I haven't called my daughter for ages. She must think I've fallen off the planet. But I'll call Lizzie first." Her long-time friend would understand her taking a date if no one else would.

Lizzy was the kind to accept of any sort of mood, personality, or whatever Martha was into. They'd been intimate friends for a long time, but during her short marriage to Bob and living farther away in another city, they hadn't been as close. But lately, with the resurgence of her alter personality, she needed the zany comfort of her friend more than ever.

Martha continued to hold a debate with herself during what remained of a long, tortuous night. Part of her feared the growing strength of Serena, part of her welcomed the thought of dating a handsome guy like Ed.

Martha fought this internal battle until she heard the slamming of a car door outside. She wanted it to be Lizzie and it was.

"Get in here, you wonderful girl!" With tears streaming down her cheeks, she ran out to the big, shiny, black Cadillac and reached inside to take her best friend in the world in her arms. "I can't stop crying, Lizzie. I'm so unbelievably glad you're here."

The slim, very trim woman moved her streamlined body out of the car and hugged Martha in return. "Let's get inside and make some coffee. Then you can tell me everything. It's good to see you, too, Martha, but I certainly don't want to hear you're in trouble again. I tell you, it just breaks my heart to know you lost that wonderful Bob." She gave her throaty, knowing laugh. "That guy kept your wild half in line."

Martha hugged her friend. "He certainly did, and that's what scares me more than anything." She helped Lizzie with her coat. "But I want to know how things are with you. We'll have time enough for all my sordid details later."

Once inside, Martha put the coffee on and, after a few general comments from Lizzie, she told her dearest friend some of what she'd been up to. "I'm afraid I've been busy, Liz, and on top of that, I've met a new guy." She waved Liz's startled questions away. "Yes, it's too soon, but I'm afraid I've made a date with him. It's almost impossible to even think about it and not feel like a damned floozy." A half laugh escaped. "I'm also a tad worried about somebody else in here, too, if you know who I mean." She pointed to her chest.

"Are you kidding! I thought you had that taken care of, Martha. What's happening? What are you up to, now?" Her brows wore only a mere suggestion of a wrinkle as she questioned Martha. "Are you saying more than what you told me the last time?"

"I'm not totally sure, but there are certain stirrings I can't get a handle on. I'm half afraid of her, yet she's really me. Oh God. What a mess I'm in." She laughed. "Well, I'm not in it yet, not all the way, but I'm off to a good start!"

"Well, we know what'll happen if you're not careful, don't we?" Lizzie snorted. "Hey, you've got me to talk with. Not as good as a shrink, but I'm free. Maybe you're still overwrought over losing Bob and who can blame you for that?"

Martha's eyes clouded with unshed tears, but she held them back. "Yeah, maybe that's it. You're good for me, Liz. I really needed you. Thanks for coming." She poured her friend a steaming cup and the vapor of it swirled upward, filling the air with the scent of freshly brewed coffee. Martha hauled out a jar of Biscotti with the merest touch of chocolate. "I'll fix a bit of something in a minute."

Over coffee and a great breakfast, she relayed her latest activities regarding her Internet chat line and the man in Greeley. "I wanted to do everything I did, Lizzy. But I worry I'm becoming one of *them*. Am I?"

"You'll never be one of *them,* but I worry about your future. That is, if you even have one, considering what you're doing."

They spent long hours chatting and catching up. Lizzie had a time constraint and had to leave. Disappointed at Lizzie's short stay, Martha felt like moping.

"I wish she'd been able to stay. But it's a long drive back."

She flipped on the TV, but found nothing that held her interest. To keep her head on straight, she called for a couple of shifts at Riverside. Maybe she'd learn something more about the Pederson household from that chatty male aide, Fred.

"Hi, Celeste, I'd like a shift this afternoon if one's available."

"Good. Be here at three. Is med-surg all right?

"Yes, med-surg is fine."

She hung up and fixed a late lunch. A tomato, cheese sandwich was all she felt like eating, that and a cup of coffee. But brewing it made her think of Ed Gilmore, and she felt her pulse race.

Martha didn't care what shift she took, she needed the work to clear her head from the feeling of disgust at herself for taking a date with a cop. "What were you thinking?" she chided herself continually, all the while remembering the way she felt in the man's presence. "So he's a great guy, but did you need to tie up with someone who could throw your stupid ass in the slammer?" She groaned. "I'm talking to myself again."

She pulled into the hospital parking lot and made her way into the familiar and comfortable atmosphere of the hospital. Bypassing staffing, and Angela's smiling face, she went straight to med-surg and plunked her belongings in the nearest vacant locker. Grabbing a coffee she headed for report.

Fred ambled by, hung his jacket on the back of his chair, and sat down for report. Martha's interest peaked at the sight of him. Keeping her voice low, she said, "Hi Fred, any news of the Pederson household?" She smiled benignly, hoping to sound only vaguely interested.

"Well, it's been pretty quiet over there, but the neighbor says the old lady's rulin' the roost after his injury." He sniggered. "She's heard the woman tell him off good and plenty, and more'n once." Fred snorted a bit and went on. "She also said the little four-year-old screams a lot at night and they don't know what's wrong with her."

The charge nurse and several other staff members came in and that open door of information closed for Martha. Showing no further interest, she did her best to pay close attention to the report given by the previous shift. But the child's screams in the night held an ominous threat in her mind. *Could the man be taking out his rage on that innocent child?*

Her assignment looked routine, but was very busy, and Martha worked her tail off, keeping her patients comfortable, clean, and satisfied. She dealt with family members when she could and, after many long hours on her feet, found a moment for coffee. Sitting in the staff lounge, she realized how greatly her work had healed and soothed her troubled spirit.

It was after eleven when she left the hospital and, driving through the quiet streets, felt peaceful and relaxed after the hectic pace of her profession. "Thank you, God, I feel normal again. Serena, you had no hold on me tonight and I'm better for it," she said to her inner self. "I wonder who's got the hots for Ed, me or you." She laughed at that statement because she knew it was her. "I'm so damned mixed up anymore, and there's no end in sight!"

Is that a car following me? Martha peered in the rear view mirror, watching a small dark vehicle moving apace with her. *Could that be Munson, or someone he's hired to do me in?* She saw a coffee shop and drove into the parking lot. With all lights off, she peered out the window and saw an elderly woman driver continue her way down the street.

"Whew, I've got to quit being paranoid!" she scolded herself. "I want to be normal again, but considering everything, how can I be after the things I've done? Things were handled when Bob was with me. Now I'm alone, facing this strange, double person that I am, all over again." Trying to believe her own words, she drove home, pulled into her garage, and went into the house. Passing the landline phone, she saw it blinking. "Who on earth knows this number? I never use it!"

She pressed the button to receive the message. "Hey, lady, where were you? I hoped we could have a chat over the phone. I guess I just miss you—everything about you."

In a panic, she failed to notice the softness in his voice, only wondered if he was getting too close for comfort. *How on earth did Ed Gilmore ever get this number? It's unlisted.*

An uneasy sensation crept over her. "That guy's a cop and a sharp-eyed devil as well. If he wants, he can find out everything I've ever done." Martha frowned. "I wonder if that detective in Colorado Springs made a report on me. If he did, I'm cooked!"

Martha sought her bed but, in a torrent of wild thoughts, lay awake for long hours. *If Mapus in Colorado Springs didn't want to prosecute me, would he have bothered to make out a report on suspicions alone? Of course, he would!*

Sleep continued to evade her and she got up to pace about the house. While making a cup of tea, she switched on the TV. A newscaster in his excited voice exclaimed.

"This just in, a small child was brought by ambulance to Riverview Hospital in critical condition. At first report, the child is not expected to survive her injuries. The name is being held for the time being, and Child Protective Services are on the case."

The reporter went on to another topic, but Martha's blood ran cold. *It's little Aliya, I know it!* She knew for certain she'd never sleep after hearing that report. *I'd like to call the ER to find out who the child is. They'd never tell me and showing that much interest might point a finger my way.* She shook her fist in frustration.

"I guess we didn't do enough to that evil bastard, Serena." Martha hated the sorrow and defeat in her own voice, but it was there. "It would take a thousand Serenas to solve the problem of child abuse! There's no way I can do it alone or even make a dent!" She huffed out an exasperated breath. "And what do I do about this poor child? Is there ever enough anyone can do?"

e/ɔe/ɔ

In the morning she dragged herself from a bed that lay torn and twisted. "What a horrible night!" she commented, looking at the mess. "Where did those crazy dreams come from?"

She knew instantly that some of it stemmed from the abuse she'd suffered in her very young childhood. *Why now?* she wondered. Shivering with old memories, she hoped the light of day would dispel them.

She made a small breakfast, had no appetite, but forced herself to take a few bites of toast along with her coffee. "Wonder if I need to see a psychiatrist about these things? Something is making me doubt myself."

Serena, I need your extra strength. I know exactly what I'm doing these days—all the way—and I am the one to blame.

CHAPTER 13

Martha prepared for her date with Ed Gilmore. Actually she'd started in the early afternoon and felt like a silly teenager doing it. Overly nervous, she tried to placate herself, insisting that she was merely going out for a nice dinner with a really great guy. After all, it *was* just a dinner date.

Doing her best to overcome other misgivings she'd detailed in her mind, she checked her appearance in the full length mirror. Her thin, gauzy, green-print dress brought out the color of her eyes and complemented her gleaming, chestnut-hued hair. The skirt was rather short on her tall frame, but her legs were long, slim, and well-shaped. She figured he wouldn't mind seeing a lot more of them, anyway.

The soft chimes of her doorbell sent shivers up her spine as she squared her shoulders and walked to the door. "Hi there, won't you come in—Ed?" She noted the hesitation in her voice and wondered why she felt that way.

"Wow, Martha, you look fabulous!"

He stepped inside and she took in his big frame clad in a dark suit, white shirt, with a red splashed tie that seemed slightly out there. *There's a certain kind of flair about this dude, that's for sure.*

"You look darned wonderful yourself."

Martha felt a flush creeping slowly upward as she looked at him. He wore a wide smile across his rugged features and she saw a twinkle in his eye. *Damn, if this man isn't handsome as hell*! Serena had also taken a good look at this fine-looking man standing in her living room. Martha knew that by the heated, wild stir she felt within her body. *I'd better soft peddle this business.*

"Well, shall we?" He gestured at the door. "I've made some reservations, if you're all set."

He held out his arm, and she grabbed the frosty little purse that looked nice with her dress and, with a small navy wrap to cover her shoulders in the cool mile-high night air, walked proudly beside the man to his car. He drove a small Mercedes, and a nice one at that. She fleetingly admired the sleek look of it as he ushered her in.

"Hey, sharp looking car, Ed." Inside her mind, she wondered where he got the money for a jazzy car like that on a cop's pay.

"Thanks. It's got a lot of miles on it but these things never wear out." He put his big paw on the stick shift, worked it, and they sped away.

"So where are we going?" She giggled slightly. "You've made reservations, you say?"

His masculine odor was definitely enhanced by his liberal use of a very expensive cologne. She knew it had cost a bundle.

"Ever hear of Andre's Hideaway? They say the food's good and I've never been there so I took a shot at it. Okay with you?"

Martha hesitated, but only for a moment, remembering how she overheard Munson in there planning his wife's murder. "I think so, but I haven't ever been there that I recall. Bob and I didn't eat out that much." She'd just lied to him and wished she hadn't mentioned her deceased husband, but—too late—she had.

Ed drove on without further comment. Martha hoped she hadn't dampened the evening between them. But when he flashed his wide smile in her direction, she relaxed and vowed to keep from mentioning Bob's name or anything else about her previous husband. The memories of him belonged deep in her heart and there they'd stay. He'd been worthy of the respect she bore him.

At the restaurant, she walked proudly at Ed's side as they entered. She gazed all about, seeing the luxuriously appointed place with new eyes. It had stone, green-hued glass, copper plating, and deep magenta hues as the primary colors. The floor was a magnificent stone-quarried tile with variegated shades of copper, greens, and beiges. When she'd been here before, she hadn't seen anything but Munson. He'd been her only interest and she hadn't eaten much, either.

After a short delay, the hostess seated them in a secluded booth beautifully surrounded with tropical plants and copper wall ornaments. Some areas sported a rich, copper-printed wall covering that complemented the overall décor.

The waiter arrived to take their drink orders and his polite bow only added to the luster of the night. Martha felt like a million bucks. His French-tinged accent, whether real or practiced, made Martha want to giggle, but she held herself in check. After all, this was the place for something like that and it seemed right.

She ordered her favorite, a pale white wine, preferably an Italian selection and hoped the waiter was not insulted by her choice. Ed took a whiskey sour and when the drinks arrived, he raised his glass to her and murmured low, "To a most lovely lady."

"Thank you, Ed," she said and sipped her drink along with him.

"Okay, let's see what we can order." Ed had a grin on his face as he scanned the menu written totally in French.

"How about *Coquille St Jacques*?" he asked, struggling happily through the pronunciation.

"Or *Fletan Provencal*?" She giggled, having no idea what it was.

"Well, there's *Duarade Grille*."

Ordering had gotten out of hand, but she enjoyed it immensely. Ed's face had taken on a rosy glow from his drink, and he laughed his way through the menu.

Neither of them could really pronounce what they ordered, but in good humor, they took chances, or rather, wild guesses and were greatly pleased with what arrived. With dinner, he ordered a very nice pale, rosè wine. Was the wine order correctly done? Neither of them knew for sure, or cared.

Martha enjoyed the evening immensely and, by the expression on Ed's features, she believed he did, too. She looked into his eyes at times, trying to read some deeper force she saw there, but his thoughts remained hidden from her. She found this man rather mysterious, an enigma in many ways.

For desert, they both enjoyed *Baba au Rhum*. "It's a *brioche*. It says here, soaked with rum, topped with fresh fruit and a thick crème topping." Martha laughed joyously as she read the fine print. "What's a *brioche*?" Part of her good humor was the pale wine, but good company and fine spirits topped off the leisurely meal. "Ed, thank you for a lovely dinner. I haven't been anywhere for a very long time and this has been a lovely treat." She reached across for his hand as she voiced her appreciation.

"Every moment spent with you is my treat, dear lady, and don't ever mistake it." Then he added, "I enjoyed the food myself. I don't think Benson, Arizona, has a French restaurant. Actually, I know they don't." He laughed and she caught the devilish smile that had struck her deeply too many times already.

His words made Martha wonder how this evening might end. The thoughts of what this man might expect from her later tonight made her shiver inwardly though she remained calm and assured with him.

They left the restaurant, and Martha wondered what he had in mind to follow a great dinner like that. She didn't want the night to end, not just yet.

"I know this great little place with country western music. Interested?" he asked.

"Sounds nice, Ed." She looked at him as he drove the car away from the French restaurant. "Been there before, have you?"

"Several times, but it'll be better tonight with you along, a whole lot better." His voice held that soft crooning tone that hit her way down deep.

Ed wheeled his car into a wide graveled parking lot and stopped. Martha saw a large, rangy-looking building loaded with flashing, neon-lighted beer signs and a cowboy outlined in wild neon colors, dancing in jerky movements. She held her comments, but heard Ed chuckling.

"So what'd you think?"

She heard the slurring of alcohol in his speech and it surprised her. He'd been so together—until now. Her curiosity rose as she contemplated attending this dance hall.

"I'll wait and see, Ed. Might be a lot of fun." She smiled at him and grabbed the door handle. "Let's go, then, partner." The Serena side of her was more than ready to kick up her heels and she figured if everything else about the man held true, he'd be one hell of a dancer.

Martha heard the pounding of the drums, wailing of fiddles, and a horn or two grinding out a familiar old country song as they neared the entrance. It sounded like fun and she was ready.

She hung on Ed's muscular arm as he paid the entrance fees and led her to a secluded table near the back of the seating area. He ordered more drinks as the bar maid came by before he got up and held out his hand. "Ready, partner? Let's give it a go, shall we?"

"You bet!" She rose to follow him to the dance floor already crowded with fancy, two-stepping couples. Some of them appeared heavily involved and clinging to each other and some happily exhibited a great deal of dancing know-how.

Martha, enclosed snugly in Ed's powerful arms, found herself quickly twirled and whipped about the floor. She was rusty so it took her by surprise that he moved her about with such great ease. He took every move upon himself and she enjoyed the feeling of competence he gave her. She felt almost like a dancing pro in short order.

"It's nice holding you like this, Martha."

During a slow dance he had the chance to get closer and took full advantage of it. Though she began feeling crowded by his closeness, she didn't want to spoil such a great evening and went along with it.

"You're a great dancer, Ed." She smiled into his eyes, but looking closer, she saw something so deadly hidden there, it chilled her to the point she no longer wanted to be held in his arms. Puzzled and alarmed, she couldn't figure out what gave her that feeling. *He's such a great guy. What is it?*

His wide grin reduced the icy tremor she'd felt. She relaxed as he swung her wide and the dance ended with a low dip, which made her giggle.

"Enjoying yourself?" Ed escorted her to their table with his arm around her waist and leaning part of his big frame against her.

Martha suspected the last three drinks were taking their toll and began to think of leaving. "I sure am. You're a fabulous dancer and good company, but I have a shift tomorrow afternoon. Shouldn't we be heading back, it's getting rather late."

"Sure thing, Martha, we'll take off right away." He quickly tossed off the rest of his drink and rose to assist with her wrap. As he placed it around her shoulders, he leaned against her back and whispered in her ear, "I'll be happy to take you home, anytime, anywhere, lady."

Martha knew he meant far more than a handshake or quick kiss goodnight on the door step. Alarmed, she realized Ed had deeper plans for her when they reached her home. The alcohol fumes from his breath told her he'd imbibed too much to be reasonable if she refused his advances. She and her inner helper decided to play this situation out.

The drive home quickly became a frightening event. When he swerved and barely missed a car, Martha tried not to scream, but gasped loudly.

"Wassa matter hon?" He laughed and hiccupped. "Don't like my drivin'?"

"Could you go a bit slower, Ed? I'd like to see the sun come up this morning." Martha tried to be gentle with him, while wondering if they'd make it to her home in one piece.

"Aw, now, don' be afraid. I'm a good driver. I'c'd make the Indy 500, wanna see me try it?"

"No, I don't want to see—Ed!" She stifled a scream as he swerved wildly to miss an oncoming car. "I just want to make it home alive, if that's all right with you!"

The anger in her voice sobered him. "Sorry, Martha. Din' mean to scare you."

Maudlin sorrow had crept into his voice and she realized this fine-looking gent had a problem with alcohol. *Oh, God, tears will be next. What a rotten way to end a fabulous date.*

With a great sense of relief to Martha's frazzled nerves, they reached her home. She'd wondered if he'd be able to find it in his drunken haze. They pulled to a stop and he slowly got out, using the door frame for support.

He came to her side of the car and took her arm as she rose from the seat. Together they walked to the front door. *Oh oh, here it comes!* She prepared herself for unwelcome advances from a man well into his cups. Ed was a drinker and she'd never have anything to do with a man like that. Never! She'd seen too much in her career as a nurse to abide that.

"Martha, I had a great time tonight. I'd like to see more of you. You know what I mean—uh, we could do some of that right now, or maybe see each other a few times first. It'd be your say."

To Martha's surprise, he no longer sounded drunk, but sober as the proverbial judge. Ed was a tough read and a tougher man. She didn't want to anger him.

"Please, I'd like to go in now. I had a very nice time and I thank you, but I'm tired and need to get some sleep." She reached for his hand.

Ed didn't want the hand. He reached for her and swept her back for a full, hard kiss. His seeking tongue tried to enter her mouth, but she resisted with all the strength she could muster. The man had a sinewy male strength and in spite of the alcohol fumes, he still had a wonderful masculine smell about him, his skin, clothes, hair, everything. But that warning—that deep chill, came over her senses again. She rejected him, struggling and pushing against his chest. He released her.

"Aw, darling, that's no way to say g-night, now is it?"

"Maybe not, but I *am* saying it! Goodnight, Ed. Thanks for dinner and the dancing. You're a very fine dancer, and I enjoyed it, but I must go in."

She left him standing there as she unlocked her door and slipped inside.

She quickly locked it and heaved a deep sigh. *Whew, I'd hate to make an enemy of that guy. He's just too much!*

CHAPTER 14

Ebert and Harry worked to make some decisions regarding the two emasculation cases.

"Is there someone who could be personally connected to these men?" Harry said. "That's the key we need. The cases are far apart and the only clue is the deed itself and the bit of sand found at the scene. So far, we have no tie between the two victims, well, from what we know at this time."

"Maybe it's the crime itself, any other castration crimes around? See what the net has on it." Ebert frowned. "Maybe someone has it in for these particular men. We need to know why and what they share in common, something sexual in nature, for sure." He picked up the phone. "Best see what Greeley has to say about that man's personal life, pursuits—whatever. Maybe the man was into some shady business, you know, the motel business and all, but if this is retaliation, why?"

Harry shrugged. "And Pederson—his four-year-old daughter's doc gave us some rough information about the child that's hospitalized. The kid is in extremely critical condition and it looks like her own father is the abuser—big time. By his description of her vaginal wounds, most of the trauma is certainly sexual. The other areas are just plain abuse."

"You mean the little girl who fell down the stairs?" Ebert shook his head. "If that man isn't a damned sex pervert anymore after having his gonads clipped, he must be a plain out-n-out battering son-of-a-bitch!" He grew very quiet. "Could there be someone who wanted to avenge that little girl?" He turned to Harry. "You know, I'd like to interview every person who ever had contact with that child, in the hospital and out of it. Might be a good place to start. Babysitters, family, hospital staff, who knows."

"I'll do the same with the guy in Greeley," Harry said. "Maybe he had some funny little habits that will give us a clue. His being in a no-tell motel isn't good so far as I can see. Why was he there and who was he meeting? That that's the real question, isn't it?" He stood up. The chair had gotten too damned hard all of a sudden. He put down the phone. "How about we catch some grub?"

"Sure thing," Ebert replied, grabbing his jacket as they left the office.

❧❧❧

Martha took a shift, hoping anxiously to hear more of Aliya's fate, if she was indeed the child mentioned yesterday on the news. Her name was not mentioned in the obits, which gave her hope the child survived. She hurried her make-up, stepped into a set of crisp, clean scrubs, and left for work.

Her mind had been on Ed a great deal, finding him completely confusing. He was too much of a man to be an alcohol abuser, or at first, she'd thought of him that way. So what was it?

She had med-surg again and didn't hear Aliya's name mentioned in report. Fred wasn't on duty this evening so that avenue of information was closed. The evening went along without incident until she overheard two nurses talking.

Lena Cabot, a nursing aide, confided to Maria, another aide, "Did you hear about that little kid they brought in yesterday? She was so banged up they didn't believe she'd live. Hanging by a thread, I hear—in the units right now."

"You don't say! Wasn't she the one they had in here twice this year for some other injuries?" Maria asked. "If it's the same kid, I betcha somethin' real rotten's going on in that home. Fred told me some awful things about that place." She turned to leave. "Why aren't the police looking into her case?"

"They need to, that's for sure."

The aides parted, going about their duties. Martha felt sick. Nauseated, after hearing about the tiny girl who'd never be normal after what she'd suffered. "Bastard may as well have committed murder with the damage he's done to that child," she muttered beneath her breath.

Hearing the sad news about Aliya she felt her anger soaring to new heights. *If clipping and a broken arm wasn't enough for that sick bastard, what would be?*

Her shift ended and she hadn't learned anything new, except confirmation that Aliya was the child in question. Martha hoped she hadn't put herself out there enough to be noticed. "I'm getting paranoid. Maybe it's leftovers from the things that happened in Colorado Springs. You never know what the police might figure out. Plenty, if they dig deep enough. Male castration is pretty rare, so it could all come back on me. I can't find it in myself to be sorry for anything, and so help me, I'll do more clipping unless they catch me." She threw her hands up in frustration.

"The child brought into the emergency room last night, has succumbed to her injuries," she heard on the radio as she drove home. "The name and more details will be released pending on notification of kin."

"That poor baby!" Martha felt the salty tears flowing down her cheeks as she wheeled into her garage. Anger and futility struck home, leaving her with a feeling of hopelessness. She sat for long moments with her head against the steering wheel, seeing Aliya's big brown eyes and trying to shut out images of how her small battered little body must have looked as tears coursed down her cheeks.

৩৩৩

Harry walked up to Ebert's desk. "I put out some feelers on castration and only got one response that meant anything. Seems they had two cases in Colorado Springs, couple of years ago." He pulled up a chair close to Ebert. "Marcus, I think we need to go slowly on what we've got here. Detective from Colorado Springs, a Ryan Mapus, called me to have a chat. He filled me in on quite a tale." Harry went on to disclose the details of one Martha Lavery. Her activities in Colorado Springs gave them pause for several moments. "Mapus told me he didn't want to prosecute the woman because actually, she did the city a big favor, *fixed* two child predators and shot a drug lord in self-defense. He figured if they tried to prosecute her, she'd be hailed as a heroine and the cops, as usual, the bad guys."

"Are you saying we have this person in our community?"

"I believe we do. She's married, or was, name's Martha Chance. Her husband died recently. She works at Riverside Hospital." He sighed then added, "That's all we know regarding her past activities, but there is something current going on with the lady. She's the one that fought off that perp, Munson, in her home recently." He laughed. "Second call to her home involved the same dude. Tried to get her again just lately and she decked him with a kid's baseball bat. Man's in custody awaiting arraignment and with a bandage on his noggin to boot," Harry went on. "Otherwise, her reputation's excellent at the hospital, so I hear, and no signs of a mental problem. Mapus said it'd been resolved."

Marcus nearly scoffed. "Mental problem, what the hell are you talking about? And how would she be connected to any of our incidents?"

"Can't be sure, but I'd like to do some checking on her. Let's keep this between ourselves for the present. Mapus said she was a nice person."

"Yeah, nice, sounds like a real winner! Let's hear more about the mental problem thing. Maybe she's gone off again."

"Well, she was never 'off' in the sense of insanity, just had another person inside her making her do the things she did." Harry laughed and repeated Martha's past exploits. "Not bad for a granny, I'd say."

"Good God, Harry, a grandmother!" Ebert had an expression of disbelief on his face. "Jeeze, Louise, what the hell next?"

"She sure as hell was—is. See why we need to go slow with this business? And by the way, I talked with that doctor again regarding the Pederson child's case. He told me that the child had been molested brutally and tortured before she was admitted to the hospital. She died yesterday." Tears came into Harry's eyes. "That little girl wasn't even five years old, had broken bones, bruises, and burn marks all over her little body. Some were half-healed, some brand new." Then he cursed. "Fell down the stairs— my ass!"

Ebert threw up his hands at the futility of protecting children from their "loving" parents. "I hope they throw the key away on that son-of-a-bitch. Is Pederson in custody? If not and the doc will testify, we'll get a warrant out on him."

"No, he's not," Harry replied. "That wife of his backs his lying story all the way. Ought to arrest that miserable excuse for a mother while they're at it." He rose from his chair. "I'll request the doc's testimony. He sounded mad as hell, so I believe we can count on him. If we have that, we can arrest the sick son-of-bitch. We can always summon the doc for testimony in any case."

"Go to it," Ebert said. "And issue that arrest warrant ASAP. The sooner that monster is behind bars, the better. There're other kids in that home." He paused a moment. "Harry, get a search warrant and we'll go over the Pederson's home with a fine toothed comb."

"Consider it done, yesterday," Harry declared. "You know, we already have a great way to interview this Martha Chance without arousing her suspicions. We need her testimony on the Munson case." His curiosity had been completely aroused by what he'd learned of this woman. "I'll see to it."

e⁄ɔe⁄ɔ

The musical notes on her phone rang out and Martha pulled it from her purse. "Hello?"

"Hey, lady."

She felt her face tighten. It was a call she'd expected, but wasn't looking forward to. "Yes, how are you?"

"I'm good. But I miss you. How about we go out tomorrow night?"

"I don't think so, Ed. It's really is too soon for me. I hope you understand how I feel."

"But we had a great time, didn't we?"

"Yes, I had a very nice time, but I'd rather wait a while before I go out again." She changed the subject, hoping to defuse the situation. "And when do I get my own car back? How much forensics do you guys need anyway?"

"I'll check. You should be able to pick it up soon."

"Thanks for checking on that, Ed. And about going out again? Really, you must give me the time I need. I'm sorry to say no and I hope you understand."

She hung up and sat in Bob's old chair. Shaking inside, for some foolish reason, she needed the comfort she'd always found there.

"I sounded like a downtrodden wimp just now, and that's not me. That man's not one to take no for an answer. I hate to say it, but I feel threatened for refusing a date with him, and that's not right." She got up and paced about the room. Then she reached for her cell and speed dialed a familiar number.

"Lizzie?" She thought her voice sounded funny and, in addition, she felt completely out of kilter.

"Martha, what's wrong? Are you okay?"

"Yeah, I'm okay but something might have happened. I need to see you if you could come. You're my best medicine right now."

"I'm on my way. Don't do anything stupid until I get there."

Martha laughed. "Thanks a mil, Lizzie. You'll never know how much I love you for coming." She sighed with relief, knowing her outrageous friend and cohort was on her way.

Martha stepped to her computer and sat down. "How would I check up on Mr. Edward Gilmore, late of Benson, Arizona?"

She entered the town and his name but nothing came up so she typed in obituaries for as near to three years ago as she could. After about one hour of searching, she found an Amanda Gilmore, aged 38, who died from injuries suffered in an auto accident.

Her husband was listed as Edward so Martha believed she'd found the right Gilmore, but there was nothing further to arouse her interest and she powered down as Lizzie knocked on the door.

"Come in, you darling. You've come so far and I do appreciate that."

"So what's got your knickers in a twist this time?"

"Lizzie, I went on that date with Ed."

"Well?"

"It seemed like a good idea when I said I'd go. The guy's a dreamboat for looks and all that, you know, tall, ruggedly handsome, deep blue eyes, but there's something not right about the man. Even Serena backed off and you know how she is."

"How was the night? Did you have a good time?"

"At first, it was magical. We ordered in French, if you can imagine. The whole night was so much fun until I realized that he drinks too much. His driving was so erratic on the way home, I wondered if we'd make it alive. He slurred words one minute and sounded clear as a bell the next. His eyes are hard and cold enough to freeze an iceberg sometimes when I look into them. I don't know what's wrong with him, but some feeling inside of me makes me wary."

"Did he try anything?"

"He wanted to—tried, but I wouldn't. He wasn't too happy about it either. After only one date—I thought it was damned pushy on his part." Martha shuddered. "I don't know what it is, but sometimes when I look into his eyes, I see an icy resolve and I don't know what it means. I don't get him. He might have reminded me of Bob at first, but not now, that's for sure."

"You're afraid of him, aren't you?" Lizzie's face betrayed her worry as her handsome features crumpled. "Something sure made you call me in a midnight rush, dear girl."

"You could be right about that. Imagine it. I truly never thought I'd be afraid of any man." Martha sighed. "It was a mistake to let this happen when, as you know, I have other things going on." She recapped her adventures as *Teenie,* and the events in Greeley. "I sure don't need a pushy cop on my trail and I knew that before I went out with him. But he had that certain smile, Liz."

"And your heart ached for that same wonderful smile so like Bob's, didn't it?" Lizzie laughed and spoke to Martha's inner person. "Serena, I think you're slipping."

"Hey, she backed off before I did, but somehow I knew something wasn't right, too. Ed's so damned good looking I got lost in my thinking." She shrugged, shook her head, and smiled at Liz in frustration.

A sly look crossed Lizzie's features. "And Bob's been gone how long?"

"I know, I know, it hasn't been that long." Martha flushed. "I know it was Ed's smile, but it will never be that again, Liz."

They spent more time drinking tea and catching up on things then went to bed. But Martha lay awake for long hours, fighting those demons that had invaded her life from the day her grandson had been molested.

You sick monsters, you destroy the quality of more lives than the poor child you savage. You whine about your sick, depraved needs. *Well, you sick devils, I have* needs *too and I'll take care of every one of you.* She softly beat her fist into the pillow. *If God lets me live long enough.*

CHAPTER 15

Martha felt a deeper fatigue than usual when she awakened. Dragging herself out of a bed of twisted linens, she staggered into the kitchen in time to see Lizzie standing in the kitchen with hot coffee ready. The waffles had been beaten to a frothy batter, rich with eggs, and the waffle iron was smoking hot.

Martha made it to a chair and sat down. "Dear Liz, you're up and so early." She pushed a clump of unruly hair out of her eyes, blinked, and reached for a cup that wasn't there.

"Dear, it's after ten. You must have been tired or— what?" Lizzie directed her hazel-eyed gaze directly at Martha. "Bad dreams—big worries?"

"Big worries, I guess. I need coffee. Can't wake up."

Lizzie poured a cup and plunked it down in front of her, spilling only a few drops.

"Thanks." Martha sipped slowly, trying to get her thoughts together. "Last night, I realized all over again, my life is as changed as my grandson's, and for the same reason. The world has gone mad with the violence against our kids and we are helpless to prevent it. No wonder I couldn't get to sleep. And I have this terrible anger back again." She snorted. "Could be it never left."

Lizzie had the waffle iron steaming with batter. "You were okay as long as you had Bob, you know you were."

"Sure, with him I lived in a fool's paradise." Martha couldn't stop the stray tears that fell from her eyes. "Deep inside of me, nothing has really changed." She grabbed a tissue and blotted her face. "Sorry to be such a basket case. Now you know why I needed you so much. You're the only soul in this world I can be totally honest with, anytime, anywhere. Otherwise I'm play-acting all the way, even with my daughter and her family. They have no idea I've been busy again, and they wouldn't like it or approve if they knew."

She buttered the crusty waffle Lizzie put in front of her and, before reaching for the syrup, looked her friend in the eye. "I know it's a lot to ask when I call you the way I do, but I don't think I could make it without you. You know everything about me and you're still my friend. Why am I so lucky?"

"Martha, you'd do the same for me, I know that. Besides, what in my dull routine could be more exciting than knowing a mental case like you?" Looking at the syrup bottle, Lizzie exclaimed, "Hey, real maple stuff, love it." She topped her own waffle and dug in.

After a short breakfast, Lizzie dropped the paper in front of Martha. "Take a look at that. Isn't this guy the one you…er…clipped in the underground parking place? He kept on with his abuse anyway, so his torture of a little child couldn't have been completely sexual with him. Now he's accused of murdering her. Looks like they've finally figured out what a monster the man is."

"Finally!" Martha slapped her hand on the paper. "Aliya suffered the tortures of hell in that house and no one came to her rescue. I tried and, obviously, failed."

"Well, maybe a bit of justice has come—though too late for her." Lizzie sighed. "With his wee little fixins, the guys in prison'll have a good time with him, won't they?

I'm sure the SOB will be everybody's sweetie and I sure as hell hope he gets his full share of their loving attention." She grimaced. "I hear those guys hate a child molester above any other criminal, and they take real good care of them, too."

"I guess I told you about his equipment, didn't I?" Martha giggled and forgot her tears. "Hey, Liz, did I tell you about the guy in Greeley?"

"You told me about it, but maybe not everything. I'm waiting to hear more about that one, too." Lizzie listened intently while Martha described the massive set on the man she'd disabled in Greeley at the cheap motel. "Imagine if I'd really been a little thirteen-year-old."

"Wow, that's one sick dude." Lizzie shuddered. "Big surprise when he woke up." She got up from her chair. "Well, dear heart, I've got to get back this morning. We have an event this evening and I have to show. Heard any more news on Mr. Big's case?"

"Not so far." Martha chuckled. "Great name for that raunchy bastard. I keep my ear out, but it's pretty far away, and the guy's on the city council. Maybe he's keeping it quiet, or trying to. I know I would. That rat-faced pervert wouldn't want people to know what he was doing at that motel. If his friends knew he was into trapping innocent young girls for sex in a sleazy motel, wouldn't news like that frost the man's fine reputation?" She smiled, feeling no remorse at what she'd done to the man—only a deep satisfaction at having done it.

Lizzy left and Martha felt at loose ends. *That ditsy woman is more help than a shrink. I miss her already.* She dug farther into her morning paper. "Okay! Munson will be held for trial on several counts including attempted murder. I guess that means I'll have to testify. Sure—poor scared little me will be glad to send his dumb ass to the slammer." She let out her breath.

He should have let Judith go gracefully instead of beating the crap out of her twice a week. She chuckled in glee at reading of his fate. *I wonder how she's doing with the Navy SEAL?*

As if summoned, the phone went musical and she picked up. Hearing her friend's familiar voice, Martha cried, "Judith! Hey, I was just thinking about you."

"Duke and I were wondering if we could meet you for dinner."

"I'd love to meet you guys for dinner. Come to the house first and we'll leave from here. Have you heard any news about his trial?"

"No. What's going on?"

"Munson's up for attempted murder, tried to kill me twice now. It would have been an attempt on you, too, if you were still here. I'm sure I'll have to be in court as a witness."

"Oh God. You can tell us all about it when we see you tonight."

Martha hung up, wondering what this dinner was all about. *Maybe they're getting along even better than I thought.*

Her land line rang again and Martha wondered, *What now.* "Yes," she said as she picked up.

"This is Detective Johns with the Denver Police. I would like to come and get a statement from you on the Munson case. Is that all right?"

"Why yes, you may come here for my statement, but I gave it to Officer Gilmore that night."

"Yes, but we need a little more information."

"I see, a more in depth sort of thing, then." After a saying goodbye, she hung up. "More cops? Makes me wonder what they really know about me."

With a touch of dread, Martha awaited the home visit by Detective Harry Johns. *Why here and not at the station or wherever?* She shrugged. *All I can do is tell them what happened. For once, the truth won't hurt a bit.*

She answered his soft knock on her door. "Jeeze, a detective who can't find the doorbell." She opened it to find a tall, dark-haired man with a touch of gray at his temples. She easily remembered seeing him at the hospital. How nice, this was the same dude who was trying to solve the Pederson clipping case, too. The thought made her smile inwardly.

She stepped back to admit him. "Come in."

He wore a charcoal business suit with tiny dark stripes, and his maroon patterned tie hung loose around his big, masculine neck. She hoped her slim-legged jeans and tee shirt were adequate wear for the interview.

"I'm Detective Harry Johns, ma'am." He flashed his ID badge. "Sorry to take up your time, but your testimony is the majority of our case. His treatment of his wife isn't primary in this particular case, but may be brought in to affirm his general character. We need your testimony sorted out before Munson goes on trial, two months from today."

It seemed to Martha that those deep gray eyes missed nothing in the room. He glanced about surreptitiously and, to her increasingly guilty mindset, she knew. *He's looking for something, but what? Must be more to this visit than meets the eye.*

"I understand, sir, and want to cooperate as much as possible. Munson tried to kill me twice right here in my home—actually three times as he planted a bomb in my car, too, but I was lucky that day. If I hadn't looked out the window and seen him drive by in that Escalade pickup, I'd be dead now. Why he was out of jail after the first assault, I'll never understand."

Harry saw the anger in her eyes and tense body movements. "We fought that, Mrs. Chance, but the man pulled strings downtown. We're very sorry that happened."

She shrugged in a gesture of futility. "I wonder how those words would have sounded at my funeral." She noticed a suppressed grin at her last remark as she led him into the den.

He took the proffered overstuffed chair. Martha sat primly in a Bob's large, soft leather chair, tense and waiting for what was to come. She felt like a tightly coiled spring.

Harry, looking at the slender green-eyed woman sitting there, tried to imagine her committing those things as told by Detective Mapus of Colorado Springs. He was completely amazed at the sight of the woman before him. In no way did she look like a granny. He knew she was, but her slim figure, short cropped coppery hair, solid presence, and no-nonsense persona spoke of a solid, worthy citizen. She faced him bravely, yet her tenseness and reserve told him she didn't want him there.

"If you can, ma'am, just go through the events of that night when, as stated, he plunged a knife into the bed, believing it was you?"

He whipped out a long legal pad, ready to jot notes. Martha wondered why he didn't use a lap-top, or at the very least, a recorder.

She carefully told her tale and how she'd detected the man's presence in her home. "He's followed me at several different times in that Escalade of his, so I was edgy and couldn't sleep well. I haven't for a long time, actually..." She went on with her story, answering his questions along the way.

His eyes had a kindly glow to them, only slightly belying her suspicions that he had questions other than what he'd asked.

She remembered her car. "And by the way, what are they doing about his planting a bomb under my car? I still haven't gotten my own car back from that."

She must be a wary one, and strong as hell, to have warded this man off more than twice, Harry thought. His mind whirled with visions of her defending herself, and Munson the worse for it each time. He decided she had the strength of ten when threatened. *She's a hell of looker, too.* There was something about this woman that put him on her side. And there was nothing about her that made him believe she could commit a criminal act, certainly not in this short interview.

"Well, Mrs. Chance, I'll check on the status of your car. It might be needed as evidence. In any case, I'll let you know where we stand on that." He rose from the chair. "Thanks for your time and we will be in touch with you, maybe several times before the trial. If anything else comes to mind, give me a call." He reached into his breast pocket and withdrew a card.

Handing it to her, he touched her hand and felt a wild sensation zinging right down to his boots. It left him puzzled and a good bit flustered.

Martha felt the brief touch as well. She noted the flush that rose from his neck and flashed upward to color his neck and face. "I hope they put that crazy man away for a long time. He's a menace." She remembered to say, "Thanks for checking on my car. I miss having my own, though the rental one is nearly the same model."

"I'll look into it, ma'am. Don't you worry about your car. I'll give you a call on it."

She followed him outside and watched as he poured his tall frame into his un-marked car, catching the gleam of his smile as he drove away.

"Somehow I have the idea that man was after more than just an interview. Does he know more about me than he let on?" She kept seeing his tall, solid frame, sitting across from her and it sent a feeling of warmth through her. "I hope I'm not getting man crazy in my senior years.

He was nice, though. No hidden icebergs with this one. And here I am, talking to myself again."

She kept thinking of Ed Gilmore and how both she and Serena felt threatened by him.

ⒺⓈⒺⓈ

Harry drove to the station, his mind working over the interview he'd just had with Martha. *There's more to that woman than meets the eye and I'd like to know a whole lot more about her. I'll call a shrink friend of mine. Maybe he'll help me get a handle on this hidden personality business.* He smiled. "She's a damned fine looking woman. The finest I've seen in a long time." He broke into a soft whistle as he drove. "I'd like to interview that lady a whole lot more, and in depth."

ⒺⓈⒺⓈ

"Hi, Judith, Duke, come in." Martha ushered her friends into the den. "So, how's everything?" Her question, loaded in a dozen ways, had her body tensed as she waited for an answer.

"Everything's fine. We're back in the house, of course, and the divorce will go through in a few weeks." Judith offered this information in an evasive tone. "We…ah, well, we're staying together. You know he might still have someone trying to get me and I need a bodyguard." Her voice was defensive.

Duke's face reddened during Judith's story and Martha sent a glance at him, laughing. "All right, you two, what's really going on?" They said nothing so Martha continued. "Come on, I'm not the cops. Out with it."

"We're talking marriage, Martha. Duke is big and looks tough and all, but he's gentle as any man could ever be and I've fallen in love with him." Judith's cheeks took on a rosy hue as she told Martha of her love. "It might seem too soon after all that's happened but who knew a guy like Duke even existed?"

"So how about you, Mr.? What have you to say?"

"Best job a man ever had, Martha. I'd like to thank you for callin' on me." He nudged Judith and they both smiled.

"So where are we eating, then?" Martha got off the happy subject and waited for the answer. "Or are you too much in love to eat, these days?"

"How about the House of Joy?" Judith giggled. "It used to be a house of prostitution, but it's a restaurant these days and we got the reservations back a while. It takes forever to get in because they're always heavily booked."

Duke had nothing to say, just kept his eyes on Judith, and Martha thought he looked like a guy totally hooked. She laughed. "A restaurant with a past? Sounds like fun."

They walked out and got into Judith's new, garnet-hued Lucerne. As Martha sank into the rich leather upholstery, she exclaimed, "Wow Judith, new car? I love it." She realized she'd assumed it was not bought with Duke's money, since the man had none that she knew of. She flushed in the darkness, hoping they hadn't noticed her slip of the tongue.

Judith understood Martha's unwitting implication. "I bought it to celebrate that I'm alive and free. Without Duke, I'd be neither. It's no wonder I love the man so much. Kudos again to you, Martha."

No embarrassment for Duke in that statement and Martha realized they'd already sorted the money situation out between them. She settled into the luxurious back seat and watched the streets whiz past as Duke wheeled the big car handily through the evening traffic.

The House of Joy, a fairly small establishment situated on a gentle rise, looked weather beaten on the exterior.

Old-style, ladies lace-up boots protruded out of faux windows and coal-oil lamps burned in other windows no longer used to lure lonely men in off the streets. The effort to give the aura of an old time bawdy house had apparently paid off. By the density of cars parked around it, Martha saw that business was booming.

Upon entering, they found it gleaming with white tablecloths and brass candelabra that did their best to look ancient in design. Escorted by a bawdily-dressed girl to a quiet booth, small and very intimate, she quickly discovered Judith was a pro at ordering fine wines. She did the honors for all, including the dinner.

They enjoyed a cold vichyssoise, followed by spicy lamb and gently steamed vegetables. For dessert they scanned the menu for something light and exotic. Martha found herself totally relaxed and enchanted by these good people who had taken care of problems in their own way.

Martha expressed her thanks. "I don't know when I've enjoyed an evening out so much. Thanks for thinking of me."

"Are you kidding?" Judith said in disbelief. "Without your help, imagine where either of us would be right now."

"I'm so happy things have turned out for you, I really mean that." Martha hesitated before adding, "Your loving husband has turned his anger toward me these days, but I've been lucky so far, or I wouldn't be sitting here myself. If you two are happy together, it's worth it all." She wiped a tear from her eyes.

"I can't tell you how badly I feel about bringing that kind of trouble into your life, Martha." Judith blushed. "There's a bit more to tell." She giggled softly. "It seems that Duke and I are uh—expecting. I'd begun to believe I'd never have children, but here we are! I think he'll make a great dad, too, don't you?" She grinned. "But won't a tiny newborn be lost in those huge hands of his?" She giggled again and when she snuggled against Duke, his big arm went around her and gave her a squeeze.

"I'll do okay," he said. "Always wanted a family, but kinda gave up on the idea. I owe you a big one, Martha. Wish old Bob could've known about all this."

She thought the man was close to tears, but he managed to stay dry-eyed. The evening ended with Martha feeling easier and happier than she had in months. "At least something came out right!"

They parted with plans to meet for dinner again soon.

CHAPTER 16

Harry pulled a chair up to Ebert's desk. "Well, I've met the woman, using an interview regarding the upcoming Munson trial as my intro. I got nothing at all to indicate any sign of mental involvement. She's an enigma. I couldn't figure anything much except she's a hell of a looker for a grandmother—tall, slim, green-eyed, and sharp as hell. Funny thing though, for some reason, I had the feeling she knew damn well what I really wanted. I got nothing, Marcus," he repeated. "Not a damned thing, but I ended up wanting to know her better, even spoke with a shrink friend of mine."

"So what'd he give you?"

"Only that if she has, or had, Dissociative Identity Disorder, as he called it, it's very rare and once integrated, the host person becomes part and parcel of both entities. How that sort of thing works out is a mystery of sorts, too. He also said he'd never treated a case like that, but always wanted to, it's that rare." Harry stopped and cleared his throat. "Ever hear of Sybil? You know—the book?"

"Yeah, saw the movie, too. God, it's nothing like that, is it? She's not that bad, is she?"

"Couldn't be, not the woman I saw sitting there. She's a practicing nurse as well. You've got to have it together to do that kind of work." Harry gave a small chuckle. "The shrink and I discussed the case of Sybil. She had twenty seven different people inside her, and some of them male."

"We'll be able to watch her since she's our prime witness against Munson," Ebert offered, his brow wrinkled in thought. "The trial will put her in the limelight quite a bit and I'd imagine the woman, if she *is* our anti-child-predator perp doing her sort of deeds, she'd find that very uncomfortable, wouldn't you?"

"I wouldn't mind doing the close surveillance on that lady, myself," H admitted with a wide grin on his face.

"Better watch yourself, man. Or we'll be keeping *you* under surveillance."

ରେପ୍ର

Martha had wandered about her house since she'd gotten out of bed, trying to decide what to do for the day. "Should I call for a shift, or not?"

Upset about the public exposure she faced in testifying at Munson's trial, a situation she'd never wanted to face, she felt on edge. The soft chimes of her doorbell startled her and made her pulse rise. "What now?" she asked as she headed for the door.

She opened it to find Ed Gilmore standing there, dressed in casual tan Dockers and a soft print sport shirt, open at the neck.

"How about us going for coffee, Martha?" The tone of his voice left no room for refusal. His forceful mien set both her selves into a steely resolve. *This guy's going to be trouble!*

He looked especially handsome this morning, with his hair slicked down and a devilish gleam in his dark blue eyes. She didn't really want to, but she opened the door and allowed him into her home.

"Hi, Ed, good to see you." Her conversation, stilted and uncomfortable, betrayed the way she felt about him. She hated the way she sounded so weak and vulnerable. That wasn't her, not in any way.

"Anything wrong, Martha?" His gaze intensified. "You're on edge. It's not me, is it?" His tone held a low growl.

"No, no, Ed. I think it's that I have to testify against Munson when he goes on trial and it's coming up so soon, like in a month or less. The man hates my guts for what he thinks I did to him, not to mention what he tried to do to me. Real or imagined on his part, he blames all his personal woes on me. The whole thing is so ugly." She shivered. "It makes me nervous to have to see his ugly face in court." She actually wanted to cry. *I'm becoming a wimp!*

He offered his arm. "Maybe a coffee will settle you."

"Okay, maybe it will." She didn't want to anger the man but she'd begun to feel uncomfortable in his presence. She wanted him gone and out of her sight! *Why do I feel this way? What's wrong with him?*

She grabbed her coat and went along with him. She wasn't dressed well enough for an outing, but the coat covered her shortcomings. He ushered her into his slick little Mercedes.

She broke the awkward silence that had built up between them. "You must be having a day off?"

Ed looked into her eyes and nodded. "Once in a while, I do, yeah."

Martha had no more to say. It was Ed's prerogative to do the talking on this little outing and she waited for him to say what was on his mind. The waiting grew heavy and added to her disquiet. She had the feeling he knew things about her. His overtly threatening attitude made her paranoid.

"How about McHenry's?" he queried. "They have some mean sour pancakes. Well, for me, anyway. I love them. I hear they're Hungarian."

She couldn't have cared less. "Sure, that's fine, if the coffee's good."

It was the usual coffee house with artificial plants and uniformed waitresses. They settled into a booth and paid more attention to their menus than was necessary or usual. The waitress came to inquire about drinks. Martha asked for coffee. Ed ordered coffee, too, but requested a shot of bourbon in it and Martha felt a jolt pass through her body. *He's for sure an alky. That proves it!*

He looked at her, shrugged. "It helps some mornings. I had a rough shift yesterday." His defensiveness illuminated a weak spot in his iron-clad personality and, for some reason, she was glad to know of it.

"Did I say anything?" Martha wasn't about to comment on his alcohol use. "You're your own man and it's none of my mix what or when you drink."

"It could be, if you wanted it to be."

He leaned toward her, and she saw something like pleading in his eyes. *Damn, if the man isn't begging.*

The waitress appeared with their coffees and waited while they ordered. Ed bent his head over his menu and finally made his selection.

Martha took a waffle with fruit. When they were alone again, he said, "I really like you, Martha. You're smart, and you're sure as hell beautiful. We'd be good together, but somehow we've gotten off on the wrong path. What happened?"

"I've already said it was way too soon for me to get involved with anyone." She tried to sound sorry, but it fell flat, even to her own ears. "It doesn't feel right, not to me—not yet."

"That's not the way I see it. There's something else going on and I want to know what that is."

He fought his disappointment, but Martha caught a glimpse of a very deep anger, and it chilled her. *How could a handsome man with a great smile like Bob's turn out to be such a huge disappointment? And why does he affect me this way?*

She didn't know why she had found him lacking, but Ed was nothing compared to the man Bob had been. *I'd like to say goodbye permanently. He won't want that, either.*

Eager to finish with this meal and say goodbye to Ed, she tried another subject. "Tell me about this Benson place you come from. Were you a police officer there, too?" She had to get his mind off the topic of dating. It had turned ugly, at least to her. "I've never been that far west. Denver's about it for me."

"It's a quiet place. Not much happens there other than the drug trade from across the border. Gets pretty hot around there, not only from the summer heat, but especially when we catch a bunch of smugglers or illegals. It's thick with them running through the area. Mostly, it's just that I got tired of the heat, and Benson's not as bad temperature-wise as at some of the lower elevations. Phoenix is a hot-house all summer."

He laughed. She caught a glimpse of his smile, and it tore at her heart strings. *Bob, has your smile come back to haunt me, or is it to warn me?*

"Sounds rather rural, then." She bent to her waffle and found it very good. As Ed tackled his stack of thin, dark pancakes, she asked, "Are those the sour pancakes you mentioned?"

"Yeah, want to try some." He held out a bite on his fork.

She hated to take anything from him that had been on his plate but she did it to avoid further comment. *Serena, help me out here. I'm becoming a wimp.* She ate the sample. "Actually they're very good, Ed. How did you know about them?"

"My mom used to make them. She learned from a Hungarian family we knew." He sent another charming smile in her direction. "She's gone now, too."

"Your wife died, you said. How'd that happen?" She really wanted to know those details but wasn't sure what made her so curious.

"It was a car accident." His eyes shifted away from her face. He looked at his hands and stopped eating as well.

Seeing that, she felt her pulse rise. She shook her head in sympathy. "I'm really sorry to hear it."

"It's been three years and I've faced it the best I can." He smiled at her again and turned back to his food. "I really wanted to talk with you about our getting together. I really like you, Martha, I like you a lot."

"I think you're a very nice man, Ed. But as I've said, I just can't get into a relationship with anyone right now. I have that trial to get through, too. It's going to be hard on me facing that creep when I only tried to help his wife. You'd think I'd ruined his entire life or something."

"It could be you did. If what I hear is true, Munson had his mind on taking her home away from her. Nice guy, huh?"

She wondered how Ed would know something like that, but remembered that, as a police officer, he was privy to all sorts of information. Maybe some of what he knew concerned her past. Ed had proved again he was a man of mystery in too many ways.

"As they say, 'no good deed goes unpunished.' I guess that's me." Martha wanted this little breakfast to end and knew Ed wanted it to last all day. "Well, Ed, I must work this afternoon, and I've several things to do before I go in. Could we go, then?"

The sullen expression that flashed momentarily over his features spoke volumes, but he hid it quickly. "Sure thing. Martha, it's been a pleasure being with you again, even for so short a time." His reluctance at parting company lay carefully hidden behind his wide grin as he helped her with her coat.

The touch of his hands made her shiver. *Why? What is it?* "Thanks, Ed." She took up her purse and walked ahead of him, leaving the restaurant.

He left her at her doorstep and drove away, flashing his wonderful smile that no longer thrilled, but rather chilled her, leaving her with a cold, icy feeling. "I'd better find out all there is to know about that dude. Serena, you know more than I do, don't you? So what is he, an ax murderer?" She laughed at her own silly idea but decided she needed to know a lot more about Ed Gilmore.

She found the *San Pedro Valley News-Sun* on the Internet and carefully searched for accidents around the date of Gilmore's wife's death.

She finally found a small article written by a concerned citizen. "Oh, oh, here we go. Gilmore's wife had extensive internal injuries and there'd been an investigation." Martha's hand trembled on the computer keys. "The husband, Edward was found innocent of any wrong doing in her death."

What made them suspect him in the first place? she wondered. *They wouldn't have gone so far without a reason. Not with a city cop.*

The person who wrote the article questioned his suitability for police work, citing the investigation as his reason. She searched farther but the investigative report was not available.

Martha's suspicions made her blood curdle. "There'll be no further truck with that dude. He won't like it, but I'll not see him again and no more forced breakfasts either. And he can drink on his own. I've always hated that scene."

Martha prepared for another afternoon shift and left her home in the rental car as her frustration mounted. "Wonder when I'll ever get my car back. Enough is enough. I'd better make some noise about that, too."

CHAPTER 17

Judith and Duke came to take her for dinner again.

"Oh, how wonderful you look," Martha exclaimed, seeing the radiant, smiling young woman standing beside the huge Navy SEAL.

He was slicked up for the night out, his hair newly plastered to his head. His blue eyes sparkled and Judith must have gotten him a smashing kind of masculine cologne. It smelled wonderful.

"Hi Martha. You're lookin' good, these days. How's it goin'."

"Fine, Duke, but later on I'll have a question or two for you. For now, let's enjoy the evening. I haven't seen either of you for several days." She hugged a very happy Judith, and Duke.

At dinner, the talk centered on the plans they'd made for their life together and the new child they both welcomed. Martha felt happy she'd taken Judith into her life and that it had turned into something wonderful. But her personal future looked pretty dismal at this point in time.

"Martha, you wanted to ask me something," Duke said. "It's okay if Jude hears whatever it is. We're all friends here, ma'am."

"I'm worried about a man I've come in contact with." Martha went on to explain her worries about Ed. "He isn't one to take no for an answer and if the man's an abuser, you guys, of all people, know how I feel about that."

"Martha, you told me an abuser would never ask someone like you out for another date," Judith asked. Alarm was written across her lovely features. "So why do you think he'd be one of those? He's still asking you out?"

"He seems to know much more about me than he should. Hasn't said anything about it, but his look implies it—or maybe I'm being overly paranoid." She hesitated then went on with what she'd started. "I haven't told you anything of my past, but a cop could easily find out most everything."

"Martha, I know some of it. Bob and I had a conversation a year or so ago about it. He trusted me with what he knew, and I've never spoken a word about it to anyone. Rest assured anything you say is safe with me.

Martha saw the excitement rising in Judith's eyes, however, and it worried her until Judith laughed. "Hey, I am a nosy female, but I'll respect any secret of yours. Don't worry your head about me, dear girl. Your personal stuff is definitely safe with me."

"You can tell her, Duke. It's actually public record in some places, maybe around here, too. Who knows?" Martha went on to tell her friends about her case and what she'd done.

"No wonder you had the strength of ten when you fought off my ex. You certainly needed it!" Judith firmed her jaw. "I say, go for it, girl! We need more like you in this messed-up world. We'll have a child ourselves and be glad some of those monsters have been stopped."

"Martha, I may not look it, but I'm hell on a computer," Duke told her. "That's in our training, too and if there's anything on this Ed, guy, I'll find it. And, dear lady, if he gives you any kind of trouble, let me know—I have my ways."

His understated tone of menace did not go unnoticed by either woman sitting there. Martha watched Judith's chest swell with pride in her Rambo man and, as for Martha, she took comfort in knowing she had a solid ally in her corner. She'd already developed the feeling she needed one.

They parted ways at her door and Duke looked deep into her eyes. "Martha, I owe you my life, you know what I mean?" She knew he referred to his newfound happiness with Judith as he added, "Anytime you need me, lady, I'm here for you."

He hugged her in a crushing embrace and she welcomed the strength of it.

ෙ෧ෙ෧

Martha had barely made it out of bed before her cell sounded.

"Yes?"

"Oh, Mom, Will was kicked out of the second grade. What am I going to do?"

Martha listened with sadness. "I'm so sorry to hear that, Jeannie. How is that possible?" Her heart ached from hearing the sorrow in her daughter's voice.

"He caused too much trouble in class, and they expelled him."

"Is there anything I can do?"

"No. *We* still don't know what to do now. I'm sorry, Mom. I have to go. I just wanted you to know."

In frustration and anger at the predators of the world, Martha punched the off button. To no one in particular, she said, "No, there's nothing anyone can do to erase his hideous memories. Poor Will. Down what path is that child headed? What will become of that charming and happy little boy we once knew?"

She put the coffee on and got out a small bowl of cereal. *I'm too sick at heart to eat anything more than this. Serena, we've got to get busy. If we remove ten predators, we would save how many youngsters, male and female from Will's miserable fate?*

She heard a car pull up out front and, in another moment, a knock on her door that was solid and strong. *After that call from Jeannie, I feel lower than a snake and right now I'll give my all if this is my darling Lizzie.* In excited anticipation, she swung open the door to see who it was.

Her disappointment at seeing Ed, big as life itself standing there, made her blood boil. She didn't open the door wide enough for admittance. "Ed! What are you doing here?"

"Driving by and thought I'd stop in. You're looking good, Martha."

"Oh sure—in my robe and uncombed hair!"

"Looks wonderful to me, dear."

"I am not your dear, and you can knock off saying things like that. I'd like some privacy so I can get dressed, if you please." She moved to shut the door in his face but he quickly shoved a big shoe in the way.

"Not so fast, lady. I've got something to say and I think you'd better listen."

Martha didn't miss the threatening tone. "I can't believe you're doing this. You couldn't possibly have anything to say I want to hear, not anymore. Please remove your foot from my door!"

"I know everything about you, Martha *Lavery*. I know it all!" He pushed the door open and shouldered his way inside. She felt a sudden chill, hearing his use of her former name. He stood in front of her, anger flaring in his deep blue eyes as he moved toward her.

Her temper soared. "Stay where you are, Ed!" The power of Serena surged into her. "You are trespassing and I could report you."

"So what do you propose to do, fix me like some others I could name?" He laughed. "Yeah, I know all about what's going on with you. Those detectives got a full report on you from Colorado Springs and passed it on." His voice dripped with the acid of a man scorned. "You're really something, lady."

"I don't care what you know. You can't come busting into my house and threatening me." She gave a small laugh. "Actually, you ought to be a little bit afraid of me, don't you think?" The cunning, calculating tone in her voice clearly did not go unnoticed. "You know, Ed, if we did get together, it would definitely be against my will, and you'd have to sleep sometime." She gave a low chuckle at seeing his face whiten. "But know this, mister. A part of me *never* sleeps. Did you know that? That's right, a part of me, the stronger part, never sleeps. She doesn't need to. How do you think I took care of Munson like I did?" She laughed in his face. "He thought I was asleep, too, so take warning before you mess with me, my dearest, Mr. Gilmore."

"You threatenin' me?"

His voice had reached a higher pitch than usual. With deep satisfaction she noticed his face has gone ever paler, though red flushes of anger were there, too.

"No. I'm just telling you the truth." She opened the door for him to leave.

"You haven't heard the last of me, Martha, baby, you sure as hell haven't!"

He left the house. She heard his tires squealing and knew they were no doubt smoking as he drove away. Watching his departure through the sheer curtains of her dining room, she waited for her temper to cool.

Unsettled and restless, Martha paced about her home. Her tangle with Ed had left her feeling edgy. *No use trying to hide anything from that man. He knows everything about me. No, he doesn't. He couldn't know everything, not my latest activities, and with no evidence, he can't do a thing.*

What really set her off kilter was the fact that Ed had mentioned the detectives from Colorado Springs discussing her events. *I could be so paranoid right now. They must have spoken with Mapus. So any emasculation work around this area will immediately be laid at my door, but again, only if they have proof.* She chuckled. "I'm very careful. I left no tracks."

But doubt assailed her. Frantic to know for sure, she went to her bedroom closet and hauled out the heavy backpack she'd chucked in the far back corner. *I'd best see if everything is okay with this equipment.* She opened it, spread a towel across her bed, and carefully removed the contents. She laid out unused scalpels, sterile gloves, dressings in sterile packs, and a pack of elongated sanitary pads. Seeing the sandbag, she exclaimed, "Oh, lordy, I never sewed that open spot along the side. It drips sand all over the place." She noticed a few drops of blood smeared on the packs and used alcohol swabs to clean them off.

Her skin burned with apprehension as she watched the fine trickle of sand oozing from the tiny rip. It spread across the rough texture of the bath towel. *If I've left sand at any of my little crimes, it would certainly be of interest. And it would be rather unusual finding sand at a crime scene, wouldn't it?* That thought made her feel cold with a terrible fear. *Maybe I have left a damning trail.*

She decided to get rid of everything. "If they found this stuff here, it'd be over for me and I'd spend longer in the slammer than any child predator. They know about my past. And thanks to Ed's big mouth, I'm aware of it. Best to know your adversaries, so they say."

She packed the backpack again except for the sandbag. The contents of that, she sprinkled around her flower beds in the back of the house. *Tonight I'll make a cozy fire in the fireplace and burn that canvas bag.* It ought to be flammable enough.

She stuck her chin out. "Maybe I'll roast a weenie or two, while I'm at it." She made another pot of coffee and laughed at herself. "I know I drink too much coffee, but it helps me think."

Later, after a cup or two, she grabbed some paper from an old tablet lying around. *I think a nice note to the Greeley Police Department will help them take care of their case regarding Art Delavan. If they don't know what the man was up to, they won't know why he was taken care of.* She wanted them to know what kind of man they had on their city council, so she wrote it on her computer and printed it off on the old tablet paper, leaving it unsigned.

The ramifications of sending it through the mail bothered her. Mailing it might be dangerous.

They'd know the general area of the perp, and with the police knowing of her past, she'd be front and center of any investigation regarding the maiming of male genitalia. Greeley must be desperate for clues in the case by now, too. Her life would be a living hell from then on if they fingered her.

Rethinking the entire thing, she donned a pair of rubber gloves she'd removed from a sterile pack left around from work and, taking a clean sheet from the tablet, reprinted the letter. *They can lift prints and DNA from anything these days, even this old paper. I'd better burn this tablet, too.* She printed the address via her computer on generic, white business envelope she'd picked out while wearing gloves. She stamped it and put it into a plastic bag then into her coat pocket.

I wish I could mail it from some faraway place. Resigned to the fact she couldn't mail it right away, she took the letter out and tucked it under her mattress. She then erased the message from her computer and decided to wait until she left town to mail it. *Maybe I can drum up a computer date with another Tracker.*

She wanted to laugh at that, but her mood had grown serious and angry. Things were closing in on her. She felt the helplessness and defeat of it.

She called to check on her grandson. "Hi, Jeannie, any better news about Will?"

"We're taking him to a new therapist."

"A new one? Is that a good idea?"

"We're hoping that a new approach can help him. Nothing else seems to."

"Well, okay, maybe a newer approach *is* what's needed."

"We are also enrolling him a special school that is just for kids with his type of problems."

"You mean they have a special school for kids with his problems?" Martha cried in dismay. "There're that many?"

"I guess there must be."

"God help us! There are so many abused kids, they need a special school with trained counselors to work with them, trying to help in their recovery!"

Feeling defeated, she rang off. Her anger knew no bounds at this news. *I need to refill that sandbag and get busy! Better yet, I'll take a new one from the ward when I work Ortho again.*

CHAPTER 18

Several days later, tired from working another shift, Martha decided to fix a snack before bed. While spreading peanut butter on nearly burnt toast, she heard a loud popping sound and her window shattered. The whizzing of air past her head made her jerk back, startled. Her heart hammered in her chest, and she felt a sudden stinging on her right ear lobe. Seeing the blood dripping onto her shoulder, she realized she must have been shot.

"My God," she screamed. "A bullet came through the window. Someone just took a shot at me!" She grabbed her cell and dialed 9-1-1. "Yes, operator, someone shot at me—right through my window. It's broken. There's glass all over inside my kitchen and I'm bleeding."

After hanging up, she surveyed the damage. Her scrub top was a mess. Blood was splattered on the floor and part of the table. "Oh my God, there's blood everywhere!" She put ice on the ear wound and pressed a towel against it to stop the blood flow. Then she huddled in the den to wait for the police.

"First, Ed threatens me, now this. The police will be swarming around, and he'll be one of them." *There's evidence I might have left behind and—oh, my God, the empty sandbag's still in the bedroom!*" She ran to the bedroom, grabbed the empty canvas bag, and shoved it into the laundry hamper. Then she took the bloody towel off her head and stuffed it in on top. *If they see blood in here it's because I tried to get this wound dressed before they got here.*

She wet a wash cloth and wiped off the closet doors where she'd left a smear of blood. *Everything's going crazy on me. Who'd be shooting at me? Munson's in the slammer.*

The doorbell rang and she hurried to answer. With surprise, she saw Detective Harry Johns on her doorstep along with an ambulance, a full complement of EMTs, and two police cars with more officers. Right now, she wanted to faint dead away to remove herself from the entire mess.

She opened her door wide enough to admit them, but couldn't utter a sound. Like a woman in shock, she stood there speechless, letting blood drip from the wound on her ear.

Harry led her to a chair, knelt in front of her, and took her hand. "Ma'am, can you tell us what has happened?"

She wondered at him being here—it was midnight or later. Things seemed so crazy all of a sudden.

The EMTs bent over her and checked her bleeding ear and, she guessed by the seeking hands that pressed several areas, the rest of her. They took her pulse and blood pressure. Her ears rang and the roaring in her head occluded her thoughts.

She barely managed to answer Detective Johns. "Uh." Then, warm tears gushed from her eyes and deep wrenching sobs quickly followed.

Harry tried to soothe her. "There now, you're going to be all right."

A part of Martha knew he tried his best and, deep inside, it amused her. As a nurse, she knew traumatic shock had overtaken her. She also knew her inner self worked to bring her senses back from it. She felt a dressing applied with firm male hands to her right ear and a bandage wound around her head.

"I know," she mumbled through heavy sobs. "I know. But I can't believe this has happened." She looked at Harry. "Someone's trying to kill me? Why?"

She felt control returning as Harry pulled a chair close to her, keeping an eye on her. Being a man, he no doubt hoped she'd soon get past the tears. Somewhere in the midst of everything, she heard him issuing orders to the accompanying officers.

"Check around the front where the shot was fired. Look for evidence, footprints, whatever." The man had a soft voice for all his commanding presence.

Martha's heart rate soared as cold filled her veins. *I hope they don't notice the sand I just dumped in the flowerbed out back.*

She stopped sobbing, slowly lifted her head, opened her eyes, and sat up. "I'm sorry. I flipped out just then. It's a terrible shock knowing someone wants you dead. I don't know what to do." She sounded sufficiently helpless, and it pleased her.

The EMT leader introduced himself. "Ma'am, I'm Jake Wells. We'd like to check you out and take you to the ER for further treatment." He moved to help her out of the chair."

"Please, what about my ear? Is it still on? How bad is it?"

"Actually, ma'am, it's just a small nick and should heal in no time at all. Most head wounds tend to bleed a lot and that's scary, especially when it's your blood."

"Then I'd rather skip the ER. Sitting there all night waiting for treatment would be worse than a gunshot wound, wouldn't it?" She managed a weak laugh.

He replied, with a slight chuckle. "Well, you check out just fine, otherwise. And it's your call about the ER, if you don't mind a small notch in your ear."

Harry spoke up. "In assault cases like this, we usually like a doctor's opinion as to the severity of your injuries."

He was very sincere. Martha understood that, but now that she had her head on straight, she didn't plan to go in. From working at the place, she knew about, and hated, the gossip that would follow.

"I'd prefer not to go, Detective Johns, if it's all the same to you. Look at me. I'm a mess, all bloody, and I'm confused. I wish everybody would just go away and leave me alone." She fought tears again, but also didn't plan to mention being harassed by Ed lately. That would lead to questions she couldn't answer. But then, she suddenly remembered that this detective knew everything about her past activities anyway.

"It's for you to decide about the ER," he said. "But I believe your life is in danger. I'd like to station an officer in the house with you for now. We'll leave after the boys check outside for clues. This attempt on your life may only be the beginning. Any idea who might be after you like that?"

"The only one I can think of would be Munson, and he's locked up—or is he?" She was never sure of that, not anymore.

"He is, ma'am." His soft, deep voice held gentle tones of reassurance.

She remembered the conversation she'd overheard between Munson and someone on the phone, when he was plotting to kill his wife. If she told Harry about that, he'd know she had stalked Munson earlier and dig into that, too. Instead, she donned a puzzled expression. "I can't think of anyone, not at all."

"Well, for now, I'll leave a man here. He's a rookie who's just started with the department, but very sharp." He called one of the officers. "Martha, this is Officer Tom Burns."

The young man nodded, his features reddened. "How do, ma'am."

She took in a slimly built, man just out of his teens, with blond hair and brown eyes. Freckles stood out on his flushed features as he nodded his head at her.

"Nice to meet you, Tom." Martha smiled at him to make him welcome, but her ear had been bandaged and she wanted to get a shower and scrub herself clean again. From now on, she'd have someone to keep an eye out for her assassin, whoever he was.

She had to find out who was after her and plan her strategy. She believed she had to take care of her stalker to save her own life. *Your call, Serena. We'll have to get him before he gets us. And he will try again.*

She heaved a sigh of relief when the others finally left. "Thank God, that's over with." She left the young rookie as he moved about the home checking other windows and the door to the garage. "Pardon me while I get a quick shower. I feel grimy after being subjected to all that's happened."

ℰ৩ℰ৩

In the morning, a sleepy-eyed Harry moved his chair, settling near Ebert's desk. "Well, now somebody's taking pot shots at our mystery lady," he said confidentially. "I definitely got the feeling she knows more than she's saying about that, too." He laid his report on Ebert's desk. "One of the guys found sand poured among the flowers in the back yard. He said it didn't look like it belonged there, just laying on top and not worked in. If it matches the sand found in Pederson's car it could be something, unless sand is just sand. That's the only clue we've found in that case."

"Get that checked out. What'd you think of her—into something, is she?"

"Like I say, she's secretive as hell. Though she nearly broke in half right after the bullet clipped her ear lobe, damned near went into hysterics with blood splattered all over her and scared to death. She's a mystery all right— hiding things too. It comes through above everything else. I can feel it."

Ebert leaned closer. "Did you get a sense of anything more than you learned from the last interview with her?"

"Could be something going on there. If the sand matches up, she might have gone to work on Pederson in retaliation for brutalizing his little girl. Our records show she had care of the child a couple of months back."

Ebert shivered at the image of Martha Chance doing the job on Pederson. In no way did it fit with the woman he'd met.

"She'll need police protection with a shooter on the prowl," Harry replied. "I left young Tom out there with her for the present. She refused to go to the ER for her ear, only clipped a bit, by the looks. Bled like hell, though." He laughed softly, remembering the slender woman with greenish eyes, overwrought and in a state of shock. He hadn't missed how quickly she'd gotten herself under control, either. "She's a cool one, is my guess. Strong, too. In fact there's something hidden in her eyes I haven't figured out yet."

"Yet? You're taking an unusual amount of interest in the woman, Harry." Ebert believed Harry was already emotionally involved. *Wouldn't that be something for the solitary soul?* He smiled to himself and shuffled the papers on his desk.

"Nothing more than the usual," Harry declared. "But you've got to admit, we don't usually run into a perp like Martha Chance. Maybe that's too strong a word for now, since we've not a damned bit of evidence against her, unless the sand is worth something. She's sure as hell got an interesting history." He got up and left Ebert's desk.

ᥱᥱᥱ

Duke visited Martha and came alone. "Martha, listen to this." What he had to say set her on edge and he noticed how her hands shook as he told her what he'd gleaned off the internet. "Looks like Ed Gilmore was at best, a dirty cop, discharged discreetly from the Benson police force, and asked to leave the area."

Martha felt ice prickling her scalp. "You're not serious?"

"You bet I am," he confirmed. "And the feeling around Benson is that he had something to do with his wife's death. I couldn't get enough finite data on a thing like that to be totally sure." He leaned closer to Martha. "If I were you, I'd be damned careful of the guy. Hot tempered and devious is what one of the officers told me. A guy I knew from the SEALs. When I saw his name on their roster, I knew I was in. Hope this helps. I'd do anything at all for you, you know that." He reached out and took her hand. "I don't know how to say thanks for the change you've made in my life." He chuckled. "Some job offer."

"I'm really glad for you, and even more for Judith." She took his hand. "And thanks a bunch for the info, and the warnings about Gilmore. You know, at first he struck me as a really great guy. But I've had strange and wary feelings about him since and couldn't figure out why." She grimaced. "It seems my protective instincts are alive and well." Then she detailed her date with Ed, leaving nothing out. "He's been here twice, and when I refused to go out with him again, he made threats—said he knew all about me." Her voice broke. "Sounds like the stuff in Colorado Springs has become common knowledge and my secrets broadcast to the whole world. 'Overheard the detectives,' he said. If they know about me—and one of them has been to the house twice—they're playing a game of some kind, too. Why wouldn't they just come out and accuse me?"

"Beats me, Martha, but this levels the playing field. At least you know where Ed is coming from." Duke gave her a pat on the back then flushed, wearing a sheepish grin. "Got to get back."

Martha hugged him. "I'm so glad you two have found each other. Do you realize how precious that sort of thing is?"

He nodded. "I do now, thanks to you, lady. I owe you—big time. You're okay right now, aren't you?"

"Don't worry about me, Duke. I can handle most things. I really can, though a bullet through my window wasn't that wonderful. I'm still trying to figure out how to tackle that."

"You shouldn't try anything on your own. You could get hurt dealing with a crazy killer like that."

"How well I know. Look at the notch in my ear." She pulled her hair aside and showed him the crusted, healing spot on her ear lobe. "It's really nothing, but I had the cops, EMTs, and a big-shot detective here all at the same time. I have a police guard right now, but I think he's outside." She gasped. "Ye Gods, I hope he is, the way I've been babbling on!"

"Bet all this makes you a nervous wreck, eh?"

"Yeah, it does, Duke. That detective, Johns, was really nice but since I know he's aware of my past, I wonder what he's really after." She frowned. "How can I relax around a guy like that? He didn't hint in any way at what he knew about me. For some reason, they're keeping it quiet, maybe waiting for me to get active again. Must be tickled pink he's found a good reason to put a guard on me, right in my own home." She cast an eye around to see where her guard was, hoping he hadn't heard anything.

"Well, I'll be off, Martha. If you need me, just call, you've got my cell number." Duke left and she noticed he drove a shiny new black Toyota pickup.

Mmm, a gift from wifey to be? Martha felt warm all over that her idea to help Judith had worked out so amazingly well.

Martha checked to see where the current guard, Tom Burns, kept himself. *If he'd overheard anything, would it matter at all*? she wondered. *They know about everything so what could this kid possibly have to add*? Hearing a metallic clink in the kitchen, she saw the kid had popped open a Pepsi. He'd brought his own, she noticed as she entered the kitchen to fix herself a cup of tea.

"Say, ma'am, I think I know that guy. Isn't he the Navy SEAL that's guarding Munson's wife?" He lounged against the sink and took a good long pull on his drink. "Everybody got a kick out of that."

"Yes he is. My, how word gets around."

"Well, I've been interested in something like that for myself, just might look into it one of these days." He looked so young and untried to Martha that she wondered why he'd joined the police.

"Are you a good swimmer?" She glanced at him, medium height, slim, and athletically inclined by the looks of him. "I hear the training makes being tough and strong look like baby stuff. Endless hours under horrid conditions, submerged in icy water enough to freeze-dry a normal person. Yet, those who do make it, and most don't, are the elite of the Navy."

She watched his reaction. He firmed up his jaw and said in the softest tones, "I can do it, ma'am. If you knew how tough I've had it all my life, you'd know I could."

"In what way, tough?" She always looked for abuse and sensed it had happened to this quiet, soft-spoken young man.

He no longer looked young and innocent, carefully keeping his distance emotionally. His eyes held a deep look of pain. "I don't talk about things, ma'am. They're buried real deep, an'll be staying there." He rose. "I'm going out and check around."

He headed out the garage door, and she knew he'd leave from that outer side door. She also wondered if the guard was on twenty-four-hour duty. He'd sure been here longer than eight hours. She'd ask him when he came back in.

Martha felt the strong urge to go out and slip behind those large shrubs outside her fence. She wanted to walk along the front of the house to see if the killer still lurked about, but she decided against it. With the guard out cruising the area, it could get a bit crowded.

She made sure her shades were drawn, now that it had grown dark. "No need to make a nice target for that devil outside," she murmured. "There's a devil inside here, too, but our shooter doesn't know about that." *If we could get rid of this cop, we could take care of that fool. I refuse to be target practice.*

She paced about, stymied by having an officer under foot. "Wouldn't he flip his wig if he knew what kind of woman he guarded?" The Munson trial loomed before her and the thought of testifying before people in open court gave her the willies. "I'll never have the anonymity or the time I need for my personal activities with a spectacle like a trial going on. There'll be a newspaper write up for sure. My patience is already wearing thin," she said, babbling because it was a relief to verbalize.

Busying herself in the kitchen, she made a bit of supper. *I'll have to face the public and look old Munson square in his hate-maddened eyes.* She laughed. *I've bested the man several times, but it only makes his venom stronger. The fool has transferred his anger from his ex-*

wife to me because I've made him look like a wimp. I'm a blasted crisis magnet, these days!

Her musings were interrupted by the chimes of her doorbell. She opened it to find another officer standing there.

"Hello, Mrs. Chance, I'm Deputy Bill Harman, sent to replace Tom." He whipped out his ID for her, while looking about for Tom. "Is he here?"

She brought him into the kitchen. "The other fellow went outside to check around. I guess to see if anyone is sneaking around with a rifle or something." *Don't I sound all helplessness?* She looked him over. "Are you a rookie, too?"

"Yes, ma'am, but don't you worry. We're well trained in surveillance." She noticed the big, sandy-haired kid was dressed in plain clothes—jeans and sweatshirt—with a soft, worn denim jacket over that. "I'll go find him. Hope he won't think I'm the shooter," he said with a laugh.

He went out via the garage door as well, but she heard no sounds of doors opening or closing.

Martha heard a cruiser drive away and decided they'd transferred whatever critical information they had for each other outside. She went to the computer. The young officer was outside and now was as good a chance at she'd get.

CHAPTER 19

She searched for another Tracker by visiting several chat lines and finding one with several phony male contributors. The silly commentary on it gave her fits of humor along with nausea over the dangerous inane garbage so important to the young. *If only these innocent, lonely, unthinking girls knew how dangerous this business really is.* She quickly flipped the computer to another web site when she heard the guard re-enter the house, then powered down, and went back to the kitchen. "Anything out there?"

"Some mighty large footprints off the sidewalk in some of the softer soils, so whoever your stalker is, he's good sized." She thought the kid looked a touch pale. "We'll get some people out here to take molds in the morning," he went on. "Maybe they did already or should have by now."

"This is really scary. I'm so glad you're here, Officer Harmon." She saw him flush with her bit of praise.

He noted, with approval, the drawn shades. *Yes, sonny boy, no need to make myself a better target.* She longed to go out and do some stalking on her own, but with the guard on duty, it might look a little strange. The frustration of being confined wore on her, but she couldn't very well pace about, either.

She called her daughter, trying to keep her worry and frustration from her voice. "Jeannie, how's everything?"

"It's not good." The young woman went on for a long time, laying out her troubles with Will.

"Oh Jeannie, I love you, but I don't know how to help you with this anymore. We've tried everything." Martha felt so hopeless, all of a sudden, and changed the subject. "How is Martin coping?"

"How do you expect? We are barely hanging on." Jeannie sighed. "I'm sorry, Mom. I just can't talk about this right now."

Hurt and angry, Martha punched off. *I didn't do enough to that rotten, miserable, miscreant! Will's decent into hell is still in high gear and nothing seems to help.* She went into her bedroom and shut the door before bursting into tears.

The damning empty sandbag hiding in her laundry hamper still haunted her. Now she was trapped in her house by a shooter. *I've got to burn that damned thing when none of the guards will see me doing it.*

She decided to make a small fire in her fireplace. Then she got her shears, fetched the bag out of the hamper, and cut it into small bits to feed it into the fire slowly so it wouldn't make a lot of smoke. She carried the shredded stuff in a plastic bag to the fireplace. She saw the guard walk through the house and then go outside once again.

She opened the half door beside the fireplace, dug out a few bits of small stuff, and laid her base, then arranged small cedar logs on top. She lit the fire and watched the flames catch bit by bit. The weather outside had turned damp and foggy. It took longer than normal to get a good fire going. Her guard wasn't in sight when she got a few pieces of the sandbag and placed them in the blaze. They burst easily into flames and quickly disappeared. Repeating the process until that bit of evidence was gone, she heaved a sigh of relief.

The young officer, passing through the house again, was drawn to the cheery fire. He warmed himself by backing up against it. "Say, ma'am, you sure know how to set up a nice fire."

"Had lots of practice, son." She smiled at him. "Well, Bill, I'm tired and with you on guard, maybe I'll get a good night's sleep. See you in the morning."

Martha giggled a bit at the way the young man's chest swelled at her words. She showered and went to bed. *I may as well as get some rest with a nice guard to keep watch.*

෧෨෨

It was early when her phone chimed. Her heart rate leaped to hear it was the detective.

"Good morning, ma'am. Will you be home today so I can come and speak with you?"

"Yes, I'll be here, but I work this afternoon, how will you manage that?"

"Well then, I'll just head on over now."

Satisfied with his answer, she hurried to get herself presentable. *I hope jeans and a sweat shirt will do for the nice detective.* She laughed and fixed a breakfast for herself and the tired looking guard. "Are you allowed to eat in a case like this?"

"Sure. Sounds great," he said as he plunked down on a kitchen chair and, for a few short moments, Martha felt like the mom of a teenaged boy, but she instantly knew better by a sudden sharpness in his attitude. "Ma'am, I heard someone outside the house last night. Couldn't get close enough to see him plain, but a man was out there, looking or stalking."

"Did you see anything at all?"

"Not enough, but I'd sure like to nail that guy. He's a danger to you and the community, too." He seemed crestfallen that he hadn't made an arrest.

"Detective Johns is coming this morning. He didn't say why—thought you'd want to know that."

"I know about it. They won't send Tom out so soon, at least until the detective's done with you."

"Done with me?" She wanted to laugh, but held back. Obviously, the kid held a lot of respect for the detective. "I don't even know why he's coming out here, again."

"Probably that Munson trial, ma'am. They don't give us a lot of details, just on a need to know basis."

A soft knock alerted Martha. She saw two men at the door and opened to admit them. "Come in, Detective Johns." He seemed very serious, and it set her on edge. "Anything wrong? I mean, more than what's going on already?"

"We need to have a serious chat, ma'am." He turned to introduce the smaller, younger man. Dressed in a dark suit with nondescript tie, he had the serious look of a professional. "This is Mark Hellams, attorney for the county. He will take your deposition." Then he turned to dismiss the young officer, giving the rookie an appreciative nod. "Your ride's out there, Bill."

Her tension mounted by the second. "What's going on, Detective Johns?"

"Let's have a seat. Another guard will be along in about an hour."

Lordy, they're going to grill me for a whole hour? The detective's attitude was gentle but firm as they went to the den and took seats. Martha sat in Bob's old chair and it gave her troubled soul a little comfort. The men took other chairs scattered about.

"Can I get you fellows some coffee?"

"In a bit. For now, we need to go over certain information we've recently learned. We spoke with a detective in Colorado Springs. It seems you were active in that city, two or more years ago." He held out his hand to stop Martha's sudden rise from her chair. "No, no, we're not here about anything in your past. It's under wraps for now but what does concern us is the recent assault on one of our more prominent citizens. The similarities are close enough that we can't ignore what we know and what we suspect." He shrugged. "We found only one thing to connect this case to your past activities, well aside from the fact of emasculation." He paused and took a breath. "I wonder if you'd have anything to say about it."

"Your officer, Ed Gilmore, told me he overheard you detectives talking about me. I don't have anything to say about my past, or the present either, for that matter. However, your Officer Gilmore threatened me with what he knew." She let her anger show, firming her lips and stubbornly thrusting her chin out. "He wants to date me, and though I did go with him once, I am afraid of the man now." She felt tears fill her eyes. Her world had begun to crumble and she sat there, feeling lost in the midst of a whirlwind "Gilmore just might have a shady past. It's a wonder your department ever hired the man."

Martha saw by his raised eyebrows that Johns appeared to be completely unaware of any such information about Ed Gilmore. "What you say may be true, but does nothing to answer our questions, Mrs. Chance."

She didn't plan on making a confession. No way, would she. "You mentioned one bit of evidence. What are you speaking of, then?"

"I'm not at liberty to say what we know. Suffice it to say, your cooperation would help us out considerably. You know, of course, we refer to the Pederson case. None of us have any sympathy toward the man, especially after the death of his child." Harry sighed. "You must know that."

"If you can't tell me what you know, why expect me to incriminate myself? My life has been a disaster since my grandson Will was molested, and that's after the police let the child predator loose because they forgot to read the man his Miranda rights!" She felt her anger rising nearly out of control as she remembered her last conversation with Jeannie about Will's continued troubles. "What are we citizens expected to do? Are we to watch our kids being ruined for life by these monsters, then sit back, and wait for you people of the law to protect them?" Her voice had gotten higher, but memories of those days came back all too frequently to haunt her. "All this is too much, way too much!"

Inside herself, she watched Johns and Hellams become nervous at her approaching hysterics and tears. Though upset and feeling hunted by these men, she also noticed their increasing uneasiness and had to stifle a laugh. *Men are such wimps when it comes to a woman's tears.*

"Say, ma'am, how about that coffee you mentioned?" Johns apparently hoped to keep her from crying by distracting her. She let him.

"Sure, I'll get it. Cream or sugar?"

Her voice took on a sweeter tone and she felt completely shameless about it. Detectives or whatever, they were still men. Suddenly, she knew she was on firmer territory. She rose from her chair and sauntered into the kitchen, fully aware that the men sat there watching and appreciating her every move. She brought them the coffee and some sweet rolls. "Here you are. Help yourself, or would you like me to serve it?" At his hesitation, she poured the coffee. "Sugar, anyone?"

They both declined the sweetener. "Black is fine, ma'am." Johns took his cup and sipped it, all the while gazing at her through narrowed, deep-gray eyes. Hellams took his black, too.

Martha couldn't help seeing them as men rather than detective and attorney. Johns cut a fine figure, yet she saw something else in his eyes. He held a kind of sadness inside, some deep sorrow withheld from everyone. She wondered what his personal story would be, if he told it.

The man piqued her interest, which took her by surprise. *God help me, I'm looking at another* man—*and a cop again. Not a good idea, but, this time, I'm pretty certain he's one of the good guys.*

"Say, this is good coffee. I'm sort of a coffee nut, myself." Johns seemed embarrassed to admit it and she watched a slight flush creep up his strong, well-muscled neck. The touch of gray at the temples only added to his distinguished air. He sat with his coffee, faced her, and kept his voice very low. "Martha, if I may call you that, I'd sure like to hear about your days in Colorado Springs. Whatever you'd say would remain between us and off the record."

His query took her by surprise. She flushed at his becoming this personal. It implied a closeness neither of them had any right to feel, but Martha saw the need in his eyes. "I know you've heard just about everything from Ryan Mapus in that city, so what more can I tell you?"

"Maybe how you went about things, how you discovered your psych problem, things not really known to anyone else. Your case is a stunner in so many ways. I went as far as consulting a shrink I know. Of course, you must realize we are sitting on that knowledge."

"I know that, and I appreciate it. I'm a nurse and it came as a terrible surprise for me as well. Dissociative Identity Disorder is very rare and is most always caused by sexual trauma during childhood. I only discovered it because of what happened to my grandson, Will. Everything happened after that." She sighed. "The greatest sorrow of all is the way this sexual assault has affected him. He'll never truly be the same loving little guy he once was. He's dark and moody these days and does things at school to get himself expelled. I'll never regret what I did to the man who molested him. Not ever!" Martha felt she'd gotten too emotional, but this was an emotional subject, one she struggled with every day.

He leaned toward her and his coffee cup tilted precariously, nearly spilling the contents. "You might be surprised how many on the force applaud your activities. But, of course, we have to enforce the law, and sometimes it hurts to do so."

"I'd be in prison longer than the people I fixed if you folks had prosecuted me." She reached for the plate of biscotti she'd brought with the coffee and rolls. "Either of you want one of these?"

Harry's laugh had a silky sound to it, deep and full, and Martha felt it pass through her body like a streak of soft fire.

"I think you're one fine woman," he continued. "And it's a real shame, all the sorrows you've had to bear." After saying that, he returned to his official mien. "But it's time to get this deposition down."

The attorney set up a small recorder and the questioning began. Martha played the total innocent, beset by a vengeful, angry man whose life plans had been interrupted and all his losses were blamed on her. She answered all Hellams' questions.

"That about wraps it up, ma'am," he said. "If we need more, we'll be in touch. This should pretty much take care of your testimony and we know how to proceed with our line of questioning. If you think of any other details, please call this number." He handed her his card. "This will reach me wherever I am."

She escorted them to the door. Hellams went out but Johns lingered. "I know you've lost your husband lately, and you've a lot on your plate, Martha, maybe too much to handle." He had readied to leave, yet he stayed.

Deep down she wondered why he'd come at all. Had his presence really been necessary? This hadn't been police business, not that she could see. The whole thing belonged to the criminal prosecutor and his staff. Munson had been arrested and the case basically solved.

"Is there anything else?" She wanted to bring things to a halt. His presence was nice, but he was a detective. She craved privacy, already having tired of the surveillance.

"No, ma'am. I'll call for your guard. We can't leave you alone with the shooter prowling around." He clicked his cell and in a few short words got his message out. "It looks like Burns will be here soon."

He stood waiting, his eyes scanning the interior of Martha's home. Except for the mess in the kitchen, she thought it looked nice enough, picked up, and clean. Bob's masculine influence remained and she enjoyed the sight of that, too.

At the sound of a vehicle, Johns took her hand. "Thanks for your confidence in us, and keep in mind that you can call me any time if you feel the need, day or night."

He meant a lot more than police business, and she knew it by the look in his eyes. She smiled inwardly. *How many of these personal cards do I have so far?*

Young Tom came in for his duty. The detective and Hellams left. With Johns gone, she felt a sudden emptiness and wondered how she could possibly feel the loss of a man she hardly knew?

With the house quiet, Martha worried how to get the letter she'd written sent to the police department in Greeley. She searched through a ton of info on her computer and found an address where mail could be forwarded anonymously.

This'll do it. There won't be any DNA on anything, paper, stamp, nothing. I used gloves for all of it, and I'll put it in a plastic bag until it's mailed. She worked on that while the guard, Tom, remained outside.

She wondered what he'd do when she worked the p.m. shift and chuckled. "A guard at work would be something."

She decided to find him and ask about it. She saw him taking plaster casts of the large man's footprint found in the soft soil outside her front fence. "Wow! That dude's got big feet." Amazement and ignorance suited her cause.

"Well, ma'am it's a mess now with all the plaster, but it looks like the man wears bigger than a twelve, could be up to fourteen. You know anyone like that?"

"Can't think of anyone off hand, and whoever he is, he isn't very bright to leave a big track like that around, is he?"

Martha felt good this morning. Her interview with Johns left her feeling comfortable in some way. The detective didn't plan to expose her past. Not for now.

The sun was bright and the leaves had begun to turn in spots. She noted bright crimson on some of the maples in her vicinity. "It's hard to believe someone's out to kill you when it's such a pretty day."

"I suppose it does, ma'am. The guy worked in the dark last night when it didn't look so pretty and, being in the dark, he might not know what clues he left behind." Burns pointed to an object lying in the soft grass. "Look, the guy chews gum, left a wrapper." He whipped out a plastic bag and, using a stick, shoved the wrapper into the bag and sealed it. He wrote the info on it and tucked it into a pocket of his jacket. "The lab might get DNA off the wrapper. They've got newer ways of doing it these days, even off fabric that a person has touched."

"That's impressive," Martha commented, but she already knew about getting DNA. She'd watched TV shows that told her that much and she planned to use what she knew in mailing the letter to Greeley. "I work this afternoon. How will you handle that situation?"

"I'll call in and let them decide." Then he asked, "You're a nurse, aren't you?"

"Yes, keeps me busy and helps people some of the time." She wondered at his query. "Why do you ask?"

"I'm thinking of training in something besides police work. I like this a lot, but maybe nursing would be more satisfying than being a SEAL." He laughed. "In this work, everyone's a suspect. We look for bad guys everywhere—sort of a reverse paranoia."

"We look for problems and trouble too, Tom, and sometimes our work can be heartbreaking, especially, when you see things you can't do anything about." She often saw Aliya Pederson in her mind and mourned the loss of the child's life. She turned to leave. "I must fix lunch, are you hungry?"

"I'm fine, ma'am." He bent down, took up the plaster cast, and packed it snugly in a box with *Evidence* lettered in black on the side.

No buttering up this kid with a nice lunch. She laughed and went inside.

Later, young Tom came in with the news. "I'll go with you to work, and someone will be there to accompany you home." He took a chair in the den and ate a sandwich. "I'll see about getting your car released. They must have all they need from it by now."

While she readied herself for the upcoming shift, her phone chimed. On the ID sector she saw it was Ed. She punched "speaker" and set it down. "Say, Martha dear, when are we going to get together?"

"How about never, Ed?" Her voice sounded icy, just the way she wanted it.

"Now, is that nice? You know we need to talk. I'm coming by."

"Too bad. I'm heading out the door for work. I don't want to see you again, you know that."

"Yeah, you do." His tone held a threat, and she heard it loud and clear. "You'll see me." He rang off and Martha felt sweat breaking out.

Will that fool never leave me alone?

But she knew Ed was no fool. His eyes never missed a detail. His competence was one of the things about the man she'd found attractive. "Serena, what are we to do about that man?" she said to the image in the mirror and shivered involuntarily.

CHAPTER 20

Martha left for work with Tom driving her rental car. She left him at the entrance and, after checking with Frannie in the staffing office, hit the med-surg unit. She hadn't been around for a few days and seeing the bustling, rushing atmosphere, made her feel right again. Being shot at and guarded day and night was wrong. Working and keeping busy felt right.

"It's great to be here again," she said to a nurse passing by.

"You must be sick in the head, or bored out of your skull, then," Linda Parnell, a new nurse returned. "This place is a zoo, has been all day."

"Anything unusual?"

"Not really. You know how it can be on this ward, another hectic day with too many admissions, non-English-speaking patients—no translators—whatever." Linda laughed. "Don't mind me, I'm just tired. Can't wait to shuck this place and go home. I need a hot shower!"

"For me, I needed to get back, and busy is what I welcome right now."

"Problems?" Linda asked. Her face held the open and honest look of a person wanting to help if she could.

"Nothing I can't handle," Martha replied and grabbed a coffee. She'd never divulge her fears at work, and being shot at didn't make for relaxing small talk.

When the shift ended, Martha felt good, tired, and looking forward to going home.

When she walked out of the elevator, Ed stepped up. "I'm assigned to be your guard for this next tour."

"Like hell!" She flinched involuntarily as he took her elbow and escorted her to her car. "Hey! That's my own car. How'd you manage it?"

"It was time. I transferred your garage opener and any other items you'd left in the rental." He smiled in satisfaction and opened her door. "Everything's here, Martha."

"I don't like this, Ed. It's not right and you know it!"

"Feels right to me, lady. Get in."

She didn't miss the menace in his voice. But there was no liquor on his breath, a hopeful sign. She'd formed a deep mistrust of the man, and it was verified by what Duke had learned. She slipped behind the wheel, adjusted the seat and mirrors to her satisfaction. *Serena, don't fail me now.*

Martha drove through darkened streets in silence. Passing an all-night coffee shop, Ed asked, "Need a little snack before you tuck in to sleep?"

How cunning he was. Martha wanted no time in the house alone with Ed. She'd never fall asleep with that predatory male anywhere near. The longer she kept him away from her home, the better.

"Sure, I could eat a bite," Martha said, trying to devise a way to call Detective Harry Johns. Ed must have bribed one of the young rookies to let him take this surveillance detail. Her mind searched for a way to put a stop to this ugly travesty.

They stopped at the dinner and went in. Ed ushered her into a booth and after she refused to let him sit beside her, sat across, facing her. This entire situation had become ridiculous. She wanted to laugh, actually finding humor in this situation, but the underlying menace in his mien was not amusing. He wanted intimacy and would not hesitate to use threats to get what he wanted.

He ordered a sandwich and coffee, and Martha asked for a BLT and coffee. She noticed he didn't fortify his coffee with alcohol.

"What, no booze, Ed?"

"I'm on duty, my dear."

"In case you haven't noticed, I am *not* your dear, Ed," *And I never will be, you wife-killing bastard!*

"Now is that nice?"

Ed smiled into her eyes, but in the depths of his deep blues, the fires of hell burned with an anger that mounted rapidly at her defensiveness. Martha became apprehensive of her personal safety.

"I'm going to the little girl's room, excuse me." She hurriedly left for the restroom and once there, pulled out her cell and the card given to her by Harry Johns. She punched the numbers.

"Hello, Detective Johns." She explained the situation and her misgivings. "Is he really my guard? Please, I don't want to leave this coffee shop with that man."

"So you're at the Li'l Diner?"

"Yes, it's the Li'l Diner. We haven't eaten yet, so there's time."

"Okay. Just hang on. I'll be there soon."

Martha felt immense relief. She looked in the smudged mirror, taking extra care to repair her make-up. *Why am I doing this? For Ed? I don't think so. I must be crazy.* Shaking her head, she went back to their booth.

"Fixed up a bit, eh?"

He sounded so pleased it made her ill. The waitress came, refilled their coffees and, in another moment, brought their food. Martha quietly kept her eye out for the detective. In this situation, he'd be her rescuer. "So, why take a detail like this one when it doesn't fit with your position on the force?" she asked, trying to make conversation. "They've used rookies until now."

"I wanted to spend some time with you." He waggled his eyebrows, disgusting her further. "Keeping you safe is my top priority, Martha." He looked deeply into her eyes and leaned as far across the table as he could to capture her hand. "You're a fascinating woman, and some of your exploits in the past absolutely blow me away!"

A shadow moved across the table. She looked up as Harry Johns stepped in closer. "Well, here you are, Ed. They told me you'd switched duties with Burns."

He motioned Martha to slide over and sat down beside her. Catching his male scent and great aftershave, she felt a wondrous sense of relief as his presence flooded over her.

"Hey, Harry, nice to see you. Yeah, well, a man needs a little light duty once in a while, and I can't think of anything to beat this job right here."

He gave a small, unsure laugh while Martha relaxed. It pleased her to see Ed uneasy in the presence of Johns. *Could it be guilt?*

"I see. Nice thought, but you're needed on traffic detail over on Delano Street and Twenty-Fifth. Lot of drunks on the road, and we've got two auto accidents, one with fatalities." He handed Ed a sheet with his current assignment noted on it. "I'll see that this lady home safely and get another guard for her. Here you go, take my patrol car." He handed the keys to Ed. "I'll let Mrs. Chance drive me back."

A volcano of resentment and hate filled Ed's eyes at being demeaned in front of a woman he desperately wanted. Martha easily saw his blazing fury and almost felt sorry for him as he reluctantly moved out of his seat and stood up to take the proffered keys from Johns.

"Okay, sir. I'll get on it"

"I'd like my keys, please," Martha said as he turned to leave. She held out her hand.

He appeared near the boiling point as he handed them over and she knew it was directed at her. She felt the chill of it in her bones. *I swear this man hates me.* Smiling inwardly, she kept her thoughts to herself, remembering Duke's warning about Ed. At seeing his anger just now, she readily believed him capable of unbelievable and frightening things, including murder.

Johns moved into Ed's spot and looked at her across the table. "You've gone pale, Martha. What's happening?"

"Nothing, sir, just had a passing thought. I've worked all evening and I'm tired, too."

"You could call me Harry. We're sort of friends by now." His gray eyes bent toward her, and the warmth in his gaze set her aglow inside. *If this is police business, I'm a Tibetan lady Monk.* She wanted to giggle but dared not allow herself the privilege.

Harry ushered her out to her car. "I see you've gotten your car back." He made the gesture of helping her to the driver's seat though it wasn't needed. She guessed he was being gallant. "How'd that happen?"

"Ed—er—Officer Gilmore brought it. It was there when I got off work." She tried to sound casual, but it was difficult with Harry looking so good. His interest in her flattered her shattered soul. "I'd asked about it several times."

He said nothing as Martha drove home and into her garage. "Are you going to be my guard all night?" she asked, her slightly raised voice expressing her incredulity. Harry was a highly paid detective and wouldn't be pulling this kind of duty. She was sure of that. *Could he have another motive?*

"No, Martha, I'll call someone in after a bit." He ushered her into the house and his gentle attentions actually made her feel like a helpless little woman in need of a protector. *Mister, if you only knew—except you already do.*

They settled in the den and she turned to him. She had to know. "Harry, please, forgive me for asking, but what's your story? I know you have one. I see it in your eyes, and I'm curious." She kept her voice low, soft, and sincere, wanting to know what hidden things in his past made him find ways to spend time with her in spite of the terrible things he knew about her.

He sighed and she saw the terrible pain and hurt shining in his dark gray eyes. "It's hard for me to talk about it, but you're right, I do have a story. What you did in Colorado Springs struck a chord with more people than you know, and I'm one of them. Yours is not the only family to have suffered from child predators."

"Oh, Detective—Harry, not you, too!" She felt the wetness as hot tears started down her cheeks.

"Yes, only my child lies in her grave. We had no hope for her recovery, after what that monster did to her. In some ways it helps to know she's safe with God and can't hurt anymore." He raised his tear-filled gaze to hers. Martha saw a few tears escape those hawk-like eyes and trace down his cheeks. "But we lost her all the same. My wife never got over it and I eventually lost her, too."

She went to him and knelt in front of his chair, reaching out to him in his agony. "I don't know what to say. Did they ever catch the man?"

"No, they never did, Martha, they never did."

"I'm sorry, Harry. I know all about it. Believe me, I do."

His long arms reached down for her and drew her onto his lap. "Dear girl, I wish I'd had the guts to do what you've done. Maybe it would've helped someone else, somehow." He held her ever closer, finally putting his face into her hair and nuzzling it. "Forgive me for holding you, but it feels damned good to me and, right now, I don't know if I can let you go."

Martha still didn't know what to say. She let him hold her and felt herself sinking deeper into his arms. He had a great masculine scent and she'd become so tired of everything she faced. "It feels good to me, too."

"We've got to keep you safe, Martha. I worry about you." His grip never lessened, but she felt his face edging closer to hers. "Forgive me." He pressed his seeking lips to hers in a long deep kiss. "Oh, God, that's good—so damnably good," he whispered ever so softly.

"Yes, it is." She moved around to face him, returning his kiss. "This is insane, Detective Johns. You know it is."

"That would be Harry, my dear." He held her out a bit and looked deeply into her eyes. "You're really something. I knew it from the first time we met. I don't know where this leads us, but I'd like to see more of you—and often." He gave her a squeeze, and loosened his grip.

Martha believed she'd acted too hastily. "None of this makes a bit of sense, and I know it's wrong. It's in no way appropriate with a pre-trial hearing coming up." She flushed. "I haven't felt this way for a very long time, Harry. And I'd like to see you, too."

"You will, Martha, my dear, you sure will."

She got off his lap, hating to leave that fine, strong, warmth, but it was getting very late. Harry got up from the chair, stood close against her and placed his arms around her, his chin resting on top of her head. "You're a tall one, aren't you?" he murmured into her hair.

"I suppose so, but not as tall as you."

She nestled against him, and they walked together into the kitchen. Martha noticed the shades were not drawn and moved quickly to pull them down. Then seeing a bit of scrap from her noon meal on the floor, she bent to retrieve it just as a shot rang out. Something whizzed through the air above her, just missing her head.

"My God, another shot!" she screamed in disbelief. "If I hadn't bent down just then, I'd have had it that time!"

Harry, moving like lightning, grabbed her and shoved her into a chair. He ran out the door, his gun drawn. She heard him yelling into his phone, "Get some people out here! There's been another assassination attempt!" as he gave the particulars.

Then he moved away and she no longer heard his voice. She sat shaking with fury.

After a few moments, he returned. "Nothing out there, but somebody's really trying to do you in, and I don't think it's safe for you to stay here, not anymore. They heard the wailing sirens as the back-up force arrived. "I'll get them on this, but I'd like to get you out of here, tonight."

Martha had a pretty clear idea of her destination as she stoically went about packing a bag. Remembering the back pack laying in the back of her closet, she felt cold all over. *That's real evidence if they snoop around here while I'm gone, and they could. This place is now a crime scene.*

She made a hasty decision. Reaching into her closet, she pulled the offending pack out and shoved it into her overnight case. Without the sandbag it weighed almost nothing. *Who would ever look in there?* She placed jeans, a sweatshirt, and a few filmy under things on top and zipped it up. *Now, with the empty sandbag burned up, and this stuff with me, there's nothing for them to find.* That little bit made her feel better until she remembered the letter. She reached beneath her mattress and retrieved it. *I'll stuff this in my suitcase under everything. Can't leave that incriminating thing here, either.*

After things settled down, Harry took her out to a squad car. As they drove away, he asked, "Would you mind coming home with me?" He chuckled. "I have no wayward intentions, Martha, I'll be a gentleman."

"I don't care where you take me as long as no more shots come tearing through the windows."

"Rest assured," he said. "It'll be my greatest pleasure knowing you are safe and above that, seeing your face in the morning. I live outside of town a bit, so with my dogs out and about, I think your chances of survival are better than average."

"Are my chances of survival better with *you*, Harry?" Her voice, soft and low, relayed her unspoken feelings as an overwhelming desire to lie in this man's strong arms burned like a furnace through her body. *This crazy feeling has to be a reaction from all the excitement.* She fought for control over her frazzled nerves but in her mind, Serena was already in an uproar. *Down, you unprincipled creature.*

She'd told no one where she was going or when she'd be back. Right now, she didn't know or care. She trusted the man at the wheel. When passing streetlights flashed across his face, she caught glimpses of his strong chin and big, hawkish nose. Put together they managed to complement his intense gray eyes. He handled the unmarked patrol car with practiced competence, and she felt herself beginning to relax.

CHAPTER 21

Wondering where this thing with Harry might lead was useless at the moment. Martha closed her eyes as he drove through them through the dark streets.

"Are you all right?" he asked.

The depth and tone of his voice roused her from her musings and settled deep inside her, creating a heat so deep she couldn't help her errant thoughts. *He's a handsome devil in his rugged, yet somehow, suave way. What's wrong with me? Is it the close call I've just survived? Who knows?*

She tried to restrain her foolish thoughts, realizing he was waiting for an answer to his question. "I'm okay—scared, though. Being shot at isn't in my line of work. Who could hate me enough to want to kill me besides Munson? And if you say he's still locked up, then who?"

"We don't know who yet, but we will, and please don't be afraid of me." He laughed softly. "I'm a nice guy, Martha."

I'll bet you are. She made no reply but the sensations swirling through her body made her wonder if she'd be able to walk when the car stopped. *Why am I feeling this way?* But she had a feeling she already knew.

"Martha, is there anything that's happened lately that might have a bearing on this shooter? Anybody you've ticked off recently?" He softened the question as much as possible, but his tone was serious as he added, "It might help us figure out who's behind all this."

"Only Munson, but he's behind bars—still is, isn't he?" She was never sure about that anymore. He nodded, so she continued. "Of course, there's Ed Gilmore. He isn't too happy with me right now and he's made threats. Says he knows things about me—said he overheard you detectives talking. Is that possible?"

She saw an angry scowl cross his face as they drove past a streetlight. "It shouldn't be. He's sure as hell been out of line in any case." Then he smiled at her and his eyebrows went up. "Ed's interested in you?"

Martha didn't even want to think about Ed. "Yes, he is, but it's definitely over—was before it ever got started as far as I'm concerned." She patted his arm. "He was absolutely furious when you interrupted his escorting me home tonight. He had bigger plans in his mind than my safety. I was sure of that." She wanted to laugh at the incredulous look on Harry's face.

"You know anything else about Ed?" he demanded.

She nodded. "I think there might be. My friend's an ex-Navy SEAL. He's the one who took on the bodyguard job for Munson's wife." Martha turned to look at him. "He and Judith are getting along very well, and when they visited, he told me he'd do anything I needed. Well anything, legal," she clarified. "So I asked him to do a check on Ed after he became nasty and threatened me."

Harry scowled. "I'll have a word with Gilmore on that."

"I doubt that would stop him," Martha argued. "Anyway, my friend found out that Ed didn't leave Benson, Arizona on the best of terms. I wouldn't want to spoil the man's career, but Duke said there were questions about his wife's death. He learned that people suspected Ed Gilmore may have made his wife's death look like an accident, but it was unproven and nothing came of that investigation."

"Interesting, I'll check that out. He's been a good, straight officer since he's been here, to my knowledge."

"Ed's a drinker for another thing, and his driving scared me half to death. Another reason I refused to go out with him again. I had to have breakfast with him several mornings ago. He was so forceful, I had to—he wouldn't take no for an answer. Then during breakfast, he had a shot of whiskey in his coffee, and in the *morning*."

"You don't go for a drinker, then. Anything else?"

"No, I've never had to deal with that on a personal basis, but as a nurse you see enough of it." She remembered more of her report from Duke. "The Benson police department asked him to leave the area—everything on the QT of course."

"How could your friend have found out those things?"

"He knew someone." Martha said it off hand. She'd never tell Duke's secrets, but because of Ed Gilmore's threatening attitude, she was relieved to enlighten the detective on the man's imperfections. She also realized her mad bout of passion had dissipated. She was in full control of her emotions again.

"Thanks for the input on Ed." Harry took another tack. "It'd help solve this thing if we could get Munson to admit he hired a killer. Not much chance of that, unreasonable as he's being."

Martha had one more thing to add. "Harry, I actually shadowed Munson, and more than once." She flushed with that admission. "As I said before, I was in a restaurant and I overheard him talking to a person on the phone. He asked that person to get on the stick and take care of his wife. He threatened him if he didn't get it done. Judith told me he'd wanted her house from the time she first met him, even measured some of the rooms. Worse yet, he had a new woman ready to move in. He was at dinner with her—kept her in a fancy penthouse, too."

"Say! Want a job as a detective? Makes me wonder what else you've done lately."

She saw his dark gray eyes flash as the car sped along. "I only followed him after he nearly killed his wife," she said. "He'd beaten her half to death several times. That's why she hired Duke." She chuckled. "When that big dude came into the house, he put Munson out on the street. The coward didn't want to tangle with the SEAL. No wonder he hates me so much."

Martha smiled. She felt good about several things she'd done and that included Pederson and the rat-faced guy in Greeley. As for the ones in Colorado Springs, she could make no apology.

"You take your role as good guy all the way, don't you?" he commented.

"You know enough of my past, Harry. I confess it felt good to even the score a little. My alter ego—her name is Serena by the way—is a conscious part of me and makes me stronger if I need to be. The cruelty and abuse I see— and I swear, it's everywhere—sets me off. It's not exclusively family anymore. I have no personal excuse, not anymore." After a moment's hesitation, she added, "My husband warned me not to let 'her' out again, just before he died."

"And have you let 'her' out again?"

Alarm crept through her at how softly and smoothly he questioned, but she merely shrugged and stayed silent.

"You can tell me anything, Martha. You might feel better for it."

"You're a good man. I know that, and when I have something to confess, you'll be the first to hear it."

All her romantic notions had fled. Her blood had cooled and begun to chill. Willing herself to be strong against him, she said nothing more, worried she'd said too much already.

Silence lay in the air as he pulled down an unpaved lane. "It's sort of rustic out here, but quiet." The tones of his voice told her he regretted putting her on the defensive. "You'll be safe here, Martha."

He pulled up before a low-slung ranch style home. The car was met with two, large, mixed-breed dogs, barking and wagging their tails. "That's Max and Skunk, Max is the bigger one." Harry got out, roughed the dog's heads and coats, and then opened the door for Martha. "They won't bother you. Come in and I'll fix you something. You must be exhausted with all that's happened, especially after working all afternoon and being shot at." He sighed. "What a day, eh?"

Looking around in the darkness, she saw a well-kept home with shrubs and a few lights here and there. She got out and Harry took her bag. He ushered her up the few steps and into his home. She petted the dogs. "Why Skunk?"

"He was a nosey little pup. You can guess the rest." He tousled the smaller dog's ears. Skunk looked like an Australian Sheppard mix, where Max had more the attributes of a German Sheppard. "They're real good dogs. Make you feel safer, don't they?" he asked, chatting away while he bustled about making hot chocolate.

"I love dogs. Maybe I should have one," Martha said, as he poured the thick dark liquid in two cups. "Looks and smells wonderful, Harry. I'll sleep my head off tonight, or what's left of the night. Thanks."

"I'm sure you need it."

He wanted their time together to last longer, she knew, but the tenseness of their earlier conversation remained and she was worn out from continually being on guard.

"Show me where I sleep, if you will. I'm more than exhausted." She finished her chocolate and rose from the chair. "What time is it anyway?"

"Time for you to get some sleep, my dear." Martha heard the resignation in his voice as he led the way to a bedroom down the hall. "There's a shower in there for you, if you like. Help yourself to the towels and such, too."

The door stood open, but before she could enter the room, he caught her close in a warm embrace. "I really care about you, Martha," he declared, looking deep into her eyes. "God help me, I do."

Though reluctant to leave those warm, strong arms, Martha steeled herself and pulled away. "Thanks for what you've done for me tonight, Harry," she said, averting her eyes. "Thank God, you *are* one of the good guys." A tear escaped as she closed the door against the warmth he offered. She wanted that warmth, and she wanted him—way too much!

☙❧

Martha struggled to wake up and get out of bed. She'd slept long and deep, and by the sunlight glancing off the windows, believed it to be nearly noon. "Am I alone, here?" she asked as she scanned the room where she'd slept in such comfort and safety.

Feminine touches were everywhere. The window treatment bespoke a touch of subtle class. They were fitted with fine, Austrian-ruffled panels and silken side drapes, pulled back with tasseled cords. Gently patterned rosebud wallpaper was off-set by walnut paneling. The furniture, older and of a sturdy, finely crafted style, was not that of a child's room.

Had his wife done the decorating? Was it done for guests or planned for when their lost little girl was grown?

She remembered Harry's sorrow over his daughter's savage rape and murder and her heart ached for him.

After a quick wash, she threw on the pair of jeans she'd stuffed into her overnight bag. Her sweatshirt was a sage green that brought out the color of her eyes. The sight of the offending backpack of surgical things leaped out at her. "How will I handle this? I've got to get this letter off, too. Wouldn't it be a kick to mail it from here?" she wondered, giggling a bit as she pulled herself together before venturing out of the room.

"Is Harry here or has he left for work, today?" she murmured and went out to find him.

He was sitting in the kitchen reading the paper. The fragrant odor of coffee welcomed her.

"Good morning. I slept so well, I thought I'd never wake up." Looking about, she saw a cheery kitchen done in light shades of green with an ancient clock ticking on the wall. It was after ten, she noted.

"So did I, Martha. In fact, I was about ready to see if you'd sleep your life away."

His eyes crinkled pleasantly when he laughed and it sent a thrill charging though her. He went to the door and let the dogs in. They ran to her, wiggling and panting, their claws clicking on the parquet flooring as they scrambled across it in their eagerness to be petted and spoken to.

She stroked them and fluffed her hands in their fur. "I'd forgotten what great pets dogs are," she said, ruffling their fur as they vied for attention. After putting their noses under her hand and nudging for more caresses, they couldn't help bestowing a casual lick when they could.

He watched her, with a shine in his eyes, as she played with his animals. "I'm glad you like my boys. They're a lot of company for this lonely guy." He went to the stove. "How about a bite of breakfast?" He held out a cup. "Coffee?"

She nodded, feeling relaxed and almost carefree. "You bet—my biggest weakness." She took the cup, meeting his eyes. The glow in those dark gray depths made her feel hesitant. "Not working today?" she asked.

"I took the day off, got a lot of time coming. I let it build up." He laid strips of thick bacon in the pan. "Like eggs?"

"Sure, any way you do, Harry."

He put bread in the toaster and, later, cracked several eggs into the pan after removing the crisp strips of bacon. The dogs crowded around licking their chops, but he shooed them out the door. "Get out of here, you two. Even my dogs like company, can't get rid of them."

He chuckled softly and went back to his cooking. She watched his tall, lean body as he grabbed jam from the fridge, plates and cutlery from the cabinets, and, in no time, set a nice plate before her.

"How's that, then?"

"Looks wonderful." She dug in all the while wondering, *Where is this going and what am I doing? This is nice, but I can't stay out here.*

They ate in silence. She watched his long fingers on his utensils and how his throat worked as he drank his coffee. A fine-looking man was always a joy to watch. Too bad it had to end.

"I can't stay out here, Harry, you know that."

"I had a long chat with Ebert, my boss. He doesn't want me getting too personal with you. The plan is to put you under closer surveillance and stake out your home. We've got some good people. Whoever the shooter is, he won't see us."

"Okay, that might be best. The shooter wouldn't likely be around here, would he?" She looked at him, "Maybe I could borrow your dogs? They do make me feel safe, and wouldn't they make short work of my nemesis?"

"You could borrow me along with them if you want-ed." He laughed a bit, but he was serious as he shoved the last bit of toast in his mouth.

She knew that statement merited a reply. "I certainly feel safe enough with you around, Harry," she replied. "But I doubt it would fly with your boss." She couldn't help but imagine having him around twenty-four-seven. *It'd fly with me, for sure, but it shouldn't.* She felt tangled again with her feelings about Harry, something she'd felt quite frequently these past several days.

"Later on, we'll go back in town and check things out."

"While I'm here I'd like to look around outside," Martha countered. "I couldn't see anything last night, seems like nice country around here,"

"Say when. I've had this place a long time and I'd love to show it to you."

The gleam of pleasure that crossed his features made Martha realize the inner sadness of the man, living alone with memories of his losses. She definitely knew how that was—she suffered it, too. "Let me finish getting myself together. Only take a minute." She went to the room, fixed her make-up, and grabbed the light jacket she'd worn last night.

He waited in the kitchen and, when she appeared, gave her an appraising glance. "You're a fine-looking woman, Martha, granny or not."

He dodged her pretend blow and took her arm. To-gether they walked outside into the fresh Colorado moun-tain air. "I have about twenty acres here. Had horses a while back." He gestured at a small barn set off away from the house. "But with only me to ride them and my work, I gave up on them."

Martha saw a pasture sloping away from the ranch style home and snug fencing—which held fields of hay—groves of pines, and oak trees placed according to the vagaries of nature. "It's beautiful out here, Harry. You have a lovely place." She smiled at him. "And it makes your losses that much worse, somehow."

"Yeah." His voice had gone husky, and she hugged him without thinking. "Oh, Martha." He took her tightly in his arms. "My God, girl, I think I'm falling in love with you." He bent her back and kissed her long and deep. "You're some kind of woman, you are."

When she caught her breath, she said, "I don't know how to handle this, Harry. My husband's only been gone for a few months." She nestled against him, and it felt good. "I think you're about the finest man I've ever known, and yet, I don't really know you that much at all. Of course, you have a bit of competition in that, with my late husband Bob. He helped me through the worst months of my life." She laughed—a helpless sound. "Harry, I'm so messed up right now."

"We've both got a lot in our pasts, Martha, but you know we can't go back as much as one day. We'll take things a bit slower, but I want you in my life. I know that much."

He held her in front of him, looking into her eyes, and then reached for her lips again. His kisses made her legs so weak, she wondered if she'd be able to stand alone when he released her. They spent another happy hour walking under apple trees and through fields of high mountain grasses. Jackrabbits bounded away and a multitude of birds took flight. The two dogs happily chased after anything that stirred.

"Well, much as I hate to say it, we'd best get back and set things in motion." His regret at returning her to her home was plain enough. "You'll not be free until we nab this bird, whoever he is."

"It's been wonderful, Harry, thanks—for everything." How trite, how poor that sounded to her own ears as she said it.

She'd tensed up inside and remained silent as he drove toward Denver, knowing they were going back to her home and the same dangers as before. If the shooter awaited her arrival, could anyone protect her?

CHAPTER 22

W hat the hell were you thinking, Harry?" Ebert sat at his desk, leaned back, and looked up at Harry. "You were way out of line taking that woman out to your place." Then he grinned. "So how did it go? With her past, weren't you a little nervous being out there with a woman like that?"

"She's alive, Marcus. That's what I was thinking, and it went, fine. The woman's no danger to any normal man. She told me a lot about it." Harry wouldn't allow Ebert to put him in the wrong. "You'd have done the same if you'd been there. The woman was scared to death. Obviously, our *protection* wasn't half enough. Hell, my dogs could've done a better job than we did."

"We'd best keep something like this quiet for now. Hate to have it getting out. Hell, we'd never hear the end of it." Ebert sighed. "I'll put double guards on her for the time being. She must be nervous as hell."

Harry chuckled. "I'll be checking on her later." He went on to tell Ebert the things Martha had told him. "If Munson has a hired shooter, we need to find out if he's still out there. He may have changed his target to Martha, but why would he?

"We need to question him on that," Ebert said.

"Good luck with that," Harry mumbled as he went back to his own desk and dug into the paperwork piled in front of him. Then he called over, "Any report on that plaster cast the kid took?"

"Yeah, looks to be a thirteen or fourteen sized shoe print. We're calling him Bigfoot for now," Ebert added. "That's all we have." He came over to Harry's desk. "We did a check on Pederson's home. The bastard had a camera set-up in the little girl's room. Looks like he'd been making his own brand of kiddie porn, maybe selling it. That's what they do."

"Marcus, that's enough to get him the death penalty if we can prove it. His wife ought to get it, too. The bastard must have kept that child scared out of her wits." Harry grimaced as if in pain. "How could any mother let that sort of thing happen?"

"I don't know, Harry, I just don't know."

❧❧

Martha paced about her home. She needed to get that letter out and wondered if anyone had checked her Internet while she was gone. They'd need a search warrant for something like that and she hadn't heard of one being issued. Would they bother to tell her?

She called Duke. He came immediately, ready to go to work.

"Can you tell if anyone has been looking on my computer?" she asked.

"I'll take a look." He sat down and powered up the desktop. After several minutes, he said, "Don't look like anybody's been on here." He raised his eyebrows. "What's going on? Anything you'd like erased?"

"No, no nothing like that, Duke," she replied, knowing he referred to her predatory activities. "But could you show me the steps to erase something permanently, if is that even possible?"

"Not entirely, but to a casual looker, it would appear erased. Once you erase something it's gone unless a specialist does the looking." He had a curious look on his rugged features. "You in trouble, Martha?"

"No, not at present." She winced. "But Duke, I've been shot at twice. The police are protecting me for now until they catch the guy." Telling him about it would devastate Duke, but she decided to go ahead. "They don't have a line on the shooter but they found a foot print. So far as I know, that's it."

"I'm not leaving you here alone, lady, I'll call Judith."

Martha wanted to protest, but the stern look on Duke's face stopped her. Inwardly, she saw her plans to eradicate another child predator fading. On top of that, she wanted to go out at night and stalk her stalker. The thought of skulking about in the darkness, looking for her attacker, thrilled and excited her. But no, she had to play the part of the hapless female, hoping and praying for police protection. It only added to her deep frustration. *Serena, what are we going to do?*

"Duke, I've already got two cops covering the place. You don't need to stay, too." She saw his hesitation. "I'm sure I'll be all right, and I'm going to work, anyway. Sitting here all day with those guards underfoot is driving me buggy!" He steadily weakened as she made her case, until she was sure he was heading home. "Please, Duke, I'll be fine," she said again.

Being able to plan and take out another predator had somehow become very important. Whether it was her or Serena, she didn't know or care. Being unable to carry on what had become a life's work made her frustration mount. And having a big Rambo type underfoot along with two cops, only added to it.

She finally had Duke convinced and led him to the door. "Thanks so much for caring. I'll keep you informed about everything." With a sigh of relief, she said goodbye, patted his arm, and let him go.

She went into the kitchen, made a strong pot of coffee, and sat down with a cup. "Finally, a moment alone." She heaved a sigh and looked at the holes in her window. Both were now covered with a bit of thick, clear plastic, until new glass could be installed by the contractor. *What a mess. Wonder how long it'll take to fix them. Perhaps I should have asked for bullet-proof glass.* She laughed, though it was far from funny.

She took her coffee to the computer desk and powered up. After checking her e-mail, she went to the chat room. "Hope those cops stay outside a while," she said as she flipped through several messages. *Oh, here we go.*

She spotted Wilmer, a young teen looking for a friend. *How about 'Wilma'? He can't miss that.* Hoping to attract him, she sent a plaintive message of loneliness and abandonment by her family. *Nice come on. What'll you reply to this drivel?* She smiled to herself, wondering how this one might play out. *I've got a feeling.*

She left the computer and did a few household chores. When her phone went musical, she wondered, *Ed? Jeannie? Harry?* When the caller ID said Lizzie, she opened it almost frantically. "Hey, Liz?"

"Hey, girl, can I come over to visit for a few days?"

"Yes—please. I need you so much!"

After she clicked off, she sighed with relief. When the tears came, Martha realized how deeply stressed she'd become and let them flow. They were healing and, with the guards outside, there was no one to see her momentary weakness.

Later, she washed her eyes and went outside to speak to the guards. "Hi guys, I have company coming, so be sure to let her in."

She described Lizzie and her car. A dedicated looking pair, the men took her guardianship seriously. *I ought to be safe enough with those two eagle eyes on the job, yet they manage to allow me a little privacy.*

When Lizzie drove up, Martha had to hold herself back from running to the car and pulling her out. Instead, she sauntered out slowly when the car door opened and took Liz in her arms. "I'm under guard, right now, Liz, come inside." Her voice was low and her warning look stifled Liz's cry of alarm. Martha led her guest inside, carrying with Lizzie's overnight bag.

"Martha! What's going on? What have you done now?"

"It's not me, Liz. Somebody is taking shots at me. The police don't know who it is and they're trying to keep me from getting my head blown off. Get a look at this window. He shot through it twice."

She stared at Martha, alarm in her eyes. "Why?"

"The only one I know of who wants me dead is Munson. You know the one. I helped his wife with the Navy SEAL. Munson's tried to kill me three times already and Serena got him twice. But we don't need to worry," she quickly added. "He's in jail for now." She grimaced. "I hope." She couldn't help an amazed laugh at the deadly turn her life had taken. "Oh, Liz, it's so good to see you. I'm all tied in knots and with you around I can let it all hang out," she said, flopping into a chair and heaving a long, deep sigh.

"Tell me about it, then," Liz demanded.

Martha laid out all that had happened and later, as they sat in the kitchen watching the night shades of purple fall over the city outside, she rose to draw the shades fully over the windows. "There are some good things about it, too." She filled Lizzie in with enough details to satisfy her, mentioning the night spent with Harry.

"A detective? You're mighty brave or a damned fool, woman. And you say he knows all about that stuff in Colorado Springs?"

"Yes, he does and he has things in his past, too, even worse than mine, Lizzie." She told her friend the sad details of how Harry had lost his family.

"Sorry to hear that. It's horrible. Things seem pretty bad right now, huh?" She shook her head in sympathy as Martha's phone went off.

Martha listened and hung up. "Speak of the devil. Guess who's coming to check up on me?" She couldn't get the grin off her face.

"I can't wait to get a look at this dude. Martha, you sure attract 'em, but how are you planning to handle him along with your other little activities?"

"I haven't figured that out yet, but I don't want to stop. I'd like to take out a few more of those chat-line honeys before I hang up my scalpel." She giggled at the outrageous thing she'd just said. Then she sighed. "I'd better put on a pot of coffee. He likes it even more than I do, and it looks like you could use a cup yourself," she commented and bustled around setting it up, getting out cups, and generally fussing.

Liz watched her in amazement. "Woman, I can't believe this. You look like a silly teenager waiting for her first date, and with all the perilous plots spinning around in that screwed up head of yours. Haven't you got enough trouble?"

"I know, Lizzie, but I can't seem to change things. They just keep happening."

At the gentle knock on her door, Martha opened it slowly and peeked out before swinging it wide. "Hello, Harry, come in."

She led him to the kitchen and introduced him to her guest. "This is my very best friend in the world, Lizzie

Marin." As the big man reached out and took her friend's hand, Martha added, "She's come to visit for a few days."

"Nice to meet you, ma'am," Harry said and looked at Martha. "I'm glad you've got company to take your mind off the way things have been around here lately" He paused and hesitated. "I just came by to see how you're doing. Being shot at isn't something we take lightly and we're putting in a lot of hours on your case." He had that crinkly look around his eyes as he spoke.

Martha detected humor behind his thoughts. "It isn't exactly anything I take lightly either, Harry. Anything yet?"

"Munson wouldn't give us anything. He knows something. I could see it in that smug look on his face. Expression often says more than words. From what I see, he may be behind your shootings."

"Coffee?" Martha held out a cup. "I believe he could be, too, and I didn't see his smug look. It's got to be someone he's hired, then."

"Looks that way. He gave us nothing, however." Harry took a seat at the table across from Martha, holding his cup in both hands. He looked at her, his eyes full of questions.

Lizzie took in the intimate scene between Martha and the detective, sensing the warmth between them. *That woman gets involved with a man no matter what.* A smile played about her lips. *What a gal!*

Harry turned to Lizzie. "You're from Colorado Springs, then?"

"Yes, Martha and I go way back, Detective Johns. I believe, in this room, we don't need to stand on ceremony. We certainly have no secrets, from what Martha tells me, and you're no stranger to trouble yourself. I was sorry to hear of it." She was open and forthright, her head held high, offering no apology for having knowledge and acceptance of Martha's past.

"You're a good friend," Harry replied. "I can see that and she needs one, now more than ever,"

Martha held out a plate of biscotti. "Here, help your-self." She felt the tension in the air and laughed. "Hey, it's getting thick in here."

Harry burst out laughing. "You'll do, Martha. You're all right." Then he said, "I've been thinking. It's Friday and I wonder if you ladies would enjoy a week-end in the country?"

"What do you say, Lizzie?" Martha asked. "He's got two great dogs and it's very pretty out there. And, he's a decent cook—for breakfast anyway."

"Hey, I'm up for anything, Martha. You know me." Lizzie looked at the tall detective. "You sure it's okay for me to tag along?"

"Wouldn't have it any other way. We can go in my car," he said. "It's unmarked. Get your gear."

Martha made a hasty call to the staffing office and after clicking off, said. "I'm free, no work for me this week-end." She headed to her room to pack a moderate sized bag and Lizzie stayed in the kitchen with Harry, her bag beside her.

Martha packed her incriminating surgical things along with needed clothing and make-up. "Can't leave this stuff lying around, and where is that letter?"

She panicked, trying to remember where she'd placed it last. She looked under her mattress but it wasn't there. "I must have it on me somewhere." The she remembered. "Oh, yeah, it was in my overnight bag, but now it's in my purse."

ↄⱷↄ

Lizzie took this opportunity to suss Harry out a bit. "Martha's attracted a dangerous enemy, enough that you folks have her under guard?"

"She's got herself tangled up with someone who's out to make trouble for her."

Lizzie thought by his answer that he deliberately downplayed Martha's trouble. "*You* might call bullets whizzing past her head *trouble,* but it's a whole lot more than that," she declared, warming to her subject. "No idea who the shooter is or why he's after her?"

"Not a concrete one. Of course, I'm not at liberty to discuss the case. She'll be safe at my place, and you, too." Since he obviously wasn't going to tell her anything, she changed tactics. "You two seem rather close. Is that a good idea?"

"Sure suits me. Martha can speak for herself." He chuckled. "Looking out for her, eh?"

Seeing the light in his eyes and how fine his lean good looks were, she lightened up and decided to have a good opinion of the man. "Martha's a lucky woman in many ways, in spite of all her heartaches, and I think we'll have a wonderful time at your pla—" She broke off at the sounds of wheeled luggage across the tiles,

Martha came out with her case. She smiled at Harry. "I'm ready."

She wore slim-fitting jeans and a light green sweater with a colorful scarf twisted artfully around her neck. Her chestnut hued hair and green eyes made quite a picture to his eyes and the glow Lizzie saw in them confirmed it.

"You look wonderful, Martha," Harry murmured, his voice low and sexy.

Lizzie felt like a third wheel. She couldn't help asking. "You two sure you want me to come with you on this rural outing of yours?"

Martha giggled as a ruddy flush crept over her face. "I think you'd better."

"All right, ladies," Harry said. "Let's get moving."

With a grin wide as the Grand Canyon spread over his handsome face, he led them out the door. After a word to the two guards, they drove off in Harry's unmarked car. Lizzie took the back seat and Martha sat beside the agent of the law.

CHAPTER 23

They laughed and talked as they drove through the increasingly rugged terrain until finally Harry turned off on the graveled road and then onto the driveway of his home. "Here we are ladies." Getting out, he had to fend off the dogs to open the doors for them. He grabbed their cases and led them inside, along with two very excited dogs.

"Welcome," he said. "Anybody hungry?"

The happy lilt in his voice was unmistakable and Martha was glad this venture for the week-end had brightened his life. Being in his company had certainly brightened hers, aside from the relief of being away from the threat of gunshots fired at her in her home.

"Hey, this is nice," Lizzie said, as she bent down and ruffled Skunk's coat. "Hello, you furry creature." Looking around the ranch-style kitchen, she offered, "I'd love to help if I could."

Martha sat in a chair. Harry set the bags down and showed Lizzie what he had available. "It's late so maybe something simple will do." Then he shooed the dogs outside. "Get out of here, you two."

"I'll make egg and bacon sandwiches unless someone's having a cholesterol moment—love 'em, myself."

Lizzie looked around for comment. "Got any cheese, a to-mato or two?"

"Yeah, right here." Harry dug the stuff out and handed it to Lizzy.

He gave a healthy male laugh that went right down deep. Having his home busy with females bustling about seemed to delight the man and Martha's heart swelled at the sight of him. It was very early in her relationship with him, but she already had strong feelings for Harry. She enjoyed his company and the feeling of safety she found with him and his home so far out in the country. It had become a sanctuary to her troubled mind.

He sat across from Martha and looked into her eyes while he waited for the snacks Lizzie busily prepared. The dogs whined outside and scratched at the door.

Martha nearly giggled. "Sounds like they want in, Harry."

"If they come in, you may have to fight for your sandwiches."

Martha felt like a school girl at the glow in Harry's eyes. "Let them in. I can handle them, how about you, Liz?"

He let them in and, after a bit of petting, the dogs settled down enough to allow them to finish their meal.

Finished with the strong coffee and greasy sandwiches, Lizzie remarked, "My therapist would flip her wig if she saw me eating this stuff. She held her coffee up in a toast. "Here's to you, Monique!"

Martha loved and thoroughly enjoyed the woman's bold bravado and the way she flung her hands out in disdain. "Lizzie, I swear, you're better for me than a 'happy pill' any day."

Harry stood up. "Let's find you ladies some beds before you fall asleep at the table in spite of the coffee." He ushered them down the hall toward the back of the house. "It's been a long day for you both."

Martha put her stuff in the same room she'd used before and Harry took Lizzie farther down to another.

Martha went to see Lizzie's room. "Say, this is nice. Like it?"

"Everything around here is. What's not to like? Martha, that man is a jewel. What are you going to do about him?"

"I don't know, but I really do like him." Martha sighed. "Liz, every man I happen to marry ends up dead. I can't go through that again. I swear I'll never do it again. I'd be a death sentence to Harry if I married him." Tears burned and threatened. "My life is a constant quagmire. Where do I go from here?

"I'm sure you're wrong, but what can I say. I understand you might feel that way, I really do." Lizzie's look of concern faded as she stifled a tired yawn. "I'm dog tired, Martha. See you in the morning, eh?" She yawned and moved toward her bathroom with a towel draped over her shoulder.

Martha tossed a "Goodnight" over her shoulder and headed for that lovely room with the tiny-rosebud-flowered wallpaper. In the hallway, as she neared her room, she came face to face with Harry.

He took her in his arms and stood there, holding her, with his nose in her hair. "Oh, Martha," he murmured as he maneuvered her into her room. Embracing her tightly, he quietly closed the door.

"Harry! What are you doing?"

But she knew and had no will power to stop him. His kisses were like a powerful narcotic to her, taking her into oblivion. He moved her to the bed, put his arm beneath her knees, and gently lifted her onto it. She felt the bed sink under his weight as he moved his body close against hers.

"I won't do anything you'd not want, dear girl. You know the way I feel about you. It's early in our time together, but we're not kids anymore either." He kissed her deeply. "I want you so dammed much it's near to killing me."

"I wouldn't want you to die, Harry." She'd burned with passion for him since she first laid eyes on him. It had built up like a fire inside her and she had found no way to quench her feelings. "I feel like I'm on fire." She kissed him with all the built up passion that burned inside her. "Oh God, Harry, I think I love you, too," she cried out as his seeking hands moved over her.

Shots rang out in rapid succession, followed by several mournful yelps. Martha's blood ran cold at the sounds of those sharp staccato retorts ringing out in front of Harry's home. The heat between them turned to ashes as their minds filled with fear and anger.

With a quick kiss to her fevered lips, Harry leaped from the bed. "What the hell? Those were shots. Sorry, darling, stay here and keep low." With that, he ran out of the room fully dressed—they hadn't gotten far.

Martha crept out into the hall and met Lizzie head on.

"What was that?" her friend cried, her hastily donned robe askew. "Martha, that assassin guy knows you're here, he must!" She paused, scanning Martha from head to toe. "How come you're still dressed?"

"Never mind that." Martha hastily straightened her sweater. "Harry said it was shots and to keep low. I heard the dogs yelp." She tried not to pace, but her tired, worn out nerves were already stretched to the limit. "I wonder what's happening and if Harry's okay. It's darker than the back side of the moon out there." Then remembering Lizzie's words, she jerked to a halt. "How could the shooter *possibly* know I'm out here—how?"

"Who knows? But he's sure out to get you, and at a detective's place. He's either a mad man, or has some kind of balls!"

"He must be. Oh God, I hope Harry's okay out there." Martha wanted to run out the door, but she minded his words to stay low.

As she and Lizzie waited in the security of the hall, the kitchen door opened and Harry walked in, his face pale and tight with fury.

"Harry! What's wrong?" Martha cried, seeing the anger and desperation on his face. "What happened out there?"

He slumped down in a chair. "Some son of a bitch shot my dogs, both of them! There was nothing unusual beforehand, a bit of barking, but that's normal for the boys if they hear things prowling around at night." He paused, rubbed his face. "Whoever the dirty bastard is, he was looking for something of mine to kill."

"Are the dogs all right?" She knelt before him, already knowing the answer.

"Skunk was dead in the driveway, and Max breathed his last just as I found him. They were out a ways from the house." He looked into her eyes. "Martha, I think your shooter followed us out here. I take this killing of my dogs as a warning of some kind."

"Warning for what?" Martha had a terrible foreboding. "It's my fault, Harry. Trouble follows me wherever I go. I'm like the cartoon guy with a cloud over his head, and believe me, it rains all the time." She felt the heat of tears flowing down her cheeks. "I'm so sorry about your dogs. They were wonderful." She wanted to scream in her anger and helplessness. "It's one thing to go after me. I'm actually getting used to it, but why Max and Skunk? Why?"

"It was a message for me, Martha. Whoever the devil is, he's after me for helping you or for being with you. Bastard took it out on my dogs."

"How's this going to go with your boss, Harry?" Martha knew the man wasn't happy Harry had brought her out here the last time. She wondered how he'd handle this latest bit of news. *Has he put his job in jeopardy because of me?*

Seeing her worried expression, Harry shook his head and picked up the phone. Lizzie busied herself in the kitchen, all the shades pulled. Harry got up and looked out the kitchen window, trying to see in the dark, but he had only a porch light, which cast little illumination. "I looked around, but saw only one good-sized man's footprint. It was too dark for a good look. I'll get some people out here."

"Coffee's ready," Lizzie broke in. "Come on, have a cup. I don't know how to help any other way."

She set out cups and dug stuff out of the refrigerator. Outside, Martha noticed daylight beginning, light enough to check things out in more detail.

"Thanks Liz. You're a real trooper. God, this is so awful. I'm beginning to wonder if I'll make it to next week."

Martha felt shaky inside, wondering where this might end. Worse yet, she didn't have the freedom to do her own detective work and maybe put an end to her sniper once and for all. Inside her mind, Serena chomped at the bit, seeking a chance to take care of Martha once again.

"So much for the nice week-end in the country, ladies," Harry said. His eyes sought Martha's.

Their wonderful night together had gone so wrong. She saw his deep regret. He'd wanted her and she'd fully returned his feelings.

"We're sorry, too, Harry."

He didn't mistake her meaning and, momentarily, forgot everything, remembering how close they'd come to cementing their relationship. He enjoyed seeing the flush of heat flowing through her.

"How's about some chow, you two?"

The ever-observant Lizzie hadn't missed what passed between them, and Martha blushed even more to see that knowledge on her face. Lizzie shoveled a load of scrambled eggs on a platter and placed it on the table.

"Dig in."

They sat down to bacon, eggs, toast, and as much jam and jelly as she could dig out of the fridge.

Harry looked at Liz. "You're a wonder, ma'am. Does your husband know what you've gotten yourself into, having Martha as your friend?"

Martha nodded at Lizzie. "I told Harry about our big night at The Paradisio, Liz. He knows all about me."

In spite of the dire situation they'd faced during the night, they had a full breakfast and enjoyed each other's company. Martha felt extremely fatigued. She hadn't slept for more than twenty four hours and sighed. "I feel like I've worked an all-night double."

After they'd eaten, Harry went out to check the tracks and greet the forensics team sent out by Ebert. The man himself was in the party.

"So, Harry, you can't stay away, eh?" He tried to be severe, but his heart went out to the lonely man. "Hey, guy, I get it, and I'd like to meet this wonder woman of yours."

Harry ushered him into the house and introduced him to the two ladies. Ebert saw two solid, very-together women and liked them both immediately. Seeing Martha's handsome features, and in spite of knowing her past, he found her charming, if a bit deep. After looking into those green eyes, he smiled to himself. *This woman carries enough secrets inside her to run a war.* "Nice to finally meet you, Mrs. Chance." He took her hand, squeezing it gently.

Martha saw approval in his eyes, in spite of his knowing all about her. She believed they had evidence in the Pederson case. That miserable sandbag had leaked. The thought of it haunted her and that damming letter was in her purse, if they ever had occasion to look. She had to find a way to get it in the mail.

With the men outside, Martha chaffed at her inaction. "Here we are stuck in the house while they get to see everything. I wanted to see that big footprint, but then again, I'd hate to see his dogs like that. Poor Harry, he loved those guys." She stood at the window watching the forensics team at work.

"Martha, that nemesis of yours must have police information," Lizzy said. "Or else he couldn't have known you'd be out here. Well, unless he lives close by or was stalking you. Even then he wouldn't know where you were headed. He's got a line to the cops, dear girl. You know he has."

"I'm sure you're right, Liz. We can run that by Harry, but if I know him, he's already figured it out." She thought for a moment. "I only know one person connected with the police interested enough in my personal business to care where I went or with whom." She frowned. "Would refusing to go on another date with a man make him angry enough to commit murder?" She snorted at the ridiculous idea. "Impossible."

"Who do you mean? Who are you talking about?" Lizzie asked, all abuzz. "You mean that guy, Ed?"

"No way, couldn't be. He's a good officer, Harry told me that." Nearly exhausted, Martha added, "Don't mind my idle speculations. I'm so tired I don't know what I'm saying."

Too tired to check out the furnishings, she flopped down on the couch in the living room and pulled the throw she found there over her tired body. It bore the scent of Harry and with that pleasant scent in her nose she let go.

"That's right. Put your feet up for a while. I'll keep an eye out for you."

Lizzie was the kind who looked for excitement. Martha loved her for that.

Later in the morning, Harry roused her from a deep, dreamless sleep.

"Oh, what—what's happening?" Hair snarled, her face flushed, she worked her mind to awareness and smiled up at Harry. "Okay, I'm awake."

He stood looking down at her and she wondered how long he'd been there. "I've got to get back to Denver," he said. "I'm afraid we'll have to cut this week-end short."

She saw the regret in his eyes. "I understand, Harry. Is Liz ready?" She got up, brushed slowly past his solid body, and headed to the snug little bedroom for her things. "I'll be just a moment, then. I need to collect my things."

"I'll wait for you, my dear."

He clearly meant that in a more intimate way and, in spite of all the horror of what had happened, she was thrilled at his suggestion. He waited for the chance to hold her again. Things were just too good with him and she knew it. Wondering when everything would come crashing down around her, she had a very sick feeling. It chilled her deep inside.

CHAPTER 24

After the excitement at Harry's place, things seemed too quiet. Lizzie had gone home and the two guards stayed outside most of the time. Left to herself, Martha turned to her computer and found several eager messages from Wilmer on the teen chat line. Delighted that her insipid queries to him had attracted his fervent interest and, because of clues hidden in his messages, she decided on him as her next target.

Hi, Wilma, what r u thinking? Do u want 2 meet? Wilmer.

Ya, but not here. I can cu in Boulder. I can take a bus. What do u look like? Wilma.

Hey! I can meet u at Freestone Motel. Gr8! If u can get there. I'm x-cited! I'm 15, and skinny. OK? It'l b fun, Wilmer.

What day? Must B night. OK? Wilma.

Next Thursday? I'll get room, let u no, cu soon, I'm x cited, Wilmer.'

Martha waited two days. She had time before Thursday to send her reply. She'd formed a plan to get away from the guards, and that took a bit of doing.

She powered up, hit the web site, and found a few frantic messages from Wilmer. "He's hot to trot, and so am I."

OK, I can cu Thursday. Mom's at work all night. Oooh, I'm x cited, cnt w8t! Wilma.

She noted his eager reply after three hours of waiting. "Wonder what the bozo does for a living. He's not on the PC all the time. I'll meet this bird, but getting away from the guards will be a trick. At least, I got that letter on the way to Greeley, bless Lizzie's conspiratorial heart."

Lizzie had taken the plastic wrapped missal, with instructions not to leave a human touch on it, and posted it on her way back to Colorado Springs. The woman's love of intrigue assured Martha, it'd been done correctly. She smiled, knowing the damning thing was gone from her purse and on its way to benefit the Greeley police department without involving herself.

Martha worked out a plan. The guards stayed outside during her shift, usually in the back by the parked cars. She'd learned their routines. Those boys were sharp and it'd be hard to pull anything. After careful observation, a window of opportunity appeared about once every hour as they made their rounds and changed positions.

With a pounding heart, Martha did a test run at home, dressed as an old woman—dumpy figure, complete with a gray wig. She'd informed the guards she was going to bed and turned her lights off. It was nearly moonless as she slipped from the side door of the garage and padded softly past the wall of the building. She opened the back gate. The newly oiled hinges did not squeak as they once had.

"Good thinking," Martha murmured softly to herself as she walked down the back alley. Reaching the street, she crowed, "So, it *can* be done." She smiled with the excitement of knowing she'd found a way to get around her guards. *Maybe I can take care of another filthy predator before the hammer falls.* The familiar anger flooded her body and mind. Inwardly, she knew the time frame for her "activities" was becoming shorter.

She boldly ambled down the street, knowing she'd be conspicuous to the two guards. The bent-over position of an older female she assumed furthered her disguise. *I'm just an old lady and they may not even note my passing except to wonder why some old gal is out walking after dark.* She stifled her humor and continued another block or two before doubling back through the alley on her way to re-enter her garage.

A wild, electrical jolt of adrenalin passed through her as a large male figure slipped furtively past the end of the alley. *Oh Lord, he's out here!* She had no weapon, nothing defensive with which to surprise him. A man who wore shoes the size of a gunboat would be a strong adversary. Filled with hatred as he must be, the deadly menace of him set her on edge. *I'll bide my time. I'm getting very good at that.* Her resolve, strong and deadly, was the strength of Serena's and her own personality combined. She entered her home and sought her bed.

౮ꢂ౮

Harry and Ebert sat at Ebert's desk. "Anything going on out there?" Ebert asked, referring to Martha's surveillance.

"Just what the two guards report—boring detail. Our Martha hasn't tried anything toward hunting pedophiles as far as we know—wants to spend more time working, or so she says." Harry hunched his shoulders. "She's creative and very driven toward eliminating every child predator on the face of the earth, as you know. And I understand her feelings. She has that extra person inside her that drives her on," he added. "I wish I understood a thing like that better." He sighed. "I know you're aware of her alter ego and

I can't explain it either, but it drives her, though she won't admit it," he said, grimacing. "How will she handle the trial? It's due to start in a couple of days unless Munson finds another way to stall."

"It'll be interesting to watch Martha in the courtroom, knowing what we do about her." Ebert shuffled a few papers, dismissing Harry.

Harry went back to his own desk, fuming inwardly because he didn't have the leeway to see Martha as often as he wanted. Ebert irritated the hell out of him with his warnings to stay away from her. "Looks bad for the force, my ass," he grumbled under his breath. He checked the computer for details on the Greeley case. "Hey, Marcus, come check this out, take a look!" He pointed to an article stating the police department in Greeley had received a note from an anonymous source detailing the circumstances of the attack on Art Delevan, a member in good standing on their city council. "Sounds like Delavan turned out to be a real winner and our avenging angel did those silly chat line girls a real favor. However, they still have no lead on the perpetrator." He chuckled softly; he had a good idea about that.

"Isn't this the one where a small trace of fine sand was discovered as well?" Ebert gave him a little smile. "Ring a bell, does it?"

"Yeah, like the Pederson case—a bit of fine sand in the back seat, and even some in his wounds." Harry smiled, too. "Ouch!"

⟡⟡⟡

Ed hadn't bugged her for a while. *Has he lost interest?* Martha wondered. *Given up trying to date me?* He'd been too persistent for her to believe that. The quiet, nagging feeling he was close by at times and the size of that shadowy figure she'd seen in the alley bothered her. *Could that have been Ed? Surely the man's no stalker.*

A small niggling doubt stayed in her mind, however. Ed was very angry at her rejection of him. Remembering the icy, granite-hard look she'd seen lurking in his eyes, she shuddered. "A man like Ed could be a dangerous sort, considering his involvement in his wife's death." *And where there's smoke…*

Martha made arrangements to go to work. Her guards would take her and pick her up. "Like a chauffeur, how very nice!" She had to make the best of it to save her life as they hadn't found her shooter. Would they ever?

Wilmer rose ever higher in her sights as a new target and she laid her plans. She needed her car, yet couldn't drive away without them knowing it. So she devised another way.

She arranged the date with Wilmer in Boulder, near enough yet far enough. She'd managed to have him agree to the same arrangements as Tracker. "Damn, I don't have my sandbag." Using Will's little baseball bat could cause severe damage. She hadn't worked Orthopedics lately, so had no opportunity to cop another sandbag. She chided herself. *Dummy, you could have sewn the other one up and kept it.*

On the Thursday of the date she called her daughter. "How's Will doing these days?" After a less than satisfactory report on Will's mental progress, Martha's anger exploded and her resolve hardened. "Is Martin there?"

"Sure," Jeannie said. "Just a moment."

Her son-in-law came on the phone. "Martin? Could you move my car for me?"

"Move your car? What do you mean?"

"Yeah, I know it sounds strange but I have a good reason for asking." She gave a small laugh. "I'm having guy trouble again and this will help."

"Guy trouble? Anything I can help you with?"

"No, honey, I can handle the situation on my own."

"Well, if you're sure. So what do you need me to do?"

"Come for a visit and take my car when you leave. Park it at the Goofy Golf then have Jeannie take you home."

"Fine. I can do that. We'll see you in a bit."

Her daughter would be livid for not knowing what her mother was doing. But Martha only wanted things to stay where they were between herself and the police. *I don't need my daughter's tearful pleas ringing in my ears.*

"Whew, that's done," Martha said when she hung up, pleased with herself. "I'll go to work and walk right out of the hospital, find my car at the Goofy Golf parking lot, go forth, and do my good deed, and the police can be damned. It's for the youth of this country."

Satisfied with her planning, she didn't worry about the execution of it. The sky wouldn't fall if it didn't pan out, but she would try—she had to. *What if he turns out to be a lonely young boy looking for love?* But she knew he wouldn't.

She worried about a weapon until she remembered an old *Death Wish* movie. "A sock full of small rocks would be better and easier to get rid of." She decided on using two thick socks filled with some of the small rocks she'd used as décor in her yard. Looking around, she didn't see anyone and, hoping no one noticed, she slipped out and gathered some in a paper bag. With an anticipatory smile, she took the necessary things out of her backpack and placed them in the trunk of her car. It was a Friday, and she had no shift.

Next Monday, the trial of Munson would begin. Thoughts of it had her feeling edgy. Her heart rate leaped whenever she imagined herself sitting in front of his leering, hate-filled face, telling her story.

Martin and Jeannie arrived to help her with her car transport. She ushered them into the kitchen and made coffee. Jeannie refused it. "Who are those men out there, Mom?" Curiosity and suspicion rang in her voice.

"Well, I didn't want to tell you but I've been threatened. I have to testify against Munson, next Monday. He's been after me to the point the cops think I need guarding. It's a big pain, especially when I want to go to work. Can you imagine a guard hanging around in the halls while I tend my patients?"

"Mom! You can't just can't *stand* to live a normal life, can you?"

Jeannie had tears forming but Martha had no time to waste time with that. "Oh, stop fussing! I had to help Judith, and you know the rest. He'll be sent up and I won't have to put up with this nonsense anymore."

Martha hoped Jeannie and Martin bought her story. But she hurt terribly for Will's parents, seeing the deep shadows of pain that underlined her daughter's eyes. Their battle to save Will was never ending. They lived in fear that he'd become a molester, too, in spite of all they tried to do. Many child predators had been molested as children, a filthy crime that created a never-ending cycle of evil.

Martin hadn't said anything until now. He was more than willing to help his mother-in-law in any way he could. He faced her, hesitant and frowning. "What're you up to, Martha?"

He wanted a real answer and she knew it. He was suspicious, but she ignored it.

"My, you're so trusting. What's got you so worried?" She gave a phony laugh. "I've been just fine. I'm working and getting on with my life. I just ran into a little romantic complication, that's all." She hoped he bought it, but her son-in-law was no fool.

"If you say so, but Bob spoke to me the day before he died. He said to keep an eye on you because he was afraid you might go back to your Serena ways. Not that we couldn't use a few good vigilantes in this country." His sorrows and worries over Will's poor progress had the man completely in favor of decimating every child predator in the area.

"It's still tough, isn't it?" She put her hand on his shoulder in sympathy when he nodded. His continued distress over his emotionally damaged son only made her resolve stronger. She hugged her daughter and, with a carefree laugh, shooed them out the door.

Martin left with her car and she prepared herself for the encounter with Wilmer. Her disguises were in her car, and so was the sock full of smooth, round rocks, each about one inch in diameter. "Those should be as good as sand. They'll give a little. A bat wouldn't."

She went to the teen chat line.

Hi, Wilmer, I m so eager to c u. I cnt w8, Wilma

Cnt w8 2 cu 2 ht im on fyr eegr me. Wilmer

2 nt. my mom's gone. 2 nt. Wilma

After a few more insipid comments, Martha signed off. "It's definitely on."

About two-thirty that afternoon, in a high state of excitement as the guards drove her to the employee's entrance of her hospital, Martha told the guards. "I'll be back out here around midnight or a bit sooner, always depends on how things go, you know." She wore her scrubs, had her stethoscope around her neck, and carried a small bag. With a jacket over her arm, she walked to the hospital entrance.

Entering the hospital, she looked back to see her guards drive away. "That's a relief. They aren't going to hang around outside and wait." She slipped into the nearest bathroom and changed into jeans and a sweat shirt. Her cap pulled low, she casually sauntered out the front door of Riverside Hospital and down the street toward the Goofy Golf parking lot, with the same bag on her arm.

She found her car, quickly drove out into the street. She had a Map Quest printout in her glove compartment and reached in to retrieve it. Reaching the freeway, she went several miles until she edged her way onto highway thirty six and headed north to Boulder. The Freestone Motel sounded low key enough for her meeting. She'd agreed to the destination since a young teenage boy wouldn't have the cash for a Marriott.

With more than enough time, Martha drove leisurely, feeling the sense of freedom from police surveillance. Friendly or not, it was an impediment to her. She only had to make sure her intended victim was a predator and not some silly kid with sex on his mind. But in her heart, she knew this Wilmer was no young boy. He was a filthy child predator.

Martha lingered, stopping for a snack, until night had fallen. She needed the depth of darkness to conceal her true age from Wilmer. Driving past the motel, she continued on for two blocks. With her disguise in place, she presented the picture of healthy, youthful female—slim, baseball cap pulled down low, and long blonde braids swinging as she walked. "Not bad for a granny."

She laughed and kept on walking toward the back, after entering the motel parking lot. The flashing Freestone Motel sign threw glaring neon lights intermittently across her path but darkness aided her disguise as she ascended the cemented stairs.

She found the room he'd obtained for this night's assignation, crept inside, and slid along the wall. *Was the man in here already?* From the glow of dim street lights she noted the usual accoutrements of an inexpensive night's accommodation. Listening intently, she heard no sounds of breathing, rusting of papers, or clinking of bottles and decided he was not present.

She set her pack down, extracted the sock full of stones, gripped it tightly, and waited. Soon she heard the sounds of footsteps coming near. *No puffing from this creep. He must be in better condition than the last foul child molester*. A shiver of disquiet rippled through her. Could she handle this man?

He paused outside the door, his hand on the knob. Then he opened it. "Hey, Wilma? You here? I'm waiting to meet you."

Oh, how sweet the tones he uttered, but Martha breathed a sigh of relief as she heard the full adult male voice, filled with overheated sexual excitement.

She tensed. When he was fully inside, she gathered her strength and swung the bag of rocks against the back of his head, avoiding the temple area. A wound there could easily be fatal, and she wasn't into killing.

"Aw! Goddamn!" He clutched his head and turned his body toward Martha. She swung the bag again and, with a flood of relief, saw him drop into a crumpled heap on the floor. She flipped on a light to get a look at this teen predator. The man was built like a wrestler, and she wondered if he could be a cross country truck driver—a man who did his online chatting on his laptop then crossed the country, leaving a trail of torn and bloodied young girls behind. He was no teenager and that was enough for her. She opened her pack and went to work.

Later, after completing her task, she drove back to her hospital. She had enough time to walk out the employee's door in her uniform with no trace of guilt on her face. She waved to her guards and waited for them to pull up beside her. She didn't recognize them and figured they were new on the case. They introduced themselves as Mick and Sam.

After checking their IDs, she climbed in and rode in the back seat like a criminal behind the security screen. She felt a glow of satisfaction at how well her night's work had gone.

Monday, she would have to face the evil Munson as he stood pleading his case before his jurors, accusers, and those who were called to testify. That included her.

She entered her house and the guards stationed themselves around outside. She'd hardly put her backpack in
the bedroom closet when she heard that familiar soft
knocking and opened the door to see Harry standing there.
She reached out, pulled the man inside, and shut the door
without saying a word.

"I had to see you, Martha. Ebert advises against it but
he doesn't know how it is with us, does he?" He reached
out to take her in his arms. "God, woman, you feel good!"

Martha pressed against his big body and felt lost in his
strength. "Harry, I'm so glad to see you, I hardly know
what to say." She looked into his eyes for signs of worry.
"Will this be trouble for you?"

"No, the guys out there owe me, so we'll be all right. I
had to see if you're okay. You have court on Monday." He
held her out before him with a question in his eyes. "Will
you be able to handle that?"

"I think so. It won't be easy, looking at his hateful
face and listening to his sneering voice. But then, I've
heard it all before, haven't I?" She moved into the den with
him and urged him to sit in the big leather chair. It fit him
just right and she didn't mind seeing him there.

His eyes burned into hers. "Martha, I had to stop
things between us the other night, but my wanting you
hasn't stopped. I can't get over how I feel. I'd like to take
you to dinner or wherever you'd care to go. Would you go
with me?"

"Of course, I'll go anywhere you want to take me,
Harry." She meant that in the most intimate way and felt
the heat rising inside her. Her heart raced in her chest,
beating like a trip hammer.

He rose quickly and came to her. "Martha, I know
you've just worked a shift, but I want you to the point of
madness. I can't help it, girl."

She met him half way. "I feel the same, Harry. It's
never left my mind, either—not one bit."

She felt him wrap his arms around her and bury his head in her hair. His hands began to stroke gently down her back, making a path of fire with each pass of his fingers. She moved with him into her bedroom and they took each other into that wonderland two people can reach when things are so wonderfully right between them.

CHAPTER 25

They ate a leisurely breakfast. The guards had changed outside, and neither of them bothered to take note of it. They only had eyes for each other as Martha put coffee and a few stale rolls on the table. "Sorry, I didn't know I'd have company." She giggled like a teenager. "Think you can eat this dried up stuff?"

"No problem, my dear. Coffee's great, too."

He had the look of a man in a haze of happiness this morning. Martha felt that way herself, and the fact that she'd had something to do with his happiness filled her with satisfaction.

But something he'd said before had burned on her mind for a long while. She decided she knew him well enough to ask about it. "Harry, I hate to bring up things to make you hurt or feel uncomfortable, but could you tell me something about your little daughter?" She hesitated, sorry to bring sad memories back to him, then went on. "What I mean is, her name, what you know about what happened, just what you'd feel comfortable telling me, of course. I have a reason for asking."

"What possible reason could you have?"

"You know about Colorado Springs, Harry, but there were a few things about the second man—he had ribbons with bits of hair clinging to them hidden away in his closet." She saw his face blanch at her words. "What is it, Harry?" she asked, but in her heart, she already knew.

He fought tears as he spoke. "Her name was Helena, and she did wear ribbons. Not always, but on the last day of her life she wore pink ones. She was playing on the little playground near our home and my wife was with her—only turned her head for a moment and our little girl was nowhere to be seen. A car sped away and she heard the tires squealing that hateful day as an old greenish car went around a corner—our nightmare began then and never ended." He paused, took a deep breath, and then went on. "They found her three days later. I can't go into more of this, Martha. I just can't talk about it anymore."

He fought tears and she felt bad for him, but her neck hairs were standing at full attention. "Harry, I believe the man who did this to your little girl is paying his price and has more to come." She touched him, caressed gently, trying to sooth him. "He is probably the man I fixed on my second foray into the world of revenge, or he very well could be," she continued. "They said he had many ribbons in his possession, with hair, and sometimes blood, on them, too. Kept them as a sort of talisman of his exploits, or what have you. One of those ribbons may have been your Helena's. He'd killed and molested young girls all over this country and got away with all of them until the day he met with Serena."

Harry let loose and wept bitterly. It hurt her to hear his deep sobs but she waited, letting him get it out. She knelt against his knees. He reached for her, wrapped his arms around her, pulled her onto his lap, and turned his head into her body. As she held him, his tears warmed her chest.

He was not a weak man in any way, but Martha understood that this kind of heartache never truly left you. Because of their tragic past, they'd forged a strong and terrible bond of heartache between them. He'd born dreadful, heartbreaking losses and she had borne much the same—intimately.

"I'm sorry, Martha, it still hurts like hell," he said as his sobbing stopped. "I didn't want to hear what you had to say, but I'm glad to know that sadistic bastard has been caught. He's been neutered, you say?" He smiled down at her, crushing her tighter in his arms. "God, woman, I love you all to hell!"

"He's on death row, Harry." She said it softly, wanting him to know that additional fact as she melted even farther into his arms. He felt so good and his musky masculine scent drove her wild.

After several long moments, he said, "I'd better hit the road. I think the new guards are here and duty calls. I hate to leave you." He stopped suddenly and changed the subject. "So where were you last evening? You weren't working. No one else knows that, but I came to the hospital to see you and they told me you weren't on duty."

"You've known this since yesterday—all night, too?"

"I knew it might be one of your escapades, or thought it could be. Was it?"

Martha froze. As close as they'd become, he was an officer of the law. Dared she tell him about meeting Wilmer and cutting short the man's teen-aged-girl predatory activities? "I don't feel like sharing certain things with you just now, Harry." She sought to change the subject. "Tell me, what should I expect in the courtroom on Monday?"

"You should take up fencing, my dear. You're very good at evasiveness, such parry and thrust." He laughed and squeezed her tighter. "It'll be on the police reports, unless I miss my guess." At her look of alarm, he laughed. "Hey, my lips are sealed." Reluctantly, he let her go. "Sorry to leave, but I still have my job—well, I hope I do." He was damned good at his calling and had no worries about job security.

She ushered him out the door and saw him wave at one of the guards. "The other man must be around back," she mused. Shrugging, she sat down to read the paper, but her quiet didn't last. Her cell went musical.

"Hello." Her heart raced as she saw the caller ID and heard Ed's low, menacing voice.

"Keeping company with one of my co-workers, eh? Thought you weren't ready for such things—like an all-nighter. Lady, you are making this man right here feel damned left out. So how's about us two getting together? I'd sure like to get it on with you, Martha." His voice changed, grew slow and menacing, sliding into an ugly snarl. "I know enough about you to ruin you and your nursing career, and don't you forget it!"

The man's on the verge of calling me a raving bitch because I won't get involved with him. "Ed, I'm free to choose who I spend time with and feel no need to ask permission from you, or anyone else," she replied. "What I do is none of *your* business." She flipped her cell shut, hoping her voice hadn't betrayed the agitation she felt. If she sounded weak, an animal like Ed would be emboldened by it. *Funny how I thought he was such a great guy when I first met him, considering what I know of him now—totally amazing!*

The call had set her on edge. He wasn't through with her—she'd run up against him again, sooner or later. With all this in mind, she tried to mentally prepare herself for the court appearance on Monday morning.

The time had finally come and she was the prosecution's star witness. "Not the hot seat I ever wanted," she groused. She hated having to be so public. *Serena, we'll be under a microscope. Will we pass?*

eↄeↄ

Martha dressed carefully, wearing a medium dark green skirt with a cream-shaded, ruffled blouse under a matching green jacket. Her chestnut-hued curls had an added bounce that set off her tall, slim figure this morning. She noticed the approving glances from her police guards who drove her to the courthouse.

Her own car sat safely stowed inside her garage. She'd be accompanied by the police in any case and sat musing in the back of the patrol car behind the mesh screening again. *I hope this doesn't become a habit.* She had to smother a giggle, thinking about what she was in the eyes of the law. *If these young rookies only knew what they had in this cage.*

Harry met her at the entrance and took her arm. "I'm here with you. Even my boss concurs, if you can imagine that." He gave her an intent look. "If you aren't a gorgeous creature," he whispered soft and low.

This man makes love at the oddest times. His gentle pressure on her elbow as he escorted her through the security checks, up an elevator, and into the courtroom gave her the extra fortitude she needed to face the man who'd tried to kill her at least three times.

Harry sat beside her. The county attorney, Mark Hellams, sitting on the other side, spoke briefly with her. "I have your deposition of the day Detective Johns and I visited your home. Is there anything other than these statements we need to know?" He took more than a legally based look at Martha and she felt his eyes appraising her. She felt she looked nice enough this morning for any courtroom, but his steady gaze tended to unnerve her and she wanted to snap a quick, *What are you looking at?*

"Not really, Mr. Hellams," she replied. "It's just as I told the detective here. That man, Munson, has formed an unreasonable hatred of me because I helped his wife. I don't even know the man, otherwise." At least she could tell Hellams the truth which made it easier to speak to him.

She'd lied so much in the past few years, telling the truth was actually a relief.

"Now this is a preliminary hearing to determine if there is cause for trial. Your testimony is crucial, so be prepared to tell your story just as we have it recorded in this deposition."

"You're kidding? This isn't a for-real trial? You're saying I'll have to go through all this again?"

"Sorry, Mrs. Chance. This is usual procedure in criminal cases."

When the gavel pounded, they all rose to await the judge's appearance. A grave-faced little man entered, wearing a black robe. Martha noticed it nearly dragged on the floor as he shuffled into the courtroom. She wondered if he suffered from the short man's Napoleon Syndrome. And if he did, would it matter?

In due course, Munson was brought in between two deputies. He wore handcuffs and ankle cuffs with chains linked between them. He looked non-committal until he spotted Martha. Seeing her, his face turned into an angry scowl, growing dark red like a thundercloud at sunset. His guards murmured something to him as he sat down.

Martha had a good view of the man, and he had one of her. She sneered inwardly at Munson. *Not so good at killing were you? I'm still here.*

After the charges were read, several arresting officers were called to make their statements regarding the stabbing incidents in Martha's home. Munson's lawyer did his best to cloud their testimony until the proceedings became a nonsensical blur to Martha as she waited for her turn to testify.

"Mrs. Martha Chance, will you please take the stand?"

Suddenly, it was her turn. She complied and was sworn in.

The prosecuting attorney, the one who now had her written deposition, began his spiel. "Mrs. Chance, would you tell us the events of the night of March fourteenth when the alleged attempt on your life took place?"

As Martha carefully related the events as they had occurred, Munson screamed, "That damned bitch liked to killed me!" Ordered to be quiet or be evicted from the court, he shouted, "Go ahead, evict me. It'd be my pleasure. I'd rather be hung than sit in this damned kangaroo court," he snarled. "There's no justice for the married man anymore—damned meddling bitch!"

"Guard, escort this man out of my courtroom." The judge, his pinched face flushed at the effrontery of the prisoner, was adamant.

He pursed his lips as Munson's lawyer rushed to the bench and pleaded that his client was desperately overwrought at the loss of his marriage. The murmuring and snickering throughout the courtroom spoke of curiosity and humor over Munson's remarks. After several minutes had passed, Munson was led back in and returned to his seat.

"Continue with your testimony, Mrs. Chance," the county attorney said.

Martha felt she droned on and on. After a few more pointed questions, she was asked to step down. The defense had no questions for her—why?

"Aren't they going to ask about all three of the times he tried to kill me?" she asked Hellams, feeling deprived of justice by the omissions. "What about when he bombed my car? How about that?" she wondered. "Why haven't they brought that up?"

"Give us time, Mrs. Chance. It's all here."

He patted her knee. That act made her feel patronized. Her mind flew into an angry whirl. *Munson has a lot of pull around here. Is this guy in his pocket, too? What secrets does the man have on these people?* An unsettled feeling came over her. She'd slowly developed the notion she was the one on trial, not Munson. She sought Harry's eyes.

With a sick feeling, he saw the questions in her eyes. He'd already formed the idea this was fast becoming a phony trial, or a mockery of one. They hadn't read all of the charges and he wondered if they ever would. He made a slight nod in her direction, hoping she caught his meaning, offering what comfort and understanding he could.

The judge banged the gavel. "This court is in recess until tomorrow at ten a.m." He rose and shuffled out of the courtroom. Munson gave Martha a mocking leer as he shuffled out with the deputy. Seeing it, she felt a sick sense of futility at the day's events. What had been accomplished? To her unsettled mind—nothing. It was early in the day, barely two p.m. Why quit now?

Harry stepped up to take Martha's arm. 'Tough day, wasn't it?"

"And useless! Did anything get done today, Harry?"

He steered her to his unmarked car. "Not much."

"Where are we going?"

"First to your house—then to mine. Okay with you?"

"I'd be glad not to be alone right now." Feeling the shivers of defeat and hopelessness, she uttered between tight lips, "Something's not right, Harry. I don't trust that prosecutor, either. Judith told me that Munson owns most of the people downtown, has a hand in everyone's pocket. Looks like she was right. How can I trust any of them?"

"You've got a point. We have to see it through, though. These people are mostly elected officials, so right or wrong, we have to do what we can." He pulled out onto the street and headed toward Martha's home. "If what you say is true, I see why Munson was out after all the crimes he's committed. But I'd find it unbelievable to see him walk free after a hearing of this magnitude."

"What about my guards? Do they know where we're going?"

"They do. What concerns me is, does our shooter know where we're going? I told the boys to say nothing about this. If he shows up and takes a shot at us, I'll know who mouthed off, and to whom," he growled. "Helluva way to shake a shooter out of the bushes."

Martha quickly packed an overnight case and they left in his unmarked car again. Nearing evening, she felt soothed by the glow of the setting sun, seeing how it had the effect of coloring the turning leaves all the more brilliant. "It's so beautiful at this time of the year, look at the colors! I wish I could get this legal business over with so I could enjoy things again. The scenery of Colorado is fabulous, and I'm unable to pay it the attention it deserves."

"You will, darling. I'll call you that if I may."

Martha nodded and smiled. "Yes, Harry. I love hearing it from you. I've wanted to say those words to you as well."

"Nothing I'd love better." He grabbed her hand for a quick squeeze but didn't ask. *Why haven't you?*

They turned into his long, graveled drive. No eager dogs rushed out to greet them, and Martha saw anew how deeply Harry was hurt by their loss. "What kind of demon would take out those innocent dogs?" she demanded. "It's empty and sad not to see Max and Skunk."

"I hope I get to face the bastard that killed my buddies. It will be a sorry day for that—" His voice had taken on a menacing tone, unusual for Harry, but it underscored the depth of his feelings.

She wanted to say more but words wouldn't be enough. The shooter was after her, and someday she'd know who he was, one way or another. Her Serena side wanted to meet this sick fiend. Other than that, her *near* future looked gloomy except for Harry's exciting presence.

They went inside and pulled the blinds. "No need making a target for the bastard," Harry muttered, as he put on a pot of coffee. "Want something to eat? It's been a long day for both of us."

"Anything's okay with me. Actually, now that you mention it, I'm famished. I haven't eaten since breakfast and I was too nervous to eat much then." She sighed. "What did you think of the court today, Harry?"

"Not much. I think you may have nailed things with what you said about Munson's influence downtown. It's got to be something like that, the way he's been handled so far."

"So the fool may get off with a slap on the hands?" He couldn't mistake her feelings, seeing the set of her jaw and frown on her face.

"We'll have to see how it goes," he replied. "But like you, I'm worried as hell. The man is dangerous and should never be allowed back on the streets. He's obviously has a mental problem. Can't they see that?"

"You're right, he must have." She took a deep breath. "Do I have to die to prove the man guilty?" she exploded, fighting tears and hating the weakness of them. "Must I take the law into Serena's hands?"

"Thinking of it?"

She heard the uncertain tone in his voice. "I usually feel this way when I'm cornered or threatened. It's a part of me, you know," she said, her tone deepening. "You know what I told Ed after he threatened me?

"I hope you'll tell me."

"I told him, whatever he plans to do to me, to remember this much: a part of me never sleeps, and that part is the one to fear." She smiled. "He went white-faced when I told him that." She shrugged. "In any case, he called me a few days before the trial—still on my trail."

"So what are we eating?" Harry asked, shifting gears. He named several options and it lightened Martha's mood.

"I don't care, Harry, a grilled cheese, then?"

They'd gotten off the Serena subject and she breathed a quiet sigh of relief. Confiding such things to an officer of the law was an uncertain path. It was one she was reluctant to follow, no matter how close they'd become.

He did everything. Martha just sat where she was, enjoying his quiet efficiency in the kitchen. He set a plate in front of her and added a cup of tomato soup to go with it. "How's that?"

"It's wonderful—just what I needed." She dug in and watched him do the same. "You're a handy dude in the kitchen."

He sat across from her and she felt the tension rising between them. It had gotten dark outside. Did the shooter lay in wait? Was he out there? She didn't know about that, but what burned on Harry's mind—no great mystery there.

Harry hardly gave the shooter any thought. He'd waited a long time to find someone to love again and Martha had taken his heart by storm. He fell in love with her looks, her sad past, and her inner strength. He wanted to defend and protect her with everything he had. But at this moment, he only knew he wanted her in his big bed. "Tired, Martha?" he crooned softly.

"Subtle, aren't you, Harry dear." She went to him, "I think I've never been so tired and I don't know what to do about it." Her voice came soft and low. Desire made her legs so weak she wondered if she could walk.

"Now, who's being subtle?" He laughed and grabbed her. "Come on, clean-up can wait, but I can't."

His strong arms assisted her as they hurried down the hall. Together they entered his room and closed out the rest of the world.

CHAPTER 26

In the courtroom once again, Martha sat beside Mark Hellams. Harry sat on her other side.

Hellams turned to her. "Martha, I don't want you to be alarmed, but there is something I must tell you." Her pulse rate rose sharply at the regret in his eyes as he continued. "The case of arson has been thrown out due to lack of evidence."

"How could that be? What about his fingerprints on the gas can?"

"Inconclusive, he wore gloves it seems, or whoever the perp was."

"What about the explosives under my car, no case there either?"

"No viable fingerprints on anything and there are too many white Escalade pickups in the Denver area," he admitted. "You know how it is—ifficult to pin something on a prominent man with such flimsy evidence."

Martha scoffed. "Prominent? I happen to know he has lost his wonderful job."

"Doesn't seem to matter," Hellams said quietly. "Not one bit, I fear."

He then turned his attention to his paperwork and ignored her, but the slump of his shoulders told her plenty.

His posture allowed no further comment and although Martha said no more, she fumed inwardly. The hearing had rapidly declined into the same mockery of justice as before. The proceedings left her wondering when they'd pin a medal on Munson's lapel for bravery under fire. She snorted at the prosecuting attorney's limp attitude.

"What was that, ma'am?" he asked.

"Nothing, and I do mean, nothing," she replied as they stood to usher in the little judge and the farce began again.

The defense brought in a noted psychiatrist, who questioned Munson in detail. When Mark Hellams questioned him, it seemed to Martha he was very careful not to rile Munson in any way.

"I didn't want him to flare up like he did before. It only helps their insanity plea," he muttered to Martha when he sat down.

The legal mockery went on for three endless hours, and it was pure torture for Martha. Finally, the judge banged the gavel. "I have reached a decision." He looked around the courtroom as if to see if he had any opposition. He coughed. "This man is unfit for trial. I remand him to the private sanitarium, Forest Meadows, for treatment until such time he is deemed sane enough for prosecution."

They left the courtroom, but not until she'd seen the victorious smirk on Munson's face. She knew full well he'd be out on the streets whenever he had the desire to do so. "Harry, why did they even bother to prosecute this man?"

Harry shook his head in disgust. "Martha, two guards won't be enough for your safety after today. That particular sanitarium is nothing more than a fancy playground for people like Munson." With eyes cold as death, he clamped jaw tight. "I wonder if he'll spend more than two nights in there."

"He claims he's lost his job, yet, he still has this kind of power?"

"There's more to it than that job. I'd sure as hell like to know what he's got on these guys downtown. It's got to be something big, and rotten as hell—has to be. This whole thing reeks to the heavens, for God's sake."

❦❧❦

Martha went with Harry for one more night. She needed to return to work and her inner person chafed under the lack of freedom due to the constant surveillance. Serena chomped at the bit to go outside at night and hunt her stalker. She burned to take charge of hunting the big-footed man who'd made Martha's life a living hell.

But she couldn't tell Harry that. "Why do I have to have these guards now that the trial is over? It's expensive for the department and I can take care of things myself." She huffed. "Frankly, I'm sick to death of it. I can't make a move without those guys shagging me all day, every day."

His face tense and pale, he clutched at her hands. "Martha, you can't take a chance like that! That crazy bastard'll knock you off like a duck in a shooting gallery."

"I can't—"She paused, her fists clenched tight in frustration. Constant police presence added to her constant state of mental claustrophobia. She longed for and needed the freedom to act, yet not wanting to look foolish to Harry, she weighed her options. "You want to bet on that?"

"Good God, woman. What are you thinking?" Harry exclaimed, white-faced in his fear for her safety. "That son-of-a-bitch will kill you."

"Not if Serena finds him first." She lowered her eyes. "Sitting around like this, being protected like some weak-kneed ninny is getting on my nerves—big time."

She stood her ground and Harry knew he'd more than met his match in Martha.

Suddenly, she changed her tone, seeking to soften her stance. "I'm sorry to go off on you like that, but I'm fed up with everything and hate having you worry about me. The law hasn't been able to catch this big-footed fool who's turned my life into a living nightmare." She moved into his arms. "You're wonderful, caring, and oh so *very* good at certain things," she said, gazing into his eyes. "Except for being with you, Harry, I have no life anymore. I don't want—can't—live in fear. I have to do something."

"My God, Martha, you're a helluva woman but you can't go out and hunt down a dangerous criminal on your own, Serena or not." He flushed, remembering her previous words. "As for the other business, it's you in the bed with me that makes that difference—all the way. But, seriously, are you sure you want the guards pulled off your case?"

"Please, Harry, I'm not afraid. I want to work, drive my car, visit my family, and spend time with you." She looked into his eyes, her jaw tight. "I want my life back."

"I'll take care of it. But I hope you don't mind having *me* underfoot, shagging after you all the time." His reluctance to do her bidding was etched in his tone, but he understood her point of view. "You crazy woman." He made a grab for her, crushed her in his arms, and pulled her down the hall.

℮ᔆ℮ᔆ

The guards had been gone since yesterday and Martha had moments of panic at the loss of that security. But this was her choice, what she'd asked for. "I won't be a target, and when night falls, and I'll be on the prowl myself." She kept her shades closed and busied herself with neglected household chores until time for work. She did not venture outside. The garbage could wait and so could her flower gardens.

She dressed carefully for her shift and thought she looked brighter than usual. "Not bad for an old gal. Must be that great guy." She felt a surge of happiness, thinking of the new, tall, strong man in her life. "I think Bob will understand if he knows.

She made it to her shift without incident. But the staff met her with endless questions about the pre-trial hearing.

"Martha, we never knew you'd been shot at," exclaimed Marcie, the unit secretary.

"I didn't want to make a big thing of it. The guy only got a slap on the wrist, anyway. So much for justice around here."

"Well, it *is* a big deal, isn't it?" one nurse commented dryly. "You could have been killed and worsened our nursing shortage!"

"Thanks!" Martha giggled and headed for the report room.

She didn't want to talk about it and, in time, the queries dried up. The shift was uneventful and Martha sighed with satisfaction as she drove out of the parking lot, heading home. She noticed certain headlights maintaining a steady pace behind her and, after watching it for a time, wondered, "Is that car following me?" Her anger rose as she considered her situation and her heart rate accelerated along with her temper. "Mister Big-Foot, or whoever you are, you'd better watch it. I'm sick of this crap from you!"

Seeing a fast food place she pulled in. In short order, a car slowed, but kept moving. She didn't recognize the car at all, but took note of it. "Who drives a small, maroon compact car? Do I know anyone like that?"

After a short while she moved out and headed home. She pulled into her garage and closed it after her. Her defenses were in full-out mode. She entered her home quietly and at the ready. She turned on all the lights and believed no stranger was hiding in her house, but hearing the sound of soft knocking on her door, she froze.

She peeked through the tiny peep hole to see Harry standing there. Opening the door, she pulled him in and relocked it. "Harry! You scared me half to death!"

"You're upset and on edge. What's going on?"

"I was followed on my way home. I know it." She detailed how she'd derailed her follower. "Big-Foot's still after me. No surprise there."

"You can have the guards back. I'll see to it."

His face bore that protective look, but Martha was sick of police hanging around. "No, Harry, please don't send them back. I can't stand them under foot. I want to go out right now and see if that dude is skulking around out there."

"You crazy woman. Let's give the man a rest tonight. What do you say?"

He pulled her into his arms. Martha welcomed his strong presence and reveled in it, but again, felt the frustration of being stymied in her desire to hunt for her nemesis.

She loved Harry and welcomed him into her home. Serena liked him way too much. Martha knew her other half's wild side was on edge and let that carry over into her night with Harry.

⣷⣄⣷⣄

"Wow, lady, wow!" Harry said next morning, as he stumbled out the door. With that comment, he left for work.

Martha spent part of the day looking on her computer for another teen predator. When the phone went musical, she picked it up and looked at the caller ID. "What do you want, Gilmore?"

"You know damned well what I want." His low growl sickened her.

"Go to hell, Ed," she snarled and clicked off. "Sick, phony jackass!" *He knows I won't go out with him again. I'd be in danger, and not from his drunken driving.*

Ed's attentions had her worried, however. A very strong, together sort of guy, if he'd really done away with his wife, he was dangerous. What would another dead woman mean to a man like that? Nothing.

"I think of him as an enemy now," she mused. "He's threatened me, more than once, so it's no wonder. But somehow there's more than that to it." She grimaced. "I forgot to take a look at his feet. Wouldn't that be something if he was my shooter?" She shrugged the thought away.

She decided to call on her daughter. "Hi Jeannie, I thought I'd come by for a while."

"Not today, Mom. The new therapist isn't doing Will much good. And I'm at my wits end. I wouldn't be good company."

"Oh, I'm so sorry to hear that. I'll come another day, then." She decided to mention a thought that had been on her mind recently. "Why don't you enroll him in a Catholic school?" she suggested. "I hear those nuns won't take any kid's crap. Might do him some good, softness and kindness isn't always the answer. I always remember the old nursing axiom. 'Pity never healed anyone.'"

"You might be right. I'll talk to Martin about it. Thanks, Mom. Goodbye."

Martha clicked off. "If I could fix that devil, Callahan, all over again, I'd do it a flash!"

The hellish nightmare of Will kept on and on. That news dampened Martha's spirits and made her forget her other problems. She went to work. Reluctantly receiving an assignment in psych, she entered the ward and met a new charge nurse, Emily Beaton.

"How's it tonight?" Martha asked.

"Not so hot. We just got us a real crazy in, fighting and incoherent. He's hush hush, know what I mean? A no-info patient, high as a kite on Crystal Meth, his family's very prominent, so I'm told." Emily grabbed a chart and went down the hall a few steps. "Well, I'll spill it all in report. We'll go into the drug room for privacy. They haven't seen fit to make us a nice report room like everybody else."

She continued to grouse about working conditions until she shut the door and they sat down. "Now as to this patient, he's the son of some biggie downtown, practically runs the city, some say. Kid must be a heavy user by the looks of him. Heart's nearly gone according to the cath lab report. Between the Echo and his cardiac catheterization, he's down to twenty percent cardiac function, maybe less. We have him on oxygen at two liters to keep his O2 sats up." She put the chart in front of Martha. "Been acting out so they stuck him here for us to wrestle with, and it's been tough keeping oxygen on a nut case like that."

Her heart raced as she read the particulars. *His family practically rules Denver these days? Is this one of the secrets Munson has downtown?* She kept her face noncommittal and muttered her understanding about the course of treatment the doctor had written in his orders. The kid was on a heart monitor, with the strip being read in the telemetry department. He had leather restraints, they had to be loosened and redone every hour. She had a heavy night ahead. "Do I have a good strong aide, tonight?"

"Yeah, Jason's here. He's been with this kid before. This isn't his first admission with us either. Jason'll be a lot of help for ya'." Emily blew her nose. "Gol' durn allergies, can't get ahead of 'em." She readied herself to leave. "These folks got more problems than this one, so I hear."

Martha held her excitement in check. There was more to learn and she felt this kid held the key to some of it. She gleaned as much as possible from the chart, but found details sparse. Now she had a name. Maybe the internet would be productive, but she doubted it—maybe Duke. That man had his ways.

The shift dragged on and the glassy-eyed kid cussed her, using his foulest terms, while he struggled against his leathers. His care merely consisted of observation for the most part but Jason, the aide, did his physical care. Martha read every pertinent detail in the kid's chart. "Maybe this isn't everything, but it's a clue-in on something," she mused.

Her other patients tended to sleep for this shift and she let her mind dwell on the intricate mysteries of power behind the throne.

∽∾∽

Going home, she watched for a car following, but saw nothing to raise alarm. *Maybe Big-Foot's taking a night off.* She laughed, and the hollow sound of it echoed in her mind. Part of her knew he'd never stop until one of them lay dead or incapacitated, yet some of her agitation was the exhilaration of fight or flight. Again, she wondered, *Do I have the strength to handle someone who wears size-fourteen or -fifteen shoes.* "Serena, I need you now," she whispered.

Harry awaited her at home. Tired from her hectic evening on psych, she welcomed the strength and comfort he brought with him and collapsed into his arms. "Harry, if I'd known you'd be here tonight, I wouldn't have worked."

"I don't want to change your life, Martha. I just want to be with you and fit myself in where I can." The heat in his eyes sent a glow of contentment coursing through her body. *It's so right between us. How did I get so lucky?*

She made hot chocolate and enjoyed a cup with him. They looked into each other's eyes, thinking of what lay in store for them during the night. Chocolate dripped on her uniform, but she never noticed.

CHAPTER 27

After Harry left for work the next morning, Martha opened her cell. "Hi Duke. Can you come over for a minute?"

"Sure. No problem."

Satisfied, she straightened her home, showered and dressed. When the doorbell rang, she hurried to open it. Surprised, she stared into the face of a man she'd come to loathe.

"Ed! What are *you* doing here?" she exclaimed, sickened. She kept the door as closed against the man as she could. Hating the idea of that big bozo inside her home, she silently thanked her stars that Duke was on his way.

"Just wanted to see your good-looking face again, honey." He grinned at her, but that winning smile, once so attractive to her, looked cold and threatening. She didn't open the door any farther.

"I've company on the way over. You'd better leave right now, Ed." She gave him her best no-nonsense glare. "I've already said more than once, I have no interest in going anywhere with you."

"Have I said anything about us getting together, or going anywhere?" His eyes took on a suggestive leer as he spoke in a low, seductive voice.

"How about every other word you utter, Ed?" With grateful relief, Martha saw Duke's new pickup coming down the street. "He's here now, Ed. You'd best leave before things get ugly."

"I can handle any guy of yours, honey, and don't you doubt it."

"He's a family friend and I doubt you can handle this dude." She shrugged, feeling a burst of confidence. "Suit yourself." She wanted to sneer in his face, but turned her attention toward Duke as he eased his big body out of the shiny new Toyota truck.

"Hi, Duke, come meet someone I used to know." She watched Ed's face change as the hulking Navy SEAL came stalking toward them, exuding the sinuous grace of a mountain lion, his huge hands curled at his sides.

"Duke, this is Ed Gilmore, or rather, Sergeant Ed Gilmore."

Duke, fully informed of her problems with Ed, held out his hand. "Pleased to meet you, Ed."

She waited to see the fireworks. The men shook hands. Duke stood his ground, his chest out a bit more than usual, facing the big police officer. Martha saw Ed's face blanch as he took in his muscular and exceedingly capable adversary.

"Well, nice seeing you again, Martha," Ed said, holding his voice steady. "But duty calls and I've got to be off." With that, the man headed for his patrol car and drove away.

Martha let Duke inside and they both had a nice chuckle over Ed's cowardice, but then Duke's face grew serious. "What the hell was he doing here Martha?"

"I don't really know, but he's become a very real threat, I know that." She shivered. "He's angry with me for refusing another date with him, but it's more than that. You found out what was said about his wife's death and, knowing him as I do now, I can't shake the feeling he had a hand in that. There is something's very wrong about that man, Duke," she said, shuddering at the memories of her last date with Ed.

"Was that why you wanted to see me?"

"No, actually, it's another matter." She felt her excitement rise as she repeated what she'd heard about Munson's influence with the big boys downtown and hesitated before mentioning her patient in psych.

"It's wrong for me to tell medical details about the kid, but my life is on the line now. I really believe it is, Duke. His name is Kevin Moncrieff. I know nothing about his family or what they may be into, but this kid is a no-info patient and his addiction is very hush-hush." She swallowed and took a deep breath. "What I want to know is why. What's that family hiding? It's not like having a meth addicted son is big news these days." She smiled at Duke. "Do you think you could find out anything that would help me understand why Munson has so much power?"

"I have my ways." He laughed. "I'll let you know what I dig up."

Martha realized how handsome Duke looked these days, relaxed and happy as he was. His face had softened and his inner happiness had a glow of its own. "How's everything with Judith, these days?"

"She's doing just fine—getting bigger. We're really excited by the thought of a child. Neither of us ever expected to be parents." The big Navy SEAL almost giggled in his joy as she showed him out the door.

"Bringing those two together certainly isn't the worst thing I've ever done." She breathed a sigh and swelled inwardly with satisfaction. "I'm happy for them, even if my own life is totally screwed up. I'm being stalked and I'll have to face that creep, Munson, in court again one day, but I'm in love with a great guy."

Martha's cell rang. She opened it to speak with her daughter. "Jeannie, what's up?"

"The sisters didn't stand for Will's crap and wrapped his little knuckles with a ruler. It's totally changed his attitude."

"Oh, Jeannie, that's great! You think that school might be a positive for him, then?" Martha's heart swelled with joy at this tiny modicum of hope for the recovery of her grandson.

"Yes, I really do."

"Jeannie, keep him there. You've tried everything else." Martha wiped away a tear. "Will has to learn to live in this world and to handle the good and bad that's in it. He has to understand common ordinary rules of behavior if he's to have any sort of a normal life. Thank God, political correctness hasn't gotten too deep a hold on the sisters."

"I won't keep you, Mom. I just wanted you to know."

After hanging up, Martha felt so good she called for another shift.

"Med-surg? Sure, my favorite spot. Thanks Margie." She had time to kill before getting ready. *Watch the tube? No, I'm going to look around for tracks.*

She quietly let herself out the side garage door and went into the back alley. After reaching the street entrance, she moved quietly toward the front of her home. Checking the soft earth along the sidewalk, she stopped, feeling a chill. *He's been here recently. That track looks fresh.*

She felt her hackles rise as she moved on past her home and saw the huge footprint twice more. The last ones were older and softened by recent rains. *He's a busy boy, with all his stalking. Must not have a job.*

It made her angry and she felt her temper rising to uncomfortable heights. "Hold on, girl, don't waste your energy on thoughts," she murmured into the darkness. "We'll meet this fool face-to-face and maybe sooner than we'd like. He's got to be a big son-of-a-gun."

She continued on down the block through the alley, went back inside her house, and got ready for work.

❧❧❧

She worked her shift, enjoyed the friendship of other professionals, and, inside herself, felt the benefit of seeing her work rewarded by improvement in her patients. Those things made her work exceedingly worthwhile. '*You cannot save everyone, but you can help them and provide comfort along the way.*' Those words from one of her instructors never left her thoughts for long when she was on duty.

Martha left work and entered her car, feeling satisfied as she pulled out of the lot and headed toward the freeway. She hadn't gone more than a mile when she noticed a masculine odor in her car. Her heart leaped and begin pounding madly.

"Who's been tinkering with my car?"

Her query was answered by the ice cold muzzle of a pistol pressed against her neck. "Keep driving, my darling," Ed murmured low in her ear. "And keep on the freeway until I say to get off."

"Ed, are you crazy?" Martha firmly believed the man had completely flipped out. She kept a steady hand on the wheel and decided to mention another important fact. "Ed, I'm low on gas. How far are we going?"

"Shut up. Just keep driving and don't try any of your sweetie bull-crap on me, sister, I'm not buying." His scent was familiar. She recognized it as a rather exotic men's cologne called Savage Wonder. *How appropriate for this nut case.*

"Is this your idea of a date, Ed?" She kept her voice firm, refusing to give in to fear, yet that sick feeling clung close about her. Would she live out the night?

"Honey, you'll find out my idea of a *real* date."

She hated his emphasis on the wild, animalistic intentions he had in mind. It made her skin crawl and her temper rise. She kept driving as ordered, watching the fuel gage slip lower. She worried that when they ran out of gas, and she managed to escape him, she wouldn't have enough fuel to get back to Denver. "Come on, Ed, I'm nearly out of gas. What are we doing, hiking the rest of the way?"

She hoped to aggravate him. Anger might dull his reflexes and aid her. Remembering an unfortunate drug lord in Colorado Springs who'd met his death at the hands of Serena, Martha wondered what would happen tonight. Her inner persona was extremely devious and, with no conscience whatsoever, when she had been cornered in this way before, that situation had ended deadly. She smiled in spite of her fear and felt her pulse racing in excitement.

"Turn here, to the right, Martha dear," he said, interrupting her thoughts and indicating a trail of faint tire tracks.

She whipped the car so hard Ed fell against the back left door, but quickly righted himself. "Hey, girl, aren't you the one?" he asked, nearly cooing in his delight at her fighting spirit.

Martha fought waves of nausea. "Where *is* this you're taking me?" Her voice gained an octave or two along with her rising anger. "There's no road here, for God's sake."

"Shut your yap and keep driving. It's right up ahead. I keep me a country estate. I use it for a hunting lodge— bring all my cop friends up here." He emitted a deep throaty laugh. "Wait 'til you see how lush it is, my lady!"

Martha caught the scent of alcohol and felt a ray of hope. *If the fool gets stinko drunk, I'm home free.*

"Whoa up. Stop the car, my darling."

She saw nothing in the headlights except a densely forested area, but pulled her car to a halt. "So where are we?" She noticed the car lighten when he got out and felt the cold air envelope her as he pulled her door open.

"Come on, get out." He reached in and took her arm. "Here, let me give you a hand." With a rude jerk on her arm, he dragged her from the car to stand on gravel and sticks. Dense brush scratched at her legs and the night winds were cold against her face. No stars were visible, only a sliver of moon.

"Ed, what on earth are you thinking?" She tried reason. "This isn't right, and you know it. They say you're a good cop. A thing like kidnapping won't help your career." She knew how stupid that sounded. The man knew what he was doing, and enjoyed the fear he'd instilled in her.

"For the money I make, my career's a big joke. I have other irons in the fire and I'm planning to have a damned good time with this particular assignment." He pulled her close against his big body, pinioning her arms so she could only struggle helplessly as he pressed his mouth hard against hers. She felt his tongue force its way inside, thrusting down as far as he could reach. "Oh God, baby, that's good." He released her, murmuring softly, "Oh what I've got in store for you, baby."

She let him half-drag her along a dimly visible path, saving her strength. She'd size up and deal with the situation when they arrived at whatever destination he had in mind.

After several minutes, a cave loomed before them. She hooted, hoping she could anger him. It would help her situation is she sent Ed into an insane rage. "My God, Ed, can't you do better than a stone-age motel?"

"It's not so bad, all fixed up nice just for you."

He held her against his side and made her walk beside him. As her eyes adjusted to the dimness, she noticed a few rude furnishings, a table, a camp stool, and a crude looking camp bed.

He flung her down on it and stood over her. "You're all mine, sweetheart. I'm boss right now and your sassy lip makes it all the sweeter for me." He laughed—a gravelly, low and deadly growl. "Darlin', there's nothing I'd love more than a helluva good fight out of you."

The light was very dim, maybe from lingering moon glow, she wasn't sure. What light there was reached into the interior of the cave and her eyes had adjusted quite well to it.

Leaving her for a moment, he lit a camp lantern. When the light blazed up, she gasped at his feet. Quickly trying to hide her amazement, she realized Ed had the longest feet she'd ever seen on a man. *Could he be the shooter*? Oh yes, she knew he was.

Rising up on the camp bed, she confronted him. "You're the sick idiot who's been taking pot shots at me, aren't you?"

He laughed and she heard it ring hollow inside the cave. "None of your business, darling. I do a nice little business taking side jobs, so sue me." He advanced toward her. "I'd like us to get better acquainted tonight, before I *really* get to work."

She sat on the camp bed, waiting. "Work?"

Now she understood. He'd been hired by Munson. She was to be killed, but not before he took his pleasure with her. She knew without a doubt, he had no plans to show her any sort of kindness. He wanted her, and had for a long time. Knowing that gave her the only power available. She felt Serena rising within her. It would be a fight to the death and she was ready.

He sat beside down her. Martha did nothing as she felt his huge hands roving across her legs, arms, and breasts. He wanted a response from her. It was important to the man for whatever reason. She refused to give him one.

"Come on, honey, give me a nice hug. It won't hurt you to be a little generous." Receiving no response, his anger quickly turned to rage.

She could nearly feel it smoldering as his breath quickened and he tightened his grip.

"You've got no problem giving it to that fucking Harry." His voice rose to a tight scream. "Come on, you do, don't you? That son-of-a bitch is at it every damned night!"

If the light was better, his neck veins would be standing at full attention. Hearing him rage about his jealousy of her attachment to Harry, she realized he had a weakness.

"I love Harry, Ed. He's a wonderful man. The best I've ever known."

He struck her then. "You filthy lying bitch!"

Though only a glancing slap, he was big and strong and the blow knocked her off the camp bed onto the stone floor of the cave. Martha shook her head to clear her senses. She was shaken, but in his anger, he'd become careless.

He reached for her, tore her scrub top, sending the buttons clattering about the cave. She felt the cold air strike her bare skin.

"This is the best assignment I've ever had, baby, and you'll know how much I want you before this night is gone." His hands grasped her and threw her onto the cot. He sought the softness of her breasts, his mouth gaping open.

Horrified at his sick greed for her flesh, she twisted out of his reach, turned, aimed a solid kick into his midsection, and felt it connect.

"Uff! You fucking bitch!"

He screamed and lunged at her, but she whipped sideways and he hit his head on the rock wall behind the camp bed. When he turned back toward her, blood dripped down the side of his face. Looking at Ed, Martha saw enough evil written across his bloody features in the faint light to know she was in a desperate fight for her life.

His venom-twisted face was etched with anger and hate, making her blood run icey-cold through her veins. He advanced. She feinted and slipped downward until she saw her chance then aimed a solid kick, square into the man's crotch.

Crumpling into a quivering mass at her feet, he screamed in agony. "I'll kill you for that, you rotten bitch!"

Martha leaped up to stand over him and uttered a harsh laugh. "How about I pour this lantern fuel over you and let it light my way back to the car?" she growled, her voice low. "I warned you, Ed, I'm more than one person and you've just ticked Serena off, big time."

"I was just funning with you, Martha. You must know that."

His pleading voice sickened her, but at the same time, she realized she didn't know what to do with him. He wasn't a child predator, so that avenue was closed to Serena. But he was recovering rapidly—soon he'd rise to his feet. She had to act fast or he'd be at her throat again.

When he started to rise up, she grabbed a rock, hit him square on the head with all she could muster. He crumpled to the stone floor again.

Believing him to be unconscious, she lifted the lantern and checked around the cave. Holding it high, she spotted a pile of equipment in the back and found a length of rope. Setting the lantern on the rude looking table, she bent to grab his legs and tie him.

Suddenly he seized her with hands of steel, crushed her arms painfully behind her back, and grabbed the length of rope. "Now, you sneaky bitch, we'll see what happens when *your* hands are tied."

He wrapped the course rope tightly around her feet and hands, pinioning her arms behind her. After he finished, he threw her onto the camp bed and surveyed his captive. The tightened rope burned into the skin of her wrists and ankles, and her arms ached from the awkward way he'd tied them.

Martha faced defeat, and Serena grew deeply angry at their combined helplessness.

CHAPTER 28

S
he changed her tactics. "Ed, we could do things so much nicer if my arms aren't tied like this." Her voice dripped with honey as she smiled up at him, her eyes melting pools of heat. "I've had the hots for your big body for a long time. It's your own fault for getting drunk that night." She sniffed. "You scared me off, Ed." Her tone wheedled and went so soft he had to lean closer to hear her words. "I've wanted you real bad for a long time, Ed."

Looking down at her, his anger melted away. "God, Martha, why didn't you say so? You knew how crazy I've been for you." He knelt on the stone floor of the cave and kissed her lips. Martha swallowed her bile, yielded, and opened her mouth beneath his.

He heard her gasp as he plunged his tongue deeply into her mouth and believed she had given in. She was his. "Oh, darling, I've wanted you for so long!" In his exultation, he reached behind her and untied her ropes so she could get her arms around his neck.

Her legs were still bound but he'd be in a big hurry to remove those ropes quickly enough. She laughed inwardly at the man's weakness. *Keep it up you stupid, overheated fool!*

He tried to pull her uniform bottoms off, but her legs were tied. In his heat, he was forced to untie her legs as well until she lay before him, helpless and ready for his big body. He was wild with desire. She could smell his passion as he bent over her body.

She waited for the moment to strike. His bloodied face loomed over her as he ripped her work pants off.

Then he kneeled over her, fully engorged in spite of her earlier attempt to disable him sexually. He moved to spread her legs and force himself into her body, moaning with excitement. She felt drops of his spittle fall upon her naked abdomen.

He was blind with passion as Martha drew her knees up and, quick as lightening, kicked his male parts again with all the strength she could muster. She struck his engorged male equipment repeatedly until he'd passed out. He'd rolled off her and onto the cold stone floor. She climbed off the cot and stood over his crumpled body. "That's how much I wanted you, Ed, you stupid, sick bastard!"

She wanted to gloat but feared his returning strength and didn't waste time. He wouldn't be fooled a second time. She'd never get the upper hand again, he was too strong for her and Serena combined.

Grabbing the rope, she trussed his feet together, then pulled his hands behind his back and did the same. She stood back and surveyed what she'd done in the flickering lantern light. "There, try to get out of that, you evil son of a bitch!"

She started in alarm at clapping from the entrance. She turned from Ed's prostrate form to see Norman Munson standing there with a cocked pistol, aimed straight at her heart. His evil, leering face lit up in a mocking smile.

"Nice work, darling, now be real nice and untie the man." He waved the gun at her in his most menacing manor. At first, a smile had crossed his lips, but in an instant, he'd turned loud and angry. "Get on it, you filthy, interfering bitch!" he snarled, his voice filled with venom.

Martha turned toward Ed, seeing him fully awake. The burning hatred gleaming in his eyes sent ice screaming through her body. With the arrival of Munson, she faced utter defeat. With sinking heart, she worked his bonds loose.

As his hands were freed, he ran them up her legs and gave her a nauseating leer. "You're all mine, now, you sneaky bitch."

"Get lost, you sick bastard!" she muttered in anger and despair.

"I'll get lost—guess where?" His hands moved farther upward, groping, seeking, and his leering gestures turned her stomach.

She worked to keep her head on straight. Pure hell lay ahead unless she could figure a way to free herself from these two men. They portrayed the latest prime examples of scum of the earth.

Munson turned to Ed. "What the hell happened here? I thought you were taking care of this bitch, and here you are trussed up like a God damned turkey."

"What're you doing out of the nut house, Munson?" she asked, using her best derogative tones. "How'd you get out? Use one of your power trips?"

"Shut your sneakin', fuckin, slut-faced mouth, you rotten, interfering, bitch!" Screaming insults at Martha, he made a move to plant a solid kick at her, but she slid away and he missed. She noted he'd managed to keep his gun steady though.

Ed grabbed hold of Martha and held her, his hands roaming freely over her body. She shivered with disgust at his heavy touch. "Leave this bitch to me, Norm. I made a deal with you and I'll keep it, but I haven't had what I want from her yet. She's done a number on me and it'll take me a while, but I'll have this woman plenty, a hundred times over, and in every way a mind can imagine. Oh yeah, I'll have her until she's ready to die before she gets what's coming to her," he growled as he touched his aching privates. "She's asked for what I've got in store for her and a whole helluva lot more. And I'll do it right here in this fucking cave." He motioned for Munson to leave. "Now, if you'll do me the courtesy of giving us some privacy, we'll get right on it, won't we, Martha dear?"

His sneering tone sent ice through her veins. *Was this what his wife dealt with?*

Unbelievably, Munson left her alone with Ed. Martha could scarcely credit that act, though she saw it with her own eyes. Her spirits rose with elation, knowing she'd find a way to work it to her advantage. Her mercy level had been met long since, and there'd be no kindness from her. She steeled herself for his onslaught as he turned to her.

"I'm hurting so damned bad. I can't do a damned son-of-a-bitchin' thing I want to. You dirty bitch, you've got a lot to answer for."

He swung a heavy blow at her head. She swerved but Ed's fist landed beneath her left eye. Lights flashed inside her head as she felt it explode. Blackness took over her mind and she fell onto the camp bed. Weak, sickened, and fighting it, she felt him grab her and hammer another shot into her stomach. Losing all sense of balance, she fell off the cot and hit the stone floor. She lay there powerless, waiting for his next blow.

Martha's mind, foggy and clouded with pain, recovered enough to have a good sense of what she faced. Her ribs were broken, she was sure of that. If Ed forced himself on her now, his heavy weight would puncture one of her lungs. She thanked God he was incapacitated enough to need more time.

She kept her eyes closed, listening to his soft groaning as he sat on the camp bed. Pain emanated from her left cheek and the deep agony in her stomach filled her with the need to vomit. The intensity of her pain overwhelmed her as she fought for consciousness. Anger at her situation flooded over her and aided her in recovering strength.

She bided her time, slowly regaining a sense of control. She kept her eyes closed listening to Ed's tortured breathing. He lay on the camp bed resting, panting, regaining strength, virility, and his ability to assault her. She lay quietly on the cold stone floor, fully attuned to Ed's progress, as she regained some control of her senses and the situation.

Outside, she heard the staccato pop-pop of gunfire and alarm filled her. She wanted to get up but dared not move enough to attract Ed's attention. He groaned heavily, moved slowly off the camp bed and limped toward the front of the cave.

Another shot rang out. Deep male voices were yelling. She opened her eyes. Struggling to sit up, she wondered, *What now?*

Ed had disappeared from the cave. Martha painfully got to her feet to totter toward the entrance. The flickering lantern light cast her shadow on the rough rocky interior. Her feet hit something, became entangled and looking down, she saw her uniform bottoms. She painstakingly retrieved them and sat on the camp bed to pull them on. "At least I'll be covered." Her torn scrub top gaped open, and she had no good way to close it. The cold night air helped revive her. Half-clothed, she headed for the entrance. Exiting the cave she saw car lights and heard men yelling and talking.

"Martha! Martha? Where are you? Are you all right?"

At the sound of Harry's welcome voice, she nearly fainted with joy as she staggered forward. "I'm here. Harry? How'd you find me way out here?" She fought tears as he reached to take her battered body in those wonderful, warm, strong arms.

"Hey, darling. We had an idea what was going down. Ed's been under surveillance for several weeks but we lost track of him for a while tonight. Worst luck." He held her out a little. "God, he sure hammered the hell out of you. You all right, Martha?" He cuddled her, aware of her painful injuries. "Ed up to his old tricks, eh?"

"Yes, I think so. Had a rough time of it with both Serena and me, but he hit me hard. Harry, what were those shots?" She had to know.

"Munson got off a shot at us but we nailed him. He's in serious condition and it's a long way to a hospital. Don't know if he'll make it." He looked around the cave. "Nice accommodations!"

"Yes, isn't it? Ed's best. He disappeared when he heard the shots. Have you found him?" She'd never rest until the man was in custody. She mentioned his huge feet.

"We caught that back awhile, but needed more on the guy. I believe we have it, now, Martha."

"Enough to overcome a crooked judge?"

Harry hugged her tight but at Martha's wince, let her go. "Sorry, girl, he's hurt you really bad. I'll take a piece out of his damned hide for that!"

"He's dangerous, Harry. I wonder at his sanity. Some people seem to be filled with rage, like it seeps all through them and people get hurt. I could easily believe he had something to do with his wife's death after tonight." Then she remembered. "Harry, he was working for Munson. Hired to kill me. I learned that for certain when they were together tonight. Wanted some time with me first, though."

Harry shook with anger. "Dirty bastard!"

Martha felt a sudden let down, a surge of deadly fatigue, and wanted to faint. "Can we get out of here?"

"We've an ambulance on the way. You'll go before Munson. I guess that might be fatal for him, but you'll be taken first. We've called for a second one. Hope it's not too late." The lack of concern in his voice surprised Martha but she didn't argue. She hadn't the strength.

With his arm supporting her, they left the cave and made their way toward the cars. She saw two police cars and one that had to be Munson's. "Harry, that's the small maroon car that followed me one night." Her thinking seemed fuzzy. "I wonder if I have a concussion. I can't think and my head is killing me."

"Here, love, sit in the patrol car, until the ambulance comes." Harry helped her move unsteadily into the front seat. She noticed dials and knobs before she leaned back and closed her eyes. Far off, she heard the faint scream of a siren.

The sounds of men going about their work roused her enough from a probable state of shock to look about. A man she believed to be Munson, lay on the ground with an officer working over him.

The ambulance drew close and the attendants came to her door. Harry told them to take care of her first. Several of them took a look at Munson as well.

She followed their commands and allowed them to place her on a gurney for further inspection. "No, I wasn't raped. It never got that far." Her abdomen felt as if it was on fire and burned inside from Ed's solid blow. She wanted to vomit and winced at the lights they shone in her eyes. Then she heard someone say, "Looks like she's got a concussion, belly's tight, possible internal bleeding—we've got to get her in fast." She felt herself lifted up, but before they took her, Harry appeared, his face heavy with worry.

"Martha, they'll take you now. I'll be in as soon as I can. Be all right, darling, please."

She heard the pleading in his voice. "Harry, Ed's out there somewhere. He'll never leave off trying to kill me. Never."

He nodded. "We're on it, girl. We'll get him."

They took her away. She felt the gurney being shoved inside the vehicle by strong hands.

A young man leaned over her. "Mrs. Chance, I'm Kevin. We'll take good care of you. Just hold on until we get you to the hospital and the doc takes a look. It'll be a bit bumpy till we hit the pavement. I'm right here with you all the way."

He patted her arm and smoothed her hair. Martha saw this slightly awkward gesture as one of comfort on his part and all he could manage under the present conditions. She closed her eyes and drifted off.

She awakened again to the sounds of the siren as they sped along. When they pulled to a halt, she felt herself lifted again and heard clicking as the legs came down then felt the slight jolt as the gurney wheels hit the pavement. She gazed upward as they wheeled her between huge double doors. *I've never looked at ER doors from this angle.*

She wanted to ask where she was, but it didn't matter, really, did it? Everything seemed so hazy.

Friendly hands lifted her onto a hospital bed, placed a pillow beneath her head, and pulled a soft blanket over her. A man leaned over her with his tiny flashlight. "Just checking your pupillary reaction, Mrs. Chance." She flinched at the light as it struck her eyes. "Sensitive to light, hmm? Bad spot on the left cheek, looks clear to the bone."

"My stomach hurts the most, Doctor. He hit me square in the middle. I nearly fainted from the pain and it hasn't let up at all. I think he may have fractured a few ribs, too."

She felt his hands on her abdomen and heard him call out, "Order a CT scan set up for skull, chest, and abdomen, pronto. We've got trouble here." He bent down close to her ear. "I understand you're a nurse on staff here, Mrs. Chance."

"Yes, if this is Riverside, I am. Is everything okay?" She knew it wasn't and his expression made her worry. "That man may have killed me yet, Doc. He's been at it for a while." She couldn't say anything more. She felt like floating away.

"We can handle it, Mrs. Chance."

"Martha, I'm here now." Harry's face floated above her. "They'll take care of everything. Don't worry, darling."

An orderly came to her side. "I'll be taking you for a CT scan now, ma'am."

He drew her away from Harry. She felt the jiggle and heard the rumble of the wheels as they moved down the corridors. Every jar caused her to wince in pain.

"Shoulda give ya somethin' for pain before all this movin'." The big black kid pushing her was sympathetic, but kept her moving all the same.

സ്ലോ

She had no idea who was with her or where she was when a voice said, "Martha, we need to go into the abdomen and stop the bleeding," A nurse bent over her. "Have you any family?"

"Look in my purse if it's here. I think it was left in my car, call Jeannie, my daughter," she mumbled the numbers and things went black.

CHAPTER 29

"Mom, you awake, yet?" Martha heard the sound of her daughter's voice coming out of the mist and opened her eyes to see a bank of faces surrounding her bed.

"Is it over?" she mumbled as she felt the dressing over her abdomen. She saw her family and, searching farther, saw Harry. "Hi, honey."

She giggled slightly and went back to sleep. When she was next fully awake, Jeannie sat next to her and Martin stood at the foot of the bed. "I guess I drifted off."

"Mom, you scared us to death." Jeannie's face was stern, but concern for her mother was written there. "The doc said you'd be fine, now, but we were really shocked to find out what's been going on."

Her tone was accusatory, and Martha understood. "You've had enough on your plate without my troubles, dear." She looked for Harry. "Jeannie, this is a friend of mine." She introduced Harry to her family and, through lowered lids, furtively watched her daughter taking in the new man in her life.

"Very nice to meet you. I had no idea. Mom?" Jeannie hesitated. She'd loved Bob and this additional news gave her a jolt.

Her son-in-law, Martin stepped up and shook Harry's hand. "Glad to meet any friend of Martha's." News of her new relationship was now out and Martha offered no apology for keeping it under wraps.

A doctor she only knew in passing came to her bedside. "I'm Doctor Bledsoe. I have your case. Martha, I must tell you what was done." He looked at her visitors. "Ah—may I speak in this company?"

"Yes, Doctor. We're all family, here."

"We had to remove your spleen. It was ruptured. It shouldn't be any cause for worry as you know. I understand you're one of us here." He smiled down at her. "You have three fractured ribs. There were no perforations. You'll recover completely in spite of all your injuries, I'm pleased to say."

Martha saw the warm tracing of tears sliding down her daughter's cheeks. "Thank you for your work, Doctor Bledsoe," Jeannie said. "We're so thankful."

Martha's heart ached for her. The girl had already had so much to bear. She saw the look of relief on Harry's face. She also noticed that he stayed discreetly in the background.

The attending nurse shooed the family from the room. Martha received another dose of medication. With the room empty and quiet, Harry came to her side.

"I'm going now, lady. Call me if you need to see me. I've posted a guard outside your room. I had to do that for your protection." He grinned at her. "Serena is out of commission for now, isn't she?"

"I think she is. I love you, Harry. Big surprise to my family, weren't you?" Her state of drowsiness made her giddy, but she felt his soft, firm kiss on her lips before he left, as well as the way he gently pulled her soul into his.

When she awoke again, Duke and Judith sat at her bedside. "Oh, hi, guys. I didn't hear you come in." She blinked her eyes, trying to make them stay open while trying to decide if she was going to stay awake for a while.

"Sorry about what happened, Martha. We came as soon as we heard." Duke paused, a frown on his face. "I have some interesting news for you. Something you wanted to know."

Martha had to force her mind awake. "I hate these pain meds. I feel like I'm on some crazy trip, Duke." She focused on Judith, "How are you two getting on?"

Judith nearly gushed. "I'm doing great myself, but Duke is like a silly kid over our baby. You wouldn't believe this man!" She patted her slightly protruding stomach and Martha enjoyed the flush on the big guy's face.

"I'm very happy for you two. You both deserve something wonderful in your lives." She felt warm inside at their happiness, then remembered Duke had something for her. "What you have to tell me, big daddy?"

He took Judith by the arm. "Honey, give us a bit of privacy. Some things are definitely better unknown."

Judith's body went stiff and her face paled as she rose to comply. "Okay, honey, back in a minute." She left the room without another word.

Duke pulled his chair close to Martha's bedside. "It'd be better she doesn't hear this stuff. It's not fit for the ears of an expectant mother."

She came fully alert. "What's going on, then? You're scaring me, Duke!"

"I hacked into the elder Moncrieff's personal computer." He smiled. "Yeah, we know how it's done. It seems our esteemed big shot, Moncrieff, markets some really rank kiddie porn—his computer's full of it. Somehow, Munson must have gotten wind of it and used it every way he could. It's been his get-out-of-jail card more than once, as you know. What I don't know is where he gets his material or if local kids were used in his films but there were horrendous shots of torture involving a tiny black-haired, black-eyed girl." Duke wiped the sweat from his brow. "It was so damned sickening!"

Martha felt shock as once again she saw Aliya Pederson's battered, tortured body in her mind and fought against the horror of it.

"What's wrong, Martha? What are you thinking?"

"I might know that child." She told him the monstrous story of little Aliya. "Could Pederson have been using his child in this sickening way?" Inside her mind, she knew he was capable of exactly that. "Could you get me a picture of that particular child? Pederson's already in the slammer on murder charges for her death. If his little girl was used in those scenes, it would hook the whole lot of them together in a horrible network of child pornography. From what you've told me, it could be her, and it fits with everything else."

"I'll get it for you as soon as I get out of here. The detectives can take it from there. They'll know how to keep things legal so these sick bastards don't get away with what they're doing.

Her mind was spinning. "Does Ed fit into any of it?"

"As far as I know, he doesn't."

"Ed was hired by Munson to kill Judith, and failing in that—me. He couldn't get to Judith because of you so he was sent after me. He couldn't do it himself, though he gave it a good try."

"Could be Munson used Ed for 'odd jobs' in a lot of ways." Duke thought a moment. "He's definitely a dirty cop, then?"

"Big time."

Their interview ended and Duke left with Judith. Martha's mind was in a desperate spin, her body wracked with pain. "I can't even get out of this bed!"

She bore her frustration poorly, but her body had suffered a severe injury, and she couldn't leave her bed without the help of a nurse. *Thanks, Ed, you sick bastard!*

She dialed Harry's number. It wasn't long before the man himself appeared at her bedside. "Hi ya, Hon. What's up?" He swooped down for a quick kiss, careful to forgo the hug he wanted to give her.

"Harry, I've a lot to tell you." She motioned him close to the bedside and spent the next moments filling him in on what she knew.

"Good God, Martha! How do you know all this?"

"I have the best source in the world and now it's up to you to figure out how to bring these animals to justice. You've got to obey every little rule or they'll walk away from everything, won't they?" Martha huffed. "There's something to be said for vigilante justice—admit it."

"Hey, I can admit it all day long, and I wouldn't mind handing some out, but knowing it, changes nothing. However, hearing what you've told me changes the whole thing in our favor. Can you get me a few photos?" He looked at her in wonder. "You're really something, girl, laying here all banged up and staying right on track. You must be one stubborn woman."

"That I am—about certain things, Harry dear, but not where you're concerned. I'm way too mellow. You have that effect on me." She gave him a lazy grin, but her pain level had increased, and she rang for the nurse. "Harry, I hurt like h—I mean I really need something right now."

"I'm going, girl, but I'll see you later. The guard's outside your door. Don't worry about Ed."

When the nurse came in, Martha asked her, "Would you tell me how the man who was shot is doing? I'm referring to Norman Munson." she clarified.

"I shouldn't tell you this, but he didn't make it."

"Why not tell me? The man tried to kill me several times. I feel sorry he didn't make it, but he was at it again when the police came. I won't let on you told me. Just consider it hospital gossip." She laughed then winced as the pain hit her ribs. "Okay, give me the stuff."

ℰↃℰↃ

When Martha opened her eyes again, she sensed someone nearby, waiting. Turning her head she spied her best and dearest friend in the world, one who knew and understood all her terrible secrets.

"Lizzie! Oh God, it's so good to see you!" A few tears slipped down her cheeks. "Hey, wretch, look what you've done, making me cry."

"So lay it on me, girl. How'd you get in a mess like this?" Lizzie shook her head in wonder. "You never cease to amaze me."

Martha told her what she could, leaving out some of the worst details. "Ed's still out there somewhere, probably dreaming up his next move to do me in. There's a guard on my door while I'm in here." She flashed a grin. "Maybe they'll let me go home if you can stay a few days Liz."

"Sure, I can. No problem. So what about guards at home then? You aren't up to snuff yet, I see."

Martha smiled, and arched her brows. "Harry'll be with me when he's off work. Maybe I'll let him put a guard on me the rest of the time."

"So it's gotten that far, has it?" Lizzie giggled. "I understand completely, my dear. He's really a great guy."

"He is. He's wonderful, but when it comes to marriage, I won't try it again. I'm a black Mariah, Liz. I won't risk Harry's life like that."

"I don't know what to say to that, but I understand what you're saying. With your marital record, I can't blame you for feeling that way." Her lips firmed into a tight line. "What'll you tell him if he asks?"

"I wish I knew. I love the guy."

They were interrupted by the surgeon's visit. Lizzie stood back while he checked Martha's abdomen and shone his light in her eyes. "You're doing very well, Martha.

Would you like to go home today? We will discharge you if someone's there to stay with you." He cocked his head, waiting.

"Yes, Doc, I'd love to go home. And I've a friend right here who'll stay with me for a while." She nodded at Lizzie.

"I'll take care of it then." He left the room and Martha immediately felt concern for Lizzie's security as well as her own. The sickening truth came home to her. No one around her would be safe. Ed was out there somewhere, waiting.

"I'd better let Harry know." She grabbed her cell and punched in his number while her friend waited.

Martha settled it with Harry. "He's coming to take me home. You'll have to follow us. I don't know where my car is." She chuckled weakly at her helplessness, "God, what a mess!"

"I'll start packing," Lizzie said. She waved at the large bouquets of flowers and numerous cards setting about. "Where are your clothes?" She paled when Martha pointed to a messy, bloodied pile of scrubs in a plastic bag.

"I'll just wear what I have on. I work here, not a problem."

Harry entered later with several items of clothing, including jeans and a sweatshirt. "I brought these for you." He nodded to Lizzie. "Glad to see *you* here."

"Do you know where my car is?" Martha asked.

"It's in your garage, dear." He sighed. "Martha, some things have come up and we need to talk." He gave Lizzie a look that told her to go for a cup of coffee or something. After Lizzie faded from the room, Harry sat on her bed. "Martha, about two or three weeks ago, a trucker was attacked and *clipped,* shall we say, for want of a better word. He wouldn't say why he was at the Freestone Motel in Boulder, but his condition was bad enough to seek medical attention. He refused to identify his attacker or any other details concerning the crime. The hospital called the police. They had to, it was an assault." He tried to hide a grin. "You wouldn't know anything about that, would you?" He raised his eyebrows. "It happened the night you were supposed to be at work—and weren't."

"I'd never have admitted anything like that, but for all you've done to save my life, I'll tell you." She told Harry how she set it up on the Internet. "The man believed I was a thirteen year old girl. I think he set up meetings all along his route, and met these stupid kids. Imagine what he's done to several other little girls about that age. Is there any way you can find out how many young girls have been molested along his truck route?"

"We can try, but these devils are slippery and the kids usually won't say anything. They sneak on home and learn to live with the rape of their small bodies. It's a damned tragedy." He gave her a very careful hug. "Your secret is safe with me and I applaud what you've done," he added quietly. "Greeley was your work, too, eh?" He smiled at her nod. "Also, my dear, we tossed the sand evidence, decided it wouldn't hold water." He chuckled at his idea of a joke.

Martha flushed. She'd kept her secrets and worried about it. But now she relaxed. He knew them all and seeing he was easy with it, she shrugged. "Sorry, Harry. I couldn't confess all these things before. Glad you tossed the sand." She couldn't hold back a giggle as she squeezed his hand.

"No problem. I just needed to set things right." He gave her a conspiratorial smirk and winked. "I'm with you all the way, girl. I wish I had your guts."

"I'm two people, don't forget. I have the guts and strength of both, mostly Serena, I imagine."

They looked up when Lizzie returned. "Okay, you two?"

"Just getting this lady ready to go home, soon as her paperwork is done," Harry assured them both.

Martha couldn't wear the jeans zipped. Her tender abdomen wouldn't allow the snug fit. Within the hour, they left the hospital in Harry's unmarked patrol car with Lizzie close behind.

CHAPTER 30

After a couple of weeks at home, with Lizzie keeping close attendance, Martha regained her strength and agility. Up and about the house and becoming restless, she complained, "I'm about ready to go for a drive, Liz. We've been cooped up here for too long and I'm near stir crazy." She sat in Bob's old leather chair, swinging her foot to and fro, wondering aloud how Liz felt about taking such a daring step.

"Better wait for Harry. He'll be totally pissed if you go out and make a target of yourself after all he's been through."

"He's been through?" She frowned then reconsidered. "You're right, Liz. Well then, how about a night out at The Paradisio?" She howled at her own wit. "See, I'm going nuts, just sitting around here."

"Yeah, you're nuts all right." Lizzie became stern. "Harry can decide this detail. Maybe we can visit his country place if you're so danged restless, you nit." She tossed her head and laughed in her carefree way. "He's been here so much watching over you, no doubt everything's gone wild out there." She smirked. "Did you ever tell him about The Paradisio?"

"I've told that man just about everything." But, Martha knew in her heart, certain things she'd suffered as a little girl would never be told. Those things lay buried deep from him, her friend, and anyone else that could possibly care, and there they would stay.

"Let's have coffee, then." Lizzie got the pot.

ℰↃℰↄ

Harry pulled up a chair next to Ebert's desk. "Marcus, we've got what we need for one hell of a bust on that kiddie-porn ring. All we need is a way into the Moncrief house. My informant says there's enough on the man's computer to send him away for the rest of his miserable damned life!"

"It has to be legal and above board," Ebert said, a warning in his voice. "How you planning to go about it?"

"Moncrieff's son is a meth user. He'll have to make a score every now and then." Harry chuckled. "I'll put Chickie on that detail. She looks the part and never misses a trick." He hunched his shoulders at the thought of it. "You know, I hate this shit, Marcus. It turns my stomach and this case more than most. I wonder how big and deep this ring goes. You know damned well, he's not alone in this particular cesspool."

"Will she be all right on that detail?" Ebert asked.

"Hell, yes," Harry replied. "Chickie can look like the biggest user on the block with black rings under the eyes, bird nest hair, and stinking clothes." He laughed. "If she doesn't show those great, perfect teeth, we'll have handcuffs on that Moncrieff kid before the week is out, mark my word."

"And he'll lead us to big daddy, Nelson Moncrieff." Ebert sighed. "You know, a man has got to be a father to his kids these days. When this goes down, he'll regret going along with his kid's addiction. He's been too easy on the kid," he added. "Get on it, Harry, and take care he doesn't catch on. With what's coming down, I almost feel sorry for the man."

ᇊᇊ

Night came stealing over the sky, purple shadows deepened, and the filth on the streets lay hidden. Cars slogged past, adding their fumes to the general stink of the air. A slightly built woman limped down the sidewalk. Her hair was clumped with sweat and dirt, her face covered with crusted sores, and dark circles ringed her bloodshot eyes. Chickie knew her job and had her strategy planned out before she'd left the station.

For several nights she'd hung around a certain corner, the one where the Moncrieff kid got his stuff. After he left the scene, she sidled up to the pusher to score a tiny bag of stuff. After she got it, she scuttled slowly back along the street into a nearby alleyway and shoved the bag into her backpack as evidence.

The pusher ought to be arrested and taken in. And he would be. But she needed him where he was right now. How many others bought that death-dealing stuff that same night? Her small body shuddered at the thought.

She'd followed the kid and had seen where he entered one of the finest old mansions in Denver. That he was dealing in drugs was easily evidenced by his sneaking around the back way. Since he did this about every other night, she knew he was trying to keep his addiction hidden from his parents. And like many despairing parents, they probably clung to the forlorn hope their child had the guts to kick this devastating habit.

No doubt they believed the kid had stayed clean since his last hospitalization. She'd also noticed that his parents kept a very busy social life and were seldom at home, leaving the son alone. This was one more inducement to a lonely child's use of drugs.

Her task was to devise a way to get inside that home. For that, she'd have to beg some crap from the stupid kid. On this particular night, after he'd made his score, he nearly raced toward home. Seeing his haste, Chickie, now dressed cute and overtly sexy, knew Kevin was in desperate need.

She intercepted him, wearing a pained expression on her face. "Hi, guy, got any stuff?" She slurred her words. "I need it real bad, know what I mean?"

"Get lost, bitch!" Kevin tended toward the nasty side. Ignoring her, he turned away toward his home in desperate haste.

"I'll do anything, please—and I mean anything—you want." She let a tear escape. "Please, kid, you won't be sorry, I promise you." She tagged along beside him, clutching his arm, begging.

"Anything?" He took in her slight form, curved in all the right places. "What'd you want, anyway?"

Chickie, seeing the rise in his pants, knew she'd made it—she was in.

"I haven't got anything right here," Kevin told her.

"Yes, you have, I saw you get it. I'll come with you. I'll go anywhere. God, I need it!" She let the hungry whine in her voice and the tears in her eyes do her work.

He rose to the bait, his faced flushed as he clutched her hand. "Okay, okay, but don't make any damned noise." He led her around the house, through a smaller door, and up a back stairway, likely used by household staff. He pulled her down a hallway and halted. "Right here's my room." He jerked her inside a darkened room and switched on a soft light next to the bed.

Chickie saw a beautifully furnished room with heavy, solid dark oak, intricately carved with bold geometric designs—a masculine room for a wimp. How his parents must weep with disappointment over their pitiable excuse for a son. She pitied them as she stood trembling in the soft lamplight, waiting for a fix.

He held out a small baggie with the familiar pale shards of death, and not a lot of it. "This was all I could get."

"I'll take it." She grabbed at it, but he clutched her wrist.

He twisted her wrist, making her wince. "Not 'til I get what I want, first, and I want it all, if you get my meaning."

"Sure—sure, but it'll be a million times better if I get mine first," she wheedled, giving him a heated stare. "You look like a real stud to me, darlin'. I'm dying for some of that, too." Would he go for her velvet tones?

"Okay, bitch, but hurry it up." He handed her the baggie. "Leave some for me or you'll be sorry."

Disgusted at the whiney, nasty tone of Kevin Moncrieff's voice, she left for the bathroom. "I'll be only a minute. I'm real quick." She promised. Inside the bathroom, she whipped out her cell and made the call. "Hurry up. I'll be screaming 'rape' in a few more minutes!" She dallied a few moments before she went out to tangle with the over-heated, drug-pushing kid.

He advanced on her, ripping off his tee shirt, and unbuckling his pants. "I'm more than ready. You've kept me hanging here. Get your damned stuff off!"

"I decided I don't want to do this anymore." She sounded like a weak, soft little girl trying to get away with her scam. "I'm leaving now!"

"Hell, you say!" His voice turned harsh as he grabbed her arm and gave it a painful twist. "Get your shit off. You're not screwing me on this deal. I have to sneak around and go through hell gettin' that stuff. I'm not giving it away for nothing, bitch!"

He shoved her onto the bed, grabbed her blouse, and ripped it off exposing her small breasts.

Chickie screamed, "Help me! Oh, help me please!"

Kevin hit her across the mouth and reached down to rip her soiled bottoms off. "Come on, let's have it, and shut your fuckin' mouth before I slap it shut," he growled, keeping his voice low as he aimed another punch to her face and moved to straddle her naked young body, sprawled across his King sized bed. He never heard the sounds of footsteps on those back stairs.

His bedroom door burst open. "Hey, what's going on in here? I heard this lady screaming." A burley cop burst into the room and grabbed Kevin. Pulling him off the girl, he twisted the kid's arms behind him and, after a small scuffle, Chickie heard the click of the handcuffs. She smiled at the cop, but hid it from Kevin.

"This guy just tried to rape me. He forced these drugs on me, too," she whimpered, holding out the incriminating baggie.

"Don't you worry, little lady. This dude won't bother you anymore." The cop hoisted Kevin to his feet. "I'll call some guys in to check out this house. Looks like a drug house to me." He whipped out his cell and made the call.

Kevin's face blanched a chalky white. Speechless, he stared at the policeman in his room. His father's power in this city would be ruined from this incident. "Just wait, you bastard. My dad'll take care of this—and you, too!" Terrified, he sobbed in fear.

"I'm sure he will, son, but when we check you out, he'll have to pull in his horns. How many times you been in the hospital because of Crystal Meth, so far?" the big officer asked.

"None of your fucking business, asshole!" Defiance rang out along with Kevin's fear. He needed another fix real bad, and soon.

He looked at Chickie. She seemed so relaxed. Did she shoot up? Something wasn't right. He remembered she gave the baggie to the cop. Who the hell was she? Not some poor girl needing a fix and, too late, he knew it.

Forensics would go over the house with every imaginable tool at hand, supposedly looking for drugs, but the real goal was Moncrieff's computer, laden with kiddie porn. The officers smiled with the small bit of success gained from this night's work.

CHAPTER 31

Harry walked into Martha's home with a smile on his face. He couldn't wait to tell her something had gone down, and this time on the positive side.

"Okay, what is it? Tell me." She knew, but begged the details. "You got the computer stuff, didn't you?"

"That and a whole lot more. He's screaming set-up and entrapment, but the rotten stuff on his computer told us what we really wanted to know. The father took shots of some of the things done to that poor little girl." Tears filled his eyes. "I can't go into that and you wouldn't want me to. Suffice to say, he's facing a few new charges, including premeditated murder." Harry paused, hesitated. "I can't talk about this anymore. I can't."

Martha took him in her arms. "I know more about this than I want to. You don't need to go into it any more. I can't bear to hear it either." She thought for a moment. "It's not right to say it, I suppose, but I'm glad your child and little Aliya are in the arms of God. Neither of them could have grown up to be normal women. Not after what happened to them. My God, how could they?"

Harry shrugged and lifted his head as he changed the subject. "Martha, would you ladies want to come out to my place for a few days?"

"Great idea. Lizzie and I were talking about getting out of this house and driving around." Martha shuddered and shook her head. "We're going stir crazy staying inside, hiding like we're the criminals."

"Sounds like heaven to me," Liz said. "I love your ranch, Harry. It's a peaceful place you have, or rather it should be." She laughed. "In spite of what happened on our last visit."

"We do have to consider that Ed's still out there somewhere, but we'll have another guest with us, a very good one."

Martha exclaimed. "What? Not another guard?"

"In a way, yes. He's getting old and has served his time. They want to retire him and I said I'd like to give him a home." Harry laughed at their questions. "His name is Warrior and he's deadly on guard. That guy's been in more scrapes than any of us. If he's loose on the grounds, old Ed'll need some real heavy padding. That'd be if he's still stalking you, Martha."

"I'll be glad to see you with a good dog again, Harry."

"So when do we go, then?" Lizzie stood. "Martha should be able to withstand the trip. She's doing well enough these days."

"How about right now?" Harry replied.

They got their stuff together and, within twenty minutes, hit the road in Harry's unmarked patrol car.

"So where's this Warrior dog?" Martha queried.

"I'm picking him up at the station." He pulled into the back of his precinct and went in. He quickly returned with a huge, golden-headed German Sheppard.

"Meet Warrior." He put the dog in beside Lizzie. "He's one of the best."

"Dare I pet him?" she asked, looking at the huge dog sitting quietly beside her.

He panted with his tongue lolling out one side of his long, black muzzle. A few drops of saliva dripped on the seat beside her.

"Sure you can. He isn't used to a whole lot of it, but he's not on duty right now, and he knows that."

Harry told the dog to lie down, which took up more of the seat. Liz moved over to accommodate him. They drove out of the city with both women looking at the beautiful dog. Martha couldn't reach him so she left the petting to her friend.

"Hey, he licked my hand, so I guess he likes the petting," Lizzie said.

Harry laughed. "What guy doesn't?"

Martha snuggled closer and caressed his cheek as they sped along. The trip was relaxing, the scenery grew ever more rural, and they laughed and chatted as if they didn't have a care in the world. Finally, they drove onto Harry's long, gravel driveway.

Approaching the ranch house, Martha saw that everything seemed trimmed and kept up. "Do you keep a gardener or something?" she asked.

"Just one of the neighbor kids. He's a good one," Harry replied. "Come on in and get comfortable."

Grabbing both bags, he led the way. The dog leaped out, sniffed the air, and emitted a low growl. Martha's heart raced with apprehension. Harry came out and she told him.

"If anyone's around here, he'll let us know," Harry assured her. "It may just be that it's a new place to him. I'll see what's up with him." He ushered them inside and went out with Warrior.

Martha watched him from the window. She saw Harry take a bit of cloth out of a bag and hold it for the dog to sniff. Then he pointed his arm in an arc and said something to the dog. Warrior took off like a shot.

"What's he doing now?" Martha asked, leaning out the kitchen window.

"He's doing a sweep of the grounds right now. If anyone's out there he'll know it and so will we."

"Wow, what a dog! No wonder you wanted him with us."

Martha felt the chill in her bones. Munson had died and more than one biggie downtown had been taken out of commission. Moncrieff's life had become a total disaster from the kiddie porn they'd found on his computer.

So why am I afraid? What's out there in the beginning darkness for me to fear? Martha couldn't fight off her feelings of unease. She was very weak, and her alter ego suffered that weakness with her.

Lizzie made a light supper of things she'd scrounged from the fridge and freezer. They sat together, sipping coffee and munching on the fresh biscuits and honey she made to go along with the mashed potatoes and salmon patties. "I make these the way my mother used to when we were kids," she said.

When they'd finished, Harry shooed them into his den. Laughing in his joy at having them in his home, he assured them, "You gals relax. I'll handle the clean-up. A woman-cooked meal is a rare delight for me. You two rest now."

Martha remembered how comfortable his den had looked when she'd been here before. Tired and with a full stomach, she hoped to catch a nap. Feeling the weakness of her recent surgeries, she hated the helplessness of her situation. Her heart went out to Lizzie who'd left her husband to fend for himself, while she'd come to tend Martha during her recovery.

Liz found a big leather chair and Martha stretched out on the couch. "I'll switch on the TV. Maybe Ed's been caught. Wouldn't that be nice?" Lizzie pushed the remote. The news came on blasting forth with the latest scandal involving the big shot, Moncrieff.

"Oh, Liz, see if you can find a movie, good or bad, I don't care. I'm sick to death of hearing all this business about corrupt politicians."

It was old news these days, though, deep inside, she knew it wasn't over for her. She hadn't seen the last of Ed Gilmore. That fact chilled her bones. She didn't want to worry Lizzie or even Harry, but at times, she felt the ice flowing inside her veins, knowing it wasn't finished.

Harry joined them. He sat with Martha, holding her. In total relaxation, they were half asleep, watching a flick, when a shot rang out from somewhere outside the house.

"Oh, God! That was a shot!" Martha yelped and tried to rise from the couch.

Harry pushed her back. "Wait right here and keep down." He shot out of the room, grabbing his gun, and hit the door at a run.

Lizzie ran out of the den. "Stay put, Martha. I'll see what I can find out."

Martha, alone and nervous, knew Ed was out there. Something was going down and she couldn't do anything to help. She worked to get herself sitting up.

The evening light had faded and, in the gloom of Harry's den, she heard a small noise and caught the odor of a male presence. When she felt the cold hard nose of a revolver pressed against her neck, she knew who it had to be.

"Going somewhere?" Ed asked. She recognized those soft hissing tones that had sounded so seductive to her at one time. "Stay down, bitch!"

"How'd you get in here?" She turned and looked at him. His scruffy beard, wind chapped face, and torn clothes so dirty and wrinkled, told her that Ed was no longer the natty dresser she'd known before. Being on the run, his life had drastically changed. Worried he was up to his old tricks, she asked, "What happened to the dog out there?"

"You mean old Warrior? Him and me was good buddies or have you forgotten, I worked on the force, too." He snorted "He came right up to me, Martha honey. I was going to smash his head in with a rock, but he'd howl before he died. A gunshot was quicker and a hell of a lot surer." He laughed again. "Took care of those other two, remember?"

"Yes, it had to be you, didn't it? Who else could be so evil? Harry heard that shot. He's out there now looking for you."

"I'm not out there, am I, sweetheart?" he sneered. "Come on, my darling, you're coming with me. I have unfinished business with you, lady, and I'm in the pink of condition."

He reached down and yanked her to her feet. Martha felt burning pain shooting through her abdomen from his roughness and felt clouds of dizziness overtaking her senses.

She pulled her arm away. "I'm sick, Ed. I've had surgery, thanks to you."

"Think I give a damn about how you feel. You've destroyed my life, you sick bitch, and now I'm going to destroy yours. If it hurts, you can bet I'll be lovin' it, every fucking minute of it!" He hauled her to the hallway and headed toward the back door.

She wondered where Harry and Lizzie had gotten to and prayed they wouldn't meet Ed. He'd gone insane and would use his gun without a thought.

He was afraid of running into Harry, she realized. Her legs felt like lead and she stumbled over the rug by the back entrance. Outside, he dragged her toward the nearest clump of trees, swinging a vicious kick at her legs. "Keep up, dammit!"

She did her best to keep up with him, but he was in a hurry and dragged her nearly off her feet. He hadn't lost much strength she noted.

"Keep up, or do I have to drag you?"

He jerked her again and she thought she'd faint. "I'm trying, but I'm weak, thanks to you, you sick bastard!" Her anger had risen and it gave her added strength. She stumbled along. Her legs stung from his kick and her vision blurred. She tripped over everything. "Just let me go. I can't keep up with you!"

"I'm not done with you yet, sweetheart. Remember, you've got a real treat coming from me." He sniggered. "I owe you big time."

"Pardon me while I vomit." She hoped he'd make noise, so Harry could find her. "Did you really kill that nice dog?"

"Shut the fuck up, bitch!" He feared the noise could alert Harry and kept the gun stuck in her face.

She kept silent. Farther from the house now, Martha rapidly lost hope. With nothing to lose, she did what she could. "Ed, give me a moment to catch my breath, please." She wheedled her best, thinking he'd be a fool to fall for that again. She wanted to laugh aloud when he stopped for a rest.

"Sit down here." He offered a tree stump and shoved her down on it. The moon had risen and she could see where she was. The ranch house looked smaller, so far away. She assumed they were somewhere in the back pasture and remembered that lovely day Harry had given her a tour, proudly showing her his place.

"Ed, where you taking me?" She looked up at him. Seeing how grungy he'd become, she wondered where he'd kept himself. "You have a car, Ed?"

"None of your damned business what I've got." He laughed. "I've got hold of you, and that's all I need—for the next while anyways." He grew quiet. "We could get things going right now. How about it?"

"How about what?" she queried. She'd detected the longing in his voice. The fool still wanted her. *Play dumb, if it makes him mad, so be it. I'm in a fight for my life right now.* "I'm too tired for anything, Ed. I'm sick and in pain."

That much was the truth. But as she slumped in fatigue, she felt around until her hand came across a short, thick, piece of broken branch. Her heart leaped as she plotted how to proceed.

"Come on then, get moving. You're rested enough. We can't stick around here all night." He sniggered softly again. "We got a better place to go."

Martha got to her feet and as he turned to start off, she swung the club with all the strength she could muster and heard it smash against his skull. When she saw him slump to the ground, she screamed with all the lung power she could manage and felt darkness creeping over her as she fell to the earth.

☙❦❧

"Martha! I'm here!" She roused enough to see Harry kneeling over Ed as he snapped on a set of handcuffs. "He's secure for now and the gang's on the way. You all right?" He raised her enough to take her in his arms. "Martha dear, say something!"

"What took you so long, Harry?" Blackness took her again.

CHAPTER 32

Martha opened her eyes, realizing she lay on the leather couch in the den. Lizzie stood over her. "Did all that stuff really happen?" Martha asked.

"Yes, it did, and you had us scared to death. Harry found you when you screamed." Lizzy knelt down and gave Martha a big, but very gentle hug. "The cops took Ed in, but he wasn't feeling too good. What'd you hit the guy with?"

"It was a clump of wood, I think. When my hand hit on it, Serena took over. I was never that strong. We smacked that devil with all we had."

"He's out of your life for good now. The Benson police had a warrant out for his arrest, on top of what they had here. I guess the murder charge will win out. Harry thinks it will." Lizzie chuckled. "I've never seen a man so worried, Martha. He's really into you."

"I'm so tired, Liz. Is it all over?"

"Looks like it."

Harry came in and knelt down next to Martha. "How's my girl?" He stroked her hair with his big hands. Lizzie discreetly left the room.

"I guess I'm okay now," Martha said then remembered. "Did he kill that wonderful dog?" She feared the answer.

"Yeah, damn his rotten hide. He'd worked with Warrior before so the dog knew him. Takes a damned cruel or sick mind to do something like that." He was close to tears.

"He *was* a sick man, Harry, very sick. Did Benson, Arizona, want him for murdering his wife, then? Is that what I heard you say?"

"Right, they wanted him for murder." He got up and took her hands. "Come on, you need a good night's sleep. We can clean up everything in the morning. There're questions, paper work, all that stuff, but I held the department off until you got some rest. Unless you need to see a doctor. Do you?"

"No. You're all I need right now." She rose to go with him to his bed, stopping only long enough to take a couple pills and wash her face.

Together they shared his bed and he held her carefully until she fell asleep.

⟡⟡⟡

The next morning rose bright and sunny. After a good breakfast of waffles, syrup, ham, and coffee, Lizzie cleaned up. When they were ready to leave for town, the doorbell rang. Harry opened it to a rusty haired boy in his early teens.

"Hi, Jerry, what can I do for you?"

"Sir, would you take a look at these here puppies? Your Max was the father, we think. Some of them look a lot like him, but some sort of look like Skunk, too. We don't know what to think about that." He laughed. "Looks like our Cindy couldn't make up her mind between your guys." He held up a basket of squealing, wriggling puppies, all nestled in a flannel bed. "They're ready for weanin', Mom said. Want one?"

Martha knelt down to the baby dogs and Liz did, too. "Oh, Harry, look at them. They're too cute." She held a nearly all black pup up to her cheek and got a pink tongue on her face in return. "This one looks like Max, don't you think?"

Harry picked up a fuzzy spotted one. "Hey, this one looks like Skunk. What do you know? Jerry, I might just take these two. Okay with you?"

The deal was done and later they headed for town to finish the paperwork and whatever. Seeing Harry's place become smaller as they drove away, Martha realized she didn't want to leave his wonderful retreat. Not ever.

If he asked her to marry him, could she put the man in that kind of jeopardy? With her marital record, it was a puzzle and she had no answer.

The End

About the Author

Ramona Forrest is a retired RN. She keeps busy writing novels—and traveling whenever possible. Forrest has resided in the back country of Arizona, assisted in round-ups, worked in Saudi Arabia, and has had the pleasure of traveling extensively. She now resides in Phoenix and spends much time in gardening, writing, entertaining friends, and family.